Charcoal Joe

Also by Walter Mosley

Easy Rawlins Mysteries

Rose Gold

Little Green

Blonde Faith

Cinnamon Kiss

Little Scarlet

Six Easy Pieces

Bad Boy Brawly Brown

A Little Yellow Dog

Gone Fishin'

Black Betty

White Butterfly

A Red Death

Devil in a Blue Dress

Leonid McGill Mysteries

And Sometimes I Wonder About You

All I Did Was Shoot My Man

When the Thrill Is Gone

Known to Evil

The Long Fall

Other Fiction

Debbie Doesn't Do It Anymore

Stepping Stone / Love Machine

Merge / Disciple

The Gift of Fire / On the Head of a Pin

The Last Days of Ptolemy Grey

The Tempest Tales

The Right Mistake

Diablerie

Killing Johnny Fry

Fear of the Dark

Fortunate Son

The Wave

47

The Man in My Basement

Fear Itself

Futureland: Nine Stories of an Imminent World

Fearless Jones

Walkin' the Dog

Blue Light

Always Outnumbered, Always Outgunned

RL's Dream

Original Ebooks

Parishioner

Odyssey

The Further Adventures of Tempest Landry

Nonfiction

The Graphomaniac's Primer

12 Steps Toward Political Revelation

This Year You Write Your Novel

Life Out of Context

What Next: A Memoir Toward World Peace

Workin' on the Chain Gang

Plays

The Fall of Heaven

Doubleday | New York London Toronto Sydney Auckland

Charcoal
Joe

An Easy Rawlins Mystery

WALTER MOSLEY

www.doubleday.com

DOUBLEDAY and the portrayal of an anchor with a dolphin are registered trademarks of Penguin Random House LLC.

Book design by Michael Collica
Jacket design by Michael J. Windsor
Jacket photograph © Ysbrand Cosijn / Shutterstock

Library of Congress Cataloging-in-Publication Data
Names: Mosley, Walter, author.
Title: Charcoal Joe : an Easy Rawlins mystery / by Walter Mosley.
Description: New York : Doubleday, an imprint of Penguin Random House, 2016.
Identifiers: LCCN 2015044304| ISBN 9780385539203 (hardcover) | ISBN 9780385539210 (ebook)
Subjects: LCSH: Rawlins, Easy (Fictitious character)—Fiction. | BISAC: FICTION / Mystery & Detective / General. | FICTION / African American / General. | FICTION / Urban Life. | GSAFD: Mystery fiction.
Classification: LCC PS3563.O88456 C48 2016 | DDC 813/.54—dc23
LC record available at http://lccn.loc.gov/2015044304

MANUFACTURED IN THE UNITED STATES OF AMERICA

10 9 8 7 6 5 4 3 2 1

First Edition

Charcoal Joe

1

On Robertson Boulevard a block and a half north of Pico, just south of Whitworth Drive, on the eastern side of the street, there once stood a three-story turquoise building that had been a posh home in the thirties. But the owner died, leaving his real-estate-rich, cash-poor relatives to turn the domicile into a commercial property.

By 1968 the first floor had become an antique-furniture shop where fifty-something Mrs. Ina Holloway sold old sofas, chairs, and dining tables of dubious pedigree to middle-aged women from Cheviot Hills—women who wanted to make their interior decorations equal in style, if not in value, to their wealthier counterparts' in nearby Beverly Hills.

The second floor was occupied by an insurance brokerage firm owned and run by Harry (born Hiro) Harada. To hear him tell it, Harry sold insurance on everything from life expectancy to pet health and marriage vows. Harry's wife and daughter, son, and daughter-in-law all worked in his second-floor office. Only Harada's gaijin son-in-law no longer worked for the old man; this because he had been in prison for a crime he confessed to, embezzlement. He, Arnold "Sandy" Patterson, was convicted on evidence that was not vetted by the defense or the prosecution—evidence that would not have stood up under scrutiny.

The police detective who interrogated Sandy accepted his confession of having stolen money that Harry's strawberry-farmer client, Gentaro Takeda, had entrusted to the company: $131,247.29. The money Gentaro gave had been in cash, and the day that everyone agreed that Sandy had taken it he was under the knife at Cedars of Lebanon for an emergency appendectomy.

Indeed, it was Harry himself who had taken the money, believing that his client was senile and probably wouldn't remember anything about the transaction. So three days later, when the elderly Mr. Takeda returned with his son Ishi to ask for the money back, Harry felt that he was safe in saying he had never received the cash in question. Mr. Gentaro had once told him, Harry claimed, that he wanted to have Harry invest some money but he had never given him the cash.

After the Takedas left, Mitsue, Harry's daughter, told him that the day after Gentaro had been there he returned saying that he had not gotten a receipt from her father. Harry was at a convention in San Diego so she looked up the transaction in his day journal, saw that no receipt had been issued, and had filled out one of the pre-signed receipts that Harry kept in the safe just in case the family had to do business in his absence.

That right there was the moment of truth for Harry Harada. Gentaro didn't seem to remember any receipt and Ishi hadn't mentioned one. Harry's greed outweighed his morality; it convinced him that the dotty old man probably lost the voucher and that the money, all cash, could not be traced. He told his daughter to forget the receipt and the visit.

When Ishi pressed charges in Gentaro's name, Harry stuck to his story. But, three months later, when the receipt Mitsue provided resurfaced, a warrant was issued for Harry's arrest. He had testified under oath that he never received monies from Gentaro and had therefore broken the law.

Mitsue begged her husband to take the blame for the good of the family. Mitsue explained that even if the father was able to stay out of prison he'd lose his license and his customers, impoverishing the entire clan.

And so stout-hearted Sandy confessed. There was no trial to speak of, so the elderly Gentaro, who was indeed senile and unreliable as a witness, was not required to appear in court. Sandy admitted telling Gentaro that he was Harry, and the confused old man believed him. Sandy explained about the pre-signed receipts in the safe, saying that he was trying to get enough money to start a business of his own.

Four months after Sandy was locked away I came to the building looking for office space. Harry managed the property but his wife, Kikuyo, did all the work. The handsome middle-aged mother-in-law did not seem very interested in me as a tenant, probably because of my skin color (which is a very dark brown); that is until I told her that I was a private detective. Upon hearing this she asked me if I could help an innocent man get out of prison.

It was a delicate operation. Gentaro Takeda's mental condition had declined further. By the time I became involved his testimony could no longer be trusted. When asked who he had given the money to he replied, "My son."

The money had been returned and Kikuyo convinced Harry to give Ishi Takeda ten thousand dollars to forgo any further complaint. I went to the state's attorney with evidence that they had convicted and imprisoned an innocent man, and so Sandy was set free and the state decided not to pursue further charges.

Kikuyo, without telling her husband, gave my company, WRENS-L Detective Agency, an unheard-of fifteen-year lease at a very reasonable rent.

Harry thought I was overcompensated but he said so only once because, in spite of his dishonesty, he was a family man and freeing Mitsue's husband brought bliss to his home and his business.

———

So at 7:42 a.m. on the first Monday in May 1968, I stood out in front of the gaily colored plaster-encased building: a professional detective with a bright future and a dark past.

Ten months earlier I had received a questionable windfall of one hundred thousand dollars in ransom money that no one wanted to claim. I used part of the money to start my own little detective agency with the two best detectives I knew—Saul Lynx and Tinsford "Whisper" Natly. Saul was a Jewish detective married to a black woman who had given him two sons. He was born and raised in L.A. and was accepted, more or less, in white circles. Whisper was a Negro from St. Louis who could find anyone, anywhere, given the time and resources.

Saul, Whisper, and I were equal partners in the business and they were repaying the initial investment at three hundred dollars a month, each.

I took in a deep breath through my nostrils and smiled, thinking that a poor black man from the deep South like myself was lucky not to be dead and buried, much less a living, breathing independent businessman.

Our little agency had a separate entrance that opened onto a stairwell made only for us. I took the steps two at a time until I reached the third-floor doorway. There I stopped again, happy that I wasn't dead and that soon, if the sky didn't fall that day, I'd be engaged to the lovely Bonnie Shay.

"Good morning, Mr. Rawlins," Niska Redman greeted.

She was our receptionist. Butter-skinned, biracial, and quite beautiful—Niska had worked for Whisper after he saved her father from false charges alleged by a business partner. She was twenty-four and filled with dreams of a world in which all humans were happy and well fed.

"How you doin', Miss Redman?"

"Great!" she exclaimed, showing wide eyes and lots of teeth. "I started practicing Transcendental Meditation. You know, only twenty minutes every morning and night and you have peace of mind all day long."

"That's like prayer?" I asked.

"More like yoga or hypnosis," she said. "How are you?"

"Down to one cigarette a day and I walked to work this morning."

"Good for you."

"Whisper in?"

Her nod was vigorous and certain. "Nobody with him," she added.

His door was open but I knocked anyway.

"Come in, Easy," he said in a low tone.

Whisper's face was medium brown with no marked features. You might overlook him even if he was standing right there in front of you. He wore short-brimmed hats of gray or brown without feathers or even a hatband. His clothes were not new or old, natty or disheveled. He only spoke in a low voice, not a whisper, and no one I knew had ever seen his apartment or house. There were some that believed he was married, and one woman I knew swore that she'd seen him sitting in the last pew at Lion's Den New Baptist Church.

"How's it goin', Tinsford?" I asked, taking the straight-back pine visitor's chair set in front of his small, battered oak desk.

Instead of answering he looked at me with dark brown eyes that contained a question.

"What?" I replied to his unspoken inquiry.

"Somethin' up?"

"No. Why?"

"Somethin' happy about you this morning."

"How's that thing with, um, what's her name?" I asked, avoiding his question out of nothing but pure stubbornness.

"Lolo Bowles," Whisper said, "Keisha Bowles's daughter."

"You locate her yet?"

"Not in the flesh but I got some leads. You know anybody run one of those clinics gets you off of drugs?"

"Saul's got a guy."

Whisper nodded and I stood up.

It was often the case that we asked each other questions, most of which went unanswered. We were all private sort of men who gathered information rather than distributed it.

Our corporation had been up and running for three months but it felt like years. I had never imagined that I'd enjoy working with partners, but just that one cryptic interchange between me and Whisper felt something like belonging.

My office was at the end of the hallway behind Niska's desk. It had been the master bedroom, making it the largest office with a nice view of a few green backyards. I would have preferred a smaller room but Saul and Whisper took those options before I finished signing the papers Kikuyo Harada had placed before me.

My five-hundred-square-foot office had dark oak floors and a huge cherrywood desk given me by Jean-Paul Villard, president and CEO of P9, one of the largest insurance companies in the world. JP liked me and was my good friend Jackson Blue's boss. When Villard heard that I was going into business for myself, rather than taking the managerial security job he'd offered, he sent the desk over just to show me there were no hard feelings.

I sat down in my padded mechanical chair, leaned back, and took out the little black velvet ring box that held a brilliant-cut half-carat diamond, set in platinum and gold.

In the last year and a half I had been as close to death as a living being can get and climbed my way back up into a world that seemed new and hopeful. I had two great kids, a perfect island woman that I would soon propose to, a profession I was good at, friends that I liked, and access to powers that most people in Los Angeles (white or black) didn't even know existed.

I had built the kind of life that I wanted, and once Bonnie said yes, everything would be perfect.

The buzzer on my desk sounded.

"Yes?" I said, pressing the button on the console.

"Raymond Alexander for you, Mr. Rawlins," Niska said.

"On the phone?" I asked, maybe a little hopefully.

"No, dude," Mouse called from the background. I could hear him on the phone and through my open door. "I'm right here."

"Send him on in," I said, thinking there was a reason that optimism didn't come naturally to people like me.

2

"How you doin', Brother Easy," Mouse greeted.

I stood and we shook hands. We were old-school American men and so did not hug.

"Cain't complain," I said with an irrepressible smile. Even the presence of one of the most dangerous men alive could not extinguish my delight with life. "Have a seat."

My visitors' chairs were made from a yellowish wood that was carved to accommodate the human form.

"Damn, niggah, you done burnt a cross in the white man's lawn an' made him like it," Mouse said as he sat back. Light-skinned and light-eyed, he was wearing a straw-colored suit with a Stetson of a wheat hue, a shirt that might have been dyed in blueberries, white silk socks, and patent leather black shoes.

He crossed one leg over the other and grinned at me.

"It's just an office," I said.

"Ain't another Negro in thirty blocks got a office around here, man. You know you just walk right in the lion's den and say, 'Pussy, lay down or get the hell out.'"

"Whisper with me."

"Tinsford's a good man," Mouse half agreed, "but you the one."

"LaMarque dropped by a few days ago. He said that you, him, and Etta went down to Ensenada to do some fishin'."

"Caught me a honest-to-God swordfish. Eleven foot long. Mothahfuckah fought harder than any man I ever killed. Shit. It was easier when I had to bite out that man's windpipe when I was handcuffed behind my back."

Mouse was a colorful man, his beauty defined by the distance one had from him.

"I never knew you to go fishing," I said, in an attempt to lighten our conversation. "Not since we were kids down in Houston."

"Etta want me to retire."

"Retire?"

Retirement was a huge word for Raymond "Mouse" Alexander. To my knowledge he had not held a legitimate job in all his forty-seven years. He might have pretended to be working for a company he planned to rob. He applied for a few jobs after the one stint in prison he ever served. But Mouse never punched a clock or looked at any man as his boss.

His money-making activities over the previous several years had been working with an international heist ring as a gunman, strong-arm, and wild card when the circumstances went south. He did two to three jobs a year and once told me that he made more than the president of Bank of America.

"Yeah," Mouse said, giving me a half shrug. "Etta said that a full-grown man shouldn't be making his family worry so hard when he go off to work. I told her that cops and soldiers do that every day. But she come back sayin' that cops retire after twenty years and I been a outlaw since I was five."

Mouse snickered. The truth is often funny.

It struck me that my lifelong friend might have been there to ask for a job. This notion further diminished my good mood. Both Whisper and Saul had told me that they would not be able to enter a partnership that included Raymond.

"So," I ventured tenuously, "what would you do if you retired? I mean would you take on some other kind of work?"

"I got me quite a pile saved up," he said. "And I been thinkin' about what you did."

"Meaning what exactly?" I can honestly say that at that moment there was no cheer in my heart.

Mouse looked me in the eye and smiled. He was a psychopath who had read maybe three books in his entire life but Raymond knew human nature as well as any psychoanalyst with a lifetime of experience.

I believe that he knew what was bothering me and reveled in my discomfort.

"Milo Sweet gonna purchase twelve rental properties for me and hire Fearless Jones to maintain the buildin's and collect the rent. Every unit'll be in Etta's name and I'll sit on the front porch livin' the life of Riley."

It was the best solution that my friend could have come up with. He needed a taxable source of income while Etta, his wife and my onetime lover, had to have a nest egg.

Mouse grinned. A ruby festooned one of his front teeth. There was a thick ring of gold and onyx on the baby finger of his left hand.

Our eyes met again and he waited.

"You the one come to me," I said at last.

"You evah hear of a brother named Charcoal Joe?" Mouse asked.

"Heard of him," I admitted. "I don't really know anything about him though. Plays poker and the horses. Got more luck than a rich man askin' for a bank loan." There were a few darker stories about Joe but I had no facts to credit them.

Mouse smiled again. "You always got the right words, Easy. Even if you don't know a thing, you never say nuthin' wrong."

I nodded, accepting the compliment, and waited.

"Joe's what you call a mastermind. He makes things happen where no one else could see the possibilities. He the one told me that doin' what I did here in L.A. was bound to lead to heartbreak. He connected me with the man in Cincinnati make my work possible all ovah the continent. Joe is connected like a spider on his web. One time there was this dude gunnin' for you—"

"Me?"

"Yeah," Mouse said, "man named Grindman, Cully Grindman. He'd been hired by another man, a man named Bashir. Anyway, Grindman aksed a waitress in a restaurant near your old office if she ever saw you in there, said you was a old friend and he wanted to say hi. That was Stella Rogers. She aksed one of Joe's people if she should get involved. Joe turned around and told me—now Grindman and Bashir in a graveyard out in East L.A. sharin' space with Sadie and Tesser Klieger."

Mouse was pretty good with words, too. Bonnie had a friend who worked with her as a stewardess on Air France, Ojayit Nadkarni. Ojayit's fiancé, Bashir, had beaten her twice and so she needed to get away. I got Jackson Blue to get her work on one of P9's company jets. She took the job and moved to Chicago.

I thought that was the end of it.

"So you see," Mouse continued, "in a way Charcoal Joe done saved your life."

"Grindman was a hit man?"

"Yes he was."

I didn't need to ask why Mouse hadn't come to me with this information. For him killing was simply a tool of the trade, hardly worth discussing. And we were friends. Where we came from this was the kind of thing that one friend did for the other.

"And what can I do for Mr. Joe?" I asked.

"Last night a white man named Peter Boughman and some other guy called Ducky were shot dead in a house down on the beach at Malibu. Ducky was killed outright and Boughman was tortured before they shot him in the eye and the heart."

"And Joe is involved?"

"Not directly. But he has a friend who has a son who went to that house, by accident, and fount the body. His bad luck was that somebody heard the shot and called the police, who got there before Seymour, Joe's friend's son, could call them himself."

"Seymour what?"

"Brathwaite. Dr. Seymour Brathwaite."

"I thought you said he was a kid?"

"Twenty-two-year-old doctor of physics. Doin' what they call postgraduate work at UCLA."

"White guy?"

"Not unless Sidney Poitier's a white guy."

"And what's in it for your friend Joe?"

"What was in it for him when he saved your ass?"

"The police arrested this kid?"

Mouse nodded.

"They book him for murder?"

"Yes, sir."

"So what can I do?"

"There wasn't no gun."

"They arrested him for what then?"

"Murder, conspiracy, breaking and entering, and resisting arrest."

"Again, what does Joe want from me?"

"He wants to talk to you about the circumstances of the case and to hire you to do what he needs done."

"Like put a couple of bodies in the Jewish graveyard in East L.A.?"

"Naw, Easy, he know that ain't your speed."

"If he doesn't want me to break the law, what does he want?"

"Whatever you ain't got words for you got a question, Ease. I'm tellin' you that my friend wants to meet with you and talk with you about a friend's son been arrested for murder. Ain't no question to that."

"When can I see him?"

"Tomorrow out in Venice."

"Why not today if he's so worried?"

"He's in the Avett Detainment Facility out there. The next visitors' day is tomorrow. Hours start at eleven."

"What's he in jail for?"

"'Bout two months ago a man saw Joe's automobile and made what the lawyer called a disparaging remark about its color, which was brown. Joe's reply was two shots over the man's head. They arrested him for discharging a firearm within city limits. He got around ninety days."

I was silent for the moment, biding my time. I couldn't say no to Mouse. He'd saved my life and had put his on the line for me many times. He was mostly evil and definitely a killer but black men in America had learned centuries ago that the devil not only offered the best deals—he was the only game in our part of town.

"All right," I said after the proper pretense of waiting. "I'll go down there in the morning. Who should I ask for?"

"Rufus Tyler. Prisoner number six-two-seven-three-one-one-L."

While I wrote down the name and number Mouse pulled a thick wad of cash from his breast pocket; this he placed on my cherry-wood desk.

I looked down at the wad and asked, "What's this?"

"Fi'e thousand dollars."

"Give it back to Joe," I said. "I haven't agreed to take the case yet."

"This money is from me, Easy. I'm the one hirin' you."

"Cheddar or blue?" I asked, taking the cash.

"Say what?"

"I just wanna know what kind of cheese is in this trap."

3

After our business was concluded Mouse and I sat around for a while talking about property and the philosophies that surrounded its ownership.

"So you always gotta be fixin' shit?" he asked me at the butt end of his sixth cigarette.

"Things have to be repaired," I said reasonably. "If the roof is leaking or the furnace breaks down, the landlord is expected to put that a'right."

"Expected by who?"

"The tenant, the city."

"If my pipes bust I fix 'em myself," he said indignantly.

"You own your house, Raymond. The tenant pays rent. He's just passing through. Anyway, Milo will look after the details. You just sit back and let Etta collect her due."

Raymond scowled, crushing out the butt. Before he could take out number seven I stood and said, "I got to go out to Pasadena and see Saul." For the past six months I had only smoked one cigarette a day, but every time Raymond lit up I was tempted to break that regimen.

I went to the walnut filing cabinet next to the door and took out a pine-tar barbecue starter-nugget that I'd purchased to assist my partner in crime-solution.

Raymond was on his feet by then.

"You'll go see Joe tomorrow?"

"Did you pay me?"

"Call me if you need some help."

"If I had to call you, you wouldn't need my help."

Mouse grunted a laugh and slapped my shoulder.

I had to walk home to get my car.

Raymond offered to give me a ride in his dark gray Lincoln but I wanted away from the smoker; anyway, walking the nearly deserted sidewalks of West L.A. had become a favored pastime.

Pico Boulevard was always a pleasant stroll. Even in 1968 the police still slowed a moment when they cruised by; but rarely, in daylight, did they actually stop black and Mexican pedestrians; not on the main arteries at any rate.

I went all the way to Point View and turned right, hoofing it three more blocks to my fancy two-story home.

I didn't even go inside, just took my deep maroon 1961 Super D/500 Dodge from the driveway, wended my way north to Sunset, and then took Coldwater Canyon Road across the mountain and into the Valley.

By the time I got to Pasadena it was almost ten. Saul Lynx was sitting in his dun-colored Studebaker half a block down from 213 Crest-Martin Way. I was going to rap on the passenger's-side window but the door came open before I got there.

Looking in, I saw my partner throwing newspapers, paper bags, empty soda bottles, and some official-looking papers from the front seat into the back.

"Hey, Easy," he said as he levered back and forth, making room.

"Is your house this much of a mess?" I asked him.

"Melba keeps a clean house," he said. "I'm pretty neat too. It's just these stakeouts collect junk and trash."

I climbed in and closed the door. Crest-Martin was a lovely street, wide and lined on both sides with oak trees. The homes were for the most part single-family dwellings built for kinfolk to grow old and die and to grow up and apart. The children were at school, mothers out shopping or watching the morning shows on TV. The men were at work; all except Bruno Medina, a package delivery man who permanently damaged his back on the job at Washburn Distributors. Bruno was collecting $935 a month in lieu of his salary and receiving another $1,600 to pay his medical costs; bills footed by Reliant Insurance Company.

Harry Harada had sold Bruno the policy, signed off on the payments seven months later, and then hired WRENS-L Detective Agency to prove fraud. If we could catch Bruno and then turn him against Karl Reuben, the doctor who ran a string of at least nineteen insurance cheats, we stood to get a bonus from the insurance consortium Harada represented, and with that the likelihood of future jobs.

"Want a buttermilk doughnut?" I asked Saul.

"From Toluca Mart?"

"Center's still warm."

The private supermarket made the pastries three times a day and Saul loved them.

Saul was a smallish man in a light green cotton suit, tan shirt, and a loosely knotted dark brown tie; the tie he wore more times than not. His nose was his one outstanding feature—protruding and somehow shapeless. Otherwise he was almost as nondescript as Whisper. Most people, when referring to Saul, would say, "You know, the guy with the nose." His cap, languishing on the dashboard, was camel brown. His pale skin now and then ignited the brilliance of his green eyes.

Between bites of a chunky doughnut and sips of lukewarm coffee he asked, "What you doing out here, Ease?"

"I told you I wanted to help."

"But you said after two weeks."

"Mouse came to see me."

"Oh."

"He hired me for a job."

"A detective job?"

"You ever hear of a guy named Charcoal Joe?"

Saul stared a moment, took a bite of fried dough, and said, "One time I had a missing-persons job; a girl named Doris Frye. She'd gone up to the Sunset Strip with some girlfriends and disappeared. Then one night, when I was parked in a car, in front of the house my information had guided me to—two big guys grabbed me and dragged me somewhere nearby. They threw me on a wet concrete floor in the subbasement of a house that was boarded up.

"When I looked up I saw this little, older black man standing in front of a wooden easel jabbing at a brown piece of paper with a charcoal stick. My hands and feet were tied and so I was quiet while the little guy drew. Maybe six minutes later he turned the easel around. It was a pretty good portrait of me. I might have been impressed if I wasn't scared shitless.

" 'You have a nice face,' the old man said. 'Big nose though. What's that nose doin' in front of my friend's house?'

"I couldn't think of a plausible lie and so I explained that Don and Lena Frye had a daughter named Doris and that Doris was last seen being dragged out of a club on Sunset. She'd gone up there with friends, two of whom had been drugged and grabbed but they managed to get away. I had information that Sam 'Meatmarket' Boll had taken other young women and pressed them into prostitution.

"The man stared at me for one long minute then looked up at his henchmen, who were, by the bye, white men, and then he turned away. I was taken back to my car and told to go home and wait there.

"Early the next morning there was a knock on my door. Doris Frye was there all strung out on heroin. I told Lena and Don that there was a clinic I knew and within two months Doris was back home, more or less in one piece."

"That sounds like a big-city fairy tale," I said, wondering what kind of floor I was destined for.

"Yeah. Two months later they found Boll between two big rocks in Laurel Canyon. His skin had mummified and so they could still tell where his throat had been cut."

Saul took the last bite of his doughnut and I handed the bag over to him.

With nothing to add or ask about Mouse's friend I said, "I'm gonna ask Bonnie to marry me today."

What Saul had and Whisper lacked was the ability to smile. A beautiful Jimmy Durante grin crossed his face.

"That's great, Easy. You think Jesus and Benita will come down for the wedding?"

My adopted son along with his common-law wife and daughter had moved to Alaska so he could get professional experience as a fisherman. Juice got a job on a salmon boat and hoped to get his own one day.

"Maybe," I said, looking down the street at Medina's red and dark brown ranch house. "Any movement on your guy?"

"No."

"How many days now?"

"Nine."

"Cops stop you?"

"I been pretending to sell insurance up and down the street. Harry gave me all the papers and told me what I should say. I got three housewives to consider life policies on their husbands. One gave me tea and kissed me good-bye."

"What's the backyard like?"

"Two of the houses that border his on the next block are empty all day—two twenty-one and two twenty-three. But an old lady named Dawson lives in two twenty-five. You want to keep out of sight from her."

"You got your camera?" I asked.

Reaching between his legs on the floor, Saul came up with a Nikon that had a six-inch telephoto lens.

"Keep it ready."

Staying away from the Dawson domicile, I walked up the driveway of the rightmost house behind Bruno's. Peeking through the high redwood fence, I saw that my mark had a lush backyard and that all the windows of his home had the shades pulled. A major drawback for insurance cheats is that they can't afford to be seen.

I forced two red planks apart and squeezed my way through to Medina's yard.

There were three big green plastic cans filled with leaves and branches next to the back of the house. I took out a sturdy branch and went from one closed window to the next, pressing against the inner frames to see if any of them was unlocked—the fourth attempt was the charm. Ever so slowly I pushed the window up maybe three inches. Then I dumped out one of the plastic green cans, took the pine-tar nugget and started it smoldering. I dropped the starter in the bottom of the empty receptacle, moved that under the cracked window, and dumped the contents of another can over it.

After that I moved quickly, jumping the fence to Bruno's neighbor's yard and then out through the driveway to Saul's car.

He was in the passenger's seat now so I slid in behind the wheel. We were both grinning. Five minutes later the front door to Bruno's house flew open and he came running out with nary a limp. He was followed by a plume of fairly dark smoke.

Dense smoke from a leaf-and-wood fire is a wonderful tool for getting a man on his feet. He was standing straight up without the help of crutches or a cane, there in the front yard of his Pasadena home. It was then that he felt naked, exposed. He looked around and saw Saul snapping pictures out the passenger's window of his car.

Bruno was well named. He was the size of a brown bear, and now that he was cured he could move with nearly the same speed.

"Hit the gas, Easy!" Saul yelled.

Luckily Saul had already turned the engine over so all I had to do was press the pedal and steer. For six or seven seconds it seemed as though the hairy behemoth might have caught us. But we picked up speed and there was no traffic to hinder us.

Saul took a dozen shots of the big man chasing us.

"Damn, Easy," Saul said as we drove off, "I never knew how good it could be to have partners."

"Yeah," I agreed wryly. "Now we can get into three times as much trouble in half the time."

4

I drove us to my car six blocks from the angry man-bear. I had parked that far off because I knew how the trick would play out.

Getting behind the wheel, the sad-sack detective headed for the basement darkroom at our office to develop Harry's evidence. I drove my car to Studio City in the San Fernando Valley, where I had an appointment on Ivy Drive.

There was a diner a few blocks away from my destination and so I stopped there because I was hungry and the place looked nice: a big blue bunker with the red neon words MARVIN'S EATS standing up top like soldiers on parade.

The waitress gave me a startled look and then a fearful questioning gaze. She didn't say anything so I asked, "Am I too late for lunch?"

She, her name tag read INEZ, was about my age, mid-forties, with golden hair from a bottle, dark metal-framed spectacles, and midriff spread.

"No," she said. I couldn't tell what she meant and my expression transmitted that intelligence. "I mean yes, we are still serving . . . sandwiches and soup."

There were seven square tables and a long counter for solitary customers. At the far end of the red bar there was a pay phone on the wall. I took the seat next to it and ordered a tuna melt with chicken noodle soup, a glass of apple juice, and a cup of black coffee.

After she served the drinks I dropped a dime in the phone slot and dialed a number. Some of the newer phone booths had digital buttons but most stayed rotary through the seventies.

"Hello," he said after the seventh ring; his voice deep and grumbling.

"Hey, Melvin."

"Mr. Sugarman, what can I do for you today?"

We had agreed that whenever I contacted Mel at his office, three doors down from Chief of Police Tom Reddin, I would use the pseudonym *Sugarman*. It didn't look good for a police officer in Captain Suggs's position to be sharing information with a Negro like me.

"Last night a man named Peter Boughman and some other guy they call Ducky were murdered in a house down Malibu," I said. "A young black man named Seymour Brathwaite was arrested at the scene and charged with the killing even though no murder weapon was found. A friend has asked me to look into the crime because he doesn't believe that Brathwaite would have committed it."

"Sounds like regular police business to me," Melvin said. Melvin was deeply in my debt but he was a cop before almost anything.

"Be that as it may, can I impose on you to look into the particulars?"

Melvin's silence was his resistance so I added, "How's Mary doin'?"

Mary was the tough cop's Achilles' heel. She was a dyed-in-the-wool grifter but in spite of that he had fallen in love. When she ran away, trying to protect him from the men she worked for, I found her and fixed it so that Mel could keep her with him.

"Give me a day," he said.

I hung up the phone and a man said, "Excuse me."

It wasn't the good-mannered *excuse me* of a man who jostled your drink by mistake or cut through a line you were standing in. It was the gun-toting, badge-bearing command given by licensed sentries and officers of the law.

The motorcycle cop, replete with black leather jacket and hard white helmet, was standing next to my stool. I could smell his peppermint breath. He hadn't taken off the headgear because he might have needed both hands to subdue me.

"Yes, Officer," I said politely.

"What are you doing here?"

"Waiting for my tuna sandwich and chicken soup."

"I mean," the cop explained, "what are you doing around here—in this neighborhood."

"I had business in Pasadena and I live near La Cienega and Pico. My daughter goes to Ivy Prep and so I thought I'd grab a bite before school lets out."

"You work at the school?"

"No."

I was pleasant enough but I didn't see any reason to help him understand how a black man's child could go to a fancy private school in the Republican stronghold of the San Fernando Valley.

"Let me see some identification," he demanded.

"Why?"

"What?"

"Man, I'm just sitting in here, usin' the phone and ordering lunch. I haven't even bent a law. So why would you come in here, in a place don't even have windows, and ask me about my business?"

"Someone called, said that you looked suspicious."

Inez was standing at the swinging pink door that led to the kitchen—staring expectantly.

I held up my arms to show the policeman what was there. I had on a blue blazer, jade turtleneck shirt, and buff-colored trousers. I had been careful setting the fire and so nothing was singed, stained, torn, or out of place. In the eyes of the law I should have been no threat whatsoever.

"Suspicious of what?"

"ID."

My daughter was expecting me so I took out my driver's license, PI's ID card, and a special card that instructed LAPD officers to call a certain number before detaining me. That number was the private line of Anatole McCourt, special aide to special aide Melvin Suggs. Anatole was the most beloved police officer in L.A. He was big and strong and honest in a way that made you want to be good.

"How do you know McCourt?" the policeman asked. I never got his name.

"Call and ask him," I said. "Phone's right here. I'll even give you the dime."

"Don't get smart with me."

"One of us got to, man. I gave you everything you asked for— more. So now either call Anatole or take me in and call him from there."

The nameless cop hated me for a moment or so. He was used to being the boss on the street; especially with people like me—as if there actually were *people like me*. He made a movement with his shoulders that was in lieu of the violence he felt. Then he turned on his heel, stopped to confer for a moment with the waitress, and exited Marvin's Eats.

The woman brought my food and left it with no smile or kind word. And that was a victory for a man like me.

But it wasn't enough.

After my meal, on the way out, I stopped at the register to pay.

"That's three ninety-eight," Inez said, looking down.

"Tell me something," I said as I handed her a ten.

When she made no sound I added, "That cop told me that some-one here called and said that I looked suspicious."

Inez met my eyes then.

"What about me looks suspicious to you?" I asked.

She maintained our connection for a quarter minute or more, looking hard and deep. Finally she lowered her head again and said, "Nothing, I guess."

"Keep the change."

———

Ivy Prep was a gated school, surrounded by a large swath of desert soil. The guard, Lee Andrews, let me through with no problem and Feather was sitting on a bench with three white girls in front of the teal-colored main building.

The girls were all talking at once, laughing and swaying with the joys and dramas of their lives.

I pulled up to the parking lot that abutted the main building and waited for Feather to notice me. She didn't like me honking for her, and adolescent girls don't need their parents walking up on them and their friends.

I sat there for a few moments trying to forget the reality of the waitress and that cop; hoping that the world my daughter was headed for would be kinder, clearer, and more understanding. Bonnie and I were going to get married. We'd make a life for Feather and maybe our own children—and society would change; it would have to.

As I came to the end of this series of thoughts, Feather looked up and noticed me. There was a somber cast to her gaze but it wasn't embarrassment or discomfort at my presence. She excused herself from her friends and ran toward the car.

I got out to greet her. She threw her arms around me and hugged me tightly; her embrace catching me at the elbows, pinning my arms like a boxer trying to smother a flurry of punches.

This was unexpected. Feather was mature beyond her years and she loved me deeply—but she was a thirteen-year-old girl and cautious about any expression of love.

"Is something wrong?" I asked when she let go.

"No, Daddy, I'm just happy to see you."

"We saw each other this morning."

"I know," she said, a little discomfited. "I just missed you I guess."

On the ride home she was quiet but not still. She looked at a textbook now and then, and changed stations on the radio whenever a commercial came on. I remember a song that had the longest title, "Just Dropped In to See What Condition My Condition Was In" by

Kenny Rogers and the First Edition. Other than that, there was Otis Redding and Aretha Franklin alongside a slate of white pop artists. I tried to recall just when it was that black singers had begun to be played on white stations.

"Bonnie's coming back from France today," I said.

"Uh-huh."

"I'm going to ask her to marry me."

Feather turned to me with a stricken look on her sweet, light brown face. I thought that she was probably worried about having another female in the house. After all, Feather oversaw the greater portion of our domestic lives. She worked with our housekeeper, Alberta Hurst, on Saturdays and prepared meals at least half of the time. Whenever there was a decision to be made about furniture, parties, or even landscaping, I almost always deferred to her taste.

Bonnie getting in the middle of that might be a problem that I had not anticipated.

"When you gonna ask her?" Feather asked in a dialect she rarely used.

"Today."

"You want me to go over with you?"

"I don't think I'd have much use for help in a proposal," I said.

Feather grimaced and looked away.

At home she started making dinner.

I went to the living room and picked up the phone.

Bonnie answered after quite some time. "Hello?"

"You back, huh?"

"I came in yesterday," she said. "They put me on an early flight because one of the girls got sick."

"Oh. You should have called. I would have taken you out to dinner."

"I thought you were busy and I had all these things I had to do. The refrigerator broke down and I had to throw everything out."

"You need me to pick you up a new one?"

"How's Feather?" Bonnie asked.

"I'm not sure."

"Why not?"

"She's just acting funny. But you know kids change every day."

"I'm pretty busy, baby," Bonnie said. "A lot to clean up still."

"Can I come over a little later? I could help if you're still cleaning."

"Let me finish here," she said. "Then I'll take a shower and drop by you."

"Should I have Feather add a plate?"

"No. No, I'll just eat something here and drop by after dinner."

5

I could hear Feather walking around the kitchen. The little yellow dog, Frenchie, was standing in the doorway to the kitchen staring at me as he always did when I was away for more than half a day. When we first met I'd had vigorous and unexpected sex with his school-teacher mistress; a few days later she was killed. His canine mind associated the two events and he hated me until I'd almost died and Feather cried by my side every night.

Frenchie loved Feather and so found forgiveness, but upon seeing me anew there was a memory of hate in those button eyes.

I leaned down to scratch behind his ears and then went to a wood chair at the octangular table that dominated the dinette.

The morning had been cool and brisk and filled with joy. I was an independent businessman on the verge of getting engaged. I had partners and friends and loved ones—a future to look forward to. But after smoking out the insurance cheat, Bruno Medina, from his home, after being hired by Mouse to work for a man who might be even more dangerous than him, and then being accosted by a waitress and armed cop for my skin color, after having my daughter hug me for no reason and her dog having to forgive me my sins for the thousandth time—after all that, the only thing I could think of doing was to pick up the keys to my Dodge and drive over to Bonnie's.

_____

On the ride, I relived the time I was driving barefoot and ran head-long off a seaside cliff. I was drunk for the first time in many years and heartbroken over losing Bonnie to another man. Mouse found me and dragged me out of the bushes. My children sat by me for many weeks while I drifted in and out of consciousness. Bonnie came back to me, though until quite recently I had been unable to forgive her infidelity.

Fully shod and sober, it felt as if I was following the same disastrous path, though I couldn't have said why.

He was sitting on her front porch in a wheelchair, all hunched over with a light brown blanket draped across his shoulders. His chin was down to his chest, his head rising and falling on a derrick of labored breaths.

I approached and sat across from him on the white railing I had erected for the sweet pea vines that Bonnie cultivated in the spring.

Joguye Cham looked up at me. His face was older and less arrogant than when last we met. The loss of bravado revealed a strength in his eyes. He gazed at me for a long moment and then sat the rest of the way up. The blanket fell from his shoulders, showing that he wore a dark blue T-shirt and light cotton trousers that could be purchased at any J. C. Penney's store.

"Mr. Rawlins," he said in a deep voice that denied his decrepitude.

"Mr. Cham."

The African tribal prince took in a deep breath, found it restoring, and decided to take another.

"I was working to unite my people," he said as if answering the question *Why are you here?* "My father sent me to Oxford and I studied and I learned how the world worked. I told Bonnie that she would be my princess and that, and that I would make a new world for her in Africa, in Nigeria. I made alliances with big corporations, oil companies. There was money and weapons and a future where I believed my people could rise up and contribute to the world as we have always done for ten thousand years.

"When Bonnie told me that she was going to be with you I said, 'With that nigger?' I said those words and lost her. I said one word and lost her. Me, an African king, calling you by the white man's curse.

"That's why she left me. That's why she came to you. I went back home and shook hands with the white men who owned the oil company. We were friends. We drank together and smoked together; we had women and mapped out the future.

"And then one day I said, almost in passing, that when I was king of all the tribes I'd set up a central institution that would share the wealth that came out of the ground with all my peoples."

The dark flesh around Joguye's eyes wrinkled and tightened. I could see that the fingers of his right hand were clutched into a permanent petrified fist. Uncontrollably his left knee was bobbing up and down like a seamstress's joint working a foot-powered sewing machine. There was regret and acceptance in his visage.

"I have a cousin named Malik. His mother was my father's sister. He often drank and smoked and had women with me and the white men I worked with. I was to be the leader and he one of my trusted council.

"And then one day we were in his mother's house. He sent his servants away, closed his doors, and then he came to me with a pistol in his hand. . . ."

The blues, I thought, were not limited to the American South.

"He said to me," Joguye continued, "that I was stupid, stupid, stupid; that I had said words that could not be taken back, that I had made a vow that could only take everything from our families. I was a fool, he said, and then he shot me. I proved that I could not deal with the white oilmen, he said, and he shot me again. My father had stolen his mother's dowry, he yelled, and he shot me. He was crying and laughing and talking and shooting me until there were no more tears and no more bullets and I was dead on the floor of my aunt's home."

My mind at that time was looking for a way out of the pain and anger and loss that I and my nemesis both felt. I remember thinking when Joguye said that he was dead on the floor that this was *metaphor*, a word that Jackson Blue once tried to explain to me.

"A simile," Jackson said, "is when you say something is *like* something else. A apple is like the earth. A piano is like a hippopotamus. You see the similarity an' smile. But a metaphor is when that comparison is as close to true as it can be."

Joguye *was* dead on the floor, as I had been at the bottom of that coastal cliff.

"My cousin Jane Okeke, who loved me because I always played with her when she was a child, found me in my blood and got her husband to help take me to a white doctor and then to Air France.

"Bonnie came and found me. She took care of me the way I helped when your daughter was sick. She married me and she brought me to America because they are looking for me. As long as I am alive I pose a danger to them."

I was trying, in my mind, to make the word "married" into a simile; this instead of thinking about finding my gun and finishing the metaphor that Malik had started.

I noted then a livid scar on the left temple of the African. He'd been shot in the head, was confined to a wheelchair, and gnarled in a way that could never be straightened out. I hated him. He had taken more from me than his father had from Malik's mother but there was no recourse.

I stood up from the trellis and lifted the blanket so that it once again covered the ailing man's shoulders, then I walked off the porch and down to the sidewalk. The last time I was in that situation I tried to kill myself—but not again.

Feather must have known about Joguye; that's why she was so upset and loving toward me. She wanted to protect me, but she also loved Bonnie and respected the African prince who had brought her to the only doctors in the world that could cure her blood disease.

I owed Feather everything, and no pain would ever get in the way of that debt again.

"Easy."

6

My first instinct was to keep walking, pretending that I had not heard my name called in Bonnie's sweet, powerful voice; failing that, I stopped but didn't turn.

"Easy."

She touched my shoulder and I pushed down the desire to slap her.

"What?" I said, still with my back turned.

"Let's go somewhere and talk."

"What about your cripple up there?" I said, finally turning.

There was shock and pain in her face but that's not what caught my eye. She was wearing the snug-fitting yellow dress that always got me excited. The hem only made it to the middle of her dark brown thighs. Her figure was right out there in the bright afternoon, but that wasn't what affected me either.

There was a whole story behind that dress. Bonnie always wore it as a prelude to our lovemaking . . . and she was coming to meet me. She was coming to make love to me one last time before creating a life with the has-been prince. Her loyalties and her heart were split.

"My cousin Gerard is coming over," she said.

"Where do you wanna go?"

"There's a new teahouse up on Melrose."

Henrietta's Tea House was a quasi-hippie joint that was decked out like a large living room. Bonnie and I sat side by side on a stunted green sofa. She ordered white tea and I coffee—black.

We'd spoken to the russet-haired waitress but not to each other—not yet. Our drinks came with scones and clotted cream, blueberry jam, and sweet butter.

"You married him," I said at last.

"To get him out of the country—yes."

"That's all?"

"At first." The second word stuck a little in her throat.

"And now?" The coffee was very hot, it burned my tongue.

"His swagger is all gone," she said. "All that's left is a revolutionary and a king who is willing to fight for his people. He's become the man he was supposed to be."

"And what about me?" I asked, regretting the words even before I spoke them.

"You were a grown man at eight years old," she said, "fully grown and living on your own."

"Do you like the scones?" the coarse-haired waitress asked. She was no more than seventeen; beautiful with a goofy grin.

"I always have them," Bonnie said kindly.

"Tamara makes them," she said. "She's my sister. I'm Barbara."

Barbara wanted to engage us in conversation but we had no room. I turned to Bonnie, and Barbara walked away.

"I know things haven't been right since the first time you got together with Joguye," I said.

"You don't need me, Easy."

"I was going to ask you to marry me today."

"Cham's manhood is gone," she said as if in rebuttal. "He needs someone beside him. He gives meaning to my life."

"What about my life? What about Feather?"

She put a hand on my knee but I pushed it off.

"I can't blame you," she said.

I twisted my lips in the way I used to when I was a little boy missing my mother after she died.

"You won't," Bonnie said then, "you won't hurt yourself, will you?"

This question ignited rage in my chest and shoulders. How dare she pretend to care about my well-being when I had the ring in my pocket and the words in my throat?

"Why the yellow dress?" I said.

Bonnie winced and looked away toward the picture-window front of the teahouse. Rays of sunlight coming in through the glass struck her left hand and right elbow. She sighed and tried to turn to meet my gaze—but failed.

I waited, wanting to touch her but knowing I shouldn't.

"We're going to have to run away," she said, giving me no more than a sidelong glance. Then she turned full-face. "And I wanted to have, to take your baby with us."

That lesson was deeper than the understanding of metaphor. Bonnie taught me something about humanity right then. Here I'd been living movie plots and novel scenarios while there were men and women like Joguye and Bonnie in the world, digging their hands into the mud and making life: everyday pedestrian Christs—both frail and omnipotent.

I opened my mouth but there were too many words to say; they jammed together, wanting to be heard and to make sense at the same time.

"You don't have to say anything," Bonnie uttered. She took a sip of tea and nodded at the cup.

Everything seemed so meaningful, so painful and yet still so right.

It was at that moment that the transition came for me. I was like a little child accepting that morning had come and sleep was over.

"Mama Jo got people all over the world," I said.

The crinkling around Bonnie's nose and eyes asked me, *What are you talking about?*

"When Jesus wanted to go fishing up in Alaska she knew an Inuit shaman that took him, Benita, and their baby in. She knows witches and alchemists, lay philosophers and healers from everywhere in the world. I have no idea how she connects with them. But the people she knows ain't in no phone book or public register. They don't pay taxes, answer the census, or even have driver's licenses in their own names. They won't be found unless they want to be."

"I don't understand what you're saying," Bonnie told me.

"If I ask her to help you and your, your husband, she'll send you to a place that neither the FBI nor all the tribes of Africa could find."

It was Bonnie's turn to be amazed. She expected brutal words or even blows; she was ready for violent sex in retribution for what her man took from me—but she wasn't prepared for me to offer help. I hadn't expected it myself.

"I'm gonna be on a job starting tomorrow," I said, when my ex-girlfriend was speechless. "But I'll get word to her and she can get word to you."

"And what about the other thing?" she asked.

"You should have Joguye's child."

"That can't happen," she said with all the finality of a death notice.

There were words to say, a motel room somewhere to hire; there was all the love I felt for that woman and the genetic directive to procreate, but I said, "I can't do that, baby."

"Why?"

"Because I got to let you go . . . completely. And if I knew I might have a child out there somewhere worryin', a child hounded by assassins . . . well, I just wouldn't be able to sleep right."

Bonnie bent forward to kiss me but I leaned away.

She nodded her acceptance.

I stood up, leaving ten dollars for Barbara.

"Hello," said Jackson Blue's wife, Jewelle MacDonald, answering her own phone.

"Hey, girl." I was standing at a phone booth on Fairfax just north of Olympic.

"Easy." Jewelle had a soft spot for me. She said that it was because she liked intelligent black men, but I think she knew that I'd cross hell and high water for any friend.

"Bonnie married the prince and now there's all kinds'a people after them," I said, deciding to explain myself in broad declaratives. "I need either you or Jackson to hide them until I get a more permanent answer."

"Um . . . sure."

"Can you send a car to pick them up at Bonnie's place?"

"Okay, but how are you?"

"I don't wanna talk about it, Jewelle. What's done is done. What I need now is for you to do what you can."

"Jackson's out on Jean's yacht but I can get the company limo."

"Thanks."

"We should get together, Easy."

"Also, can you take Feather for the night?"

"I'll pick her up myself."

"How's the baby?" I asked, just to show that I wasn't completely devastated.

"Olivia is fine," Jewelle said. There was some hesitation in her voice. She probably didn't know that I knew she'd had a revenge affair after Jackson had a fling with another woman. The problem was that the baby might not have been Jackson's. I knew the whole story but kept it secret so as to spare her unnecessary pain.

Feather was my next call.

"Hello?"

"Hey, honey."

Silence and then, "Did she tell you?"

"Yeah. Yeah. Yeah, yeah, yeah."

"Are you okay, Daddy?"

"I am."

"You not gonna drink?"

"I am not. But I do need to be alone for a bit. Jewelle's gonna take you for the night. She'll get you to school tomorrow."

Adolescent girls don't like being shuttled around haphazardly. They want to be heard and in control of their environment. That's how I knew the degree to which Feather was worried about me; because instead of arguing she said, "Yes, Daddy."

Those two words told me how much pain I was going to feel.

"I'll call you later on," I said.

"Daddy?"

"What?"

"Should I take Frenchie with me?"

"Yeah, yeah. Jackson likes the dog and I might have my hands full."

7

It's a long way from West L.A. to Watts.

It's the same city but a darkness descends as you progress eastward. You pass from white dreams into black and brown realities. There were many miles to cover but distance was the least of it. It was another world, where I was going.

In West Los Angeles, when people looked at their TVs they saw themselves and what they wanted to be: James Arness and Lorne Green, Mary Tyler Moore and Lucille Ball. They had their own jokes and music and interpretations of right and wrong in the world. People in Watts saw the same shows but not their faces, their dreams, the hard facts of their lives. In Watts, people spoke the same language in different dialects and at separate schools. For darker-skinned citizens *employment* was synonymous with *toil*. The police were often the enemy, as the motorcycle cop had been for me out in Studio City.

I parked close to the curb at 114th Street and Central Avenue. There a black door was wedged between Bob's Hardware and Center Five & Dime (both looted, scorched, and then boarded up after the riots three years before). There was no sign or promise on that tar-colored door. If you didn't know what lay on the other side, you just walked on by.

It was nineteen paces up the first tier of stairs while twenty-three steps made up the second. There, at the top of the three-story structure, was another door jacketed in green metal.

I knocked and a slat in the wall slid open next to my head. Yellowy eyes anchored in dark flesh glared at me, and then the green door opened wide.

Seated on a tall brown stool was Elias Shaw—three hundred and then some pounds of muscle, hard fat, and bad intentions. His skin was only a shade lighter than mine and the crowbar in his hand was in lieu of the .45 in his back pocket. He wore overalls and a long-sleeved yellow shirt (to match, I imagined, the "whites" of his eyes).

"Easy Rawlins," he said aloud, as a vassal to royalty might announce an arrival at the king's ball.

The room was large and bright because the sun was still out and the roof was mostly skylight. There were maybe twenty-five patrons in the illegal saloon. Chuck Berry was wailing from the jukebox and John was standing behind the bar. His darkness, strength, and proportions were mythic. He was both ugly and attractive, tight-lipped with eyes that told you everything you needed to know.

I walked up to where he was drying a glass mug and took a seat there before him, again reminding me of some kind of audience with royalty.

"What's wrong with you?" he asked after just a glance.

"I'm here, ain't I?"

There was both evil and forgiveness in John's grin. He took a bottle with no label from under the mahogany bar and poured a long drink into a slender glass that he then set before me. I looked at the glass a moment and then swiveled around to take in the environs of the only kind of black business that throve in Watts in those days.

The patrons of the Black Door Bar were mostly around my age, and all black. Chesa Tambor, a Louisiana Creole, was sitting at a small blue table with Fisk Ryan. Fisk had only recently come out of prison for murdering Chesa's lover (and Fisk's best friend) Bob Stods. Fisk did six years and I was told by various acquaintances that

Chesa and he had reached a rapprochement while he served his time. After all, she'd had the clandestine affair with Bob; so in a way she was the source if not the cause of his death *and* Fisk's imprisonment.

Soul Benton had the three youngest women in the room sitting around his table. I didn't know the girls' names but I could know any or all of them for twenty dollars a head—so to speak.

Mike Twine and Hugh Short were at the pool table. They were both sharks, and John had laid down the law that they could play but could not bet on the premises.

"Hey, Easy," Louise Lash said.

She was maybe forty with a face that would be beautiful twenty years after her death. Her skin was black and flawless. Even when she wasn't talking her mouth seemed to be saying something elusive.

"Lou."

"I hear you all rich nowadays."

"I'm workin'."

"That's rich."

"How's Jackman?"

"Moved back to Texas," she said with something like a sneer on those sculpted lips. "Not before he got me pregnant—twice."

Our eyes met. Louise had always liked me. Ten years before, we'd spent three days in a cinder-block house five miles north of Ensenada.

"You know Jewelle MacDonald?" I asked my onetime paramour.

"Yeah."

"She could give you a job cleaning out apartments rented by the week to traveling businessmen."

"I need to feed my kids tonight."

Truth between men and women, after all the make-believe was over, was something that had to be recognized.

I handed her a twenty-dollar bill and John came up from his side of the bar.

"All right, Lou," he said. "You got what you need so either spend it or move on."

"You want me to make you some dinner, Easy?" she asked, ignoring the master of the house.

"Not tonight, baby. Like I said . . . I'm workin'."

The handsome and beautiful woman pushed one shoulder in my direction and then shoved off toward the door.

"You a soft touch, Easy," John chided.

"Not much joy in a rock, John."

"You right about that. You gonna drink that liquor?"

"Don't know yet."

"When you gonna find out?"

There was a small man, the color of tarnished gold or buffed bronze, sitting at a table about fifteen feet from the bar. He was older, maybe in his sixties, and nursing a beer the way my old friend Odell used to—before he died.

"My girlfriend ran off and married an African king," I said.

"Damn."

"That ain't all, man. The king crossed the white men that really own his country and they got the other kings out there trying to hunt him down."

"That sounds like a problem solve itself," John observed.

"Yeah," I agreed, "but like you said . . . I'm a soft touch."

"So why ain't that glass empty then?"

The rheumy eyes of the old man watching us seemed to be asking the same question.

"I can say it," I said to John, "but I don't feel it."

"You mean you not mad?"

"No. But worse than that, I don't feel anything at all. I mean when I saw him and she told me I was angry but you know even then it felt more like reflex than I was gonna be like Fisk there an' kill somebody. I even told her that I'd help them get away."

John's smile was better than his grin. In its glow you felt understood.

"You and me a lot alike, Easy."

"How you see that?" I asked, realizing that I was slipping into the dialect of my upbringing like a tired man putting on his favorite pair of worn house shoes.

"Somebody does somethin' wrong or gets wrong done to 'em then you go out and find out who did what and what happened where. You fix the problem after the damage been done. Me, I'm what you call a crime prevention specialist. Men and women come to me when they just about to blow. They think they comin' in for one drink, just enough fortitude to go out and kill the no-good mothah-fuckah wronged 'em. But then I give 'em another drink and we start talkin' about old times and better days ahead. Between the liquor and the talkin' you get some medicine and more times than not the crime don't happen."

"That's the glass you put in front'a me?" I asked.

John nodded.

"But what if I don't drink it?"

"That's okay. It's right here and you are too. The liquor will guide you. You got to make a choice. Now maybe in your case you already did but now you got to accept it. So either you drink or you don't . . . the answer's the same."

A man I didn't recognize walked up to the bar three stools away. John moved over to greet him and I took out my one cigarette of the day. I'd been carrying around a pack of Lucky Strikes for ten days so it was half gone. I lit the tobacco stick and took in a deep breath.

The wonderful thing about one cigarette a day is that whenever you lit up it was always the first and therefore the best smoke of the day. I loved Bonnie but I'd been smoking since I was ten years old; that tar and nicotine brought back a whole lifetime of laughter and tears.

"Excuse me, mister," someone said.

It was the old gold- or bronze-colored man that had been watching from the distance. I was sure that he was going to ask me for a cigarette.

"You gonna drink that liquor?" he asked.

"No, brother. Help yourself."

He hopped up on the stool next to me and put away the special bootlegged brew that John kept for his favorite customers.

"You Easy Rawlins, right?" my new friend asked.

"What's your name?"

"Hollis. Hollis Pressman from southern Illinois. I used to be a porter but now I play the horses on Tuesdays and Thursdays and take the bus out to the beach Mondays and Wednesdays."

"What about Fridays?"

"If I win at the horses I go ask Soul Benton for a girl and I give John two bits. If I lose John give me the beer I paid for when I was flush."

I laughed out loud, realizing that John was right; that whiskey was my medicine even if somebody else drank it.

8

I called Jewelle from John's phone in the back office.

"Hello?"

"That you, Feather?"

"Hi, Daddy! Are you okay?"

"Yeah. How come you answered the phone?"

"Jewelle's with the baby and everyone else is gone. Are you okay?"

"I wouldn't go that far, Sweet Pea, but I still got my shoes tied and I haven't had anything stronger than Dr Pepper. How's Jewelle and Jackson?"

"Olivia is beautiful. Aunt Jewelle let me hold her while she cooked and stuff. I'll do my homework after dinner and Uncle Jackson's going to take me to school in the morning."

"I'm sorry if I threw you off schedule."

"Uh-uh, Daddy. I know you got a lot on your mind."

"Tell Jackson that I'm gonna call him soon.

"Okay. I will."

"I love you."

"Me too."

John lived at his bar. There was a whole one-bedroom apartment behind the office. When business slowed down, Brawly Brown, John's stepson by his ex-wife, showed up to tend bar.

John took me into the kitchen, where he made a dish of fried sausages, new potatoes, onions, peppers, and chilies. It was a meal you wouldn't find on any restaurant menu—not even in Louisiana.

After eating he leaned back in his chrome and yellow vinyl chair and stared.

"Why you here, Easy?"

"Food and friendship."

"If that was it you'd be home with your child. You give your liquor to Hollis so you still on a wagon."

"You evah hear of a man named Rufus Tyler?"

John let his chair settle back down so that he'd be on four solid legs. That was enough to let me know the depths I'd entered.

"Charcoal Joe," John intoned.

"That's what Mouse said."

"Joe was Mouse before there was a Mouse."

I felt a tickle at the base of my skull.

"Joe," John continued, "has been in turn what they call a prodigy, an undertaker, thief, artist, grim reaper, card counter, riddle-maker like you wouldn't believe, rich as Midas, and as close to a fallen angel that a mortal man can get.

"He was born in New York City to parents from North Carolina, I believe. They all came out here in the late teens, early twenties, where Edgar Tyler started a mortuary and his wife, Sharon, stayed home while Rufus went to school. Boy could drain a corpse, play cello, and do your portrait all in the same day.

"At seventeen he got the gambling bug and won at every game he played. A white dude named Foner found out how good Rufus was and would bring him out to rich white men sayin' that he got a nigger could beat any or all of them. These was mostly oilmen from Oklahoma so their pride was threatened 'fore their billfolds got emptied out.

"One man, I forget his name, said that he was gonna kill Foner and Joe. He was known as a man of his word but Joe didn't care; he cut a deal with Foner and the oilman's wife. For twenty thousand dollars he'd kill the rich man so that nobody would evah know any of them were involved."

"And did he?" I had to ask.

"The man was killed and all three had alibis so tight that not even the KKK would have indicted Joe."

"How'd he do that?"

"I don't even wanna know, Easy. You don't either. Rufus Tyler don't play according to our rules. He got a whole other thing goin' on. If you after him—stop. If he want somethin' from you then give it up and move on."

"What if he wants to hire me?"

John met my eye and then shook his head slowly like a soothsayer reading his favorite child's bad fortune.

"Then it's like my mother used to say," he said.

"What's that?"

"When the evil eye is on you, all you can do is hope that there's a God out there with your name somewhere on his mind."

I smiled at the blessings of black mothers.

"You wanna sleep on the couch?" John offered.

It was late and I'd just lived through six or seven days rolled into one. I nodded and he went to get me a blanket.

The old red leather sofa had been with John for many years. He had it through half a dozen bars, two marriages, in storage during a three-month stint in the county jail for assault, and even for a while there when he was homeless and EttaMae Harris kept it for him in her garage.

It was worth it. That was the most comfortable couch I'd ever encountered. When you sat on it, it was both soft and supportive; when you laid down it was as if a celestial hand was holding you in inevitable sleep.

I dreamed about Bonnie.

She was naked coming out of the Caribbean ocean with water flowing down from her head and over her breasts. She smiled at me and I felt the pain of loss.

"You missed your chance, Easy," she said.

"I know."

"Are you going to do anything about it?"

Now she was wearing that yellow dress and the question took on new meaning.

I looked at her pretending, even in my dream, that I was actually considering the question.

"No," I said. "No. You were meant to be a queen and I'm just a man without a country."

"I love you more than anything, Easy."

"I couldn't ask for more than that."

Something fell somewhere.

I opened my eyes and saw a figure in the dimly lit living room. It was a young, very young, brown woman with a red towel loosely wrapped around her otherwise naked body.

"I'm sorry," she said, smiling and moving her left shoulder in an apologetic gesture.

I sat up and inhaled.

"Easy Rawlins," I said.

"Monica Fairfield," she replied.

"You with John?"

"Is that his name?" she answered.

I stood up, fully dressed.

"I was lookin' for the toilet," she said.

"Second door on the left over there," I obliged.

She smiled again. Even in the dim light I could see the beauty of her youth.

She went into the toilet and the light in the living room came on. John was standing there behind me in a blue robe that might have been as old as his sofa.

"Pretty girl," I said.

"Soul leave me some company now and then so he can do business in the bar."

"She didn't even know your name," I said.

"I don't talk much to most people, Easy," he said. "They don't understand where men like us is comin' from."

On that early morning ride from Watts to the sea I considered John's words. We came from dark skins, darker lives, and a slim chance of survival. The fact that we once knew each other in Fifth Ward, Houston, Texas, and that we were both still alive and ambulatory, was a miracle in itself. Where we came from *he's dead* was as common a phrase as *he's sick* or *he's saved*. People died in our world with appalling regularity. That child keeping him company overnight would understand the meaning but not the feeling of the words John had to say.

I got to Venice Beach at a few minutes before 7:00 a.m. The waves were lackluster and the skies still misty before the sun's full force cleared them. But the air was crisp and the breezes salty. I had come a long, long way to get there: from Jim Crow through Hitler's war to a place that would seem deadly to most but was like a refuge to me.

"Excuse me," a man asked.

"Yes, Officer?" I turned to face the two white cops that had trudged through a hundred yards of sandy beach to get to me.

"Can we help you?"

"No, sir," I said with absolutely no anger in my heart. "I'm going to visit my cousin at the Avett Detainment Facility. They got him in there for huntin' rabbits within the city limits. I'm bringin' him a carton of Lucky Strikes and news from his wife who is sick and can't come herself."

"Avett's visiting hours don't start until eleven," one cop, the one with blue eyes, said.

"I know. But you see, I live out in Compton, been out here from Texas for four years and I've only seen the ocean twice. I figured that I'd leave early and get in a few rays before sittin' down with Junior."

What could they say? It was a public beach made for loitering. I wasn't drinking or exposing myself (other than my black skin, that is).

"Stay out of trouble," the brown-eyed cop commanded.

"Yes, sir," I said, "that's what I tell myself every morning I'm blessed enough to wake up."

The Avett Detainment Facility was the most informal jail I had ever seen. It stood against a hill behind a salmon adobe wall that was maybe four feet high. There was a sentry at the gate but no barbed wire, restless German shepherds, or armed guards on raised turrets.

I drove my car up to the wire fence thinking I could ram right through with four armed confederates and free or kill anyone I wanted.

"Yes, sir?" the middle-aged, paunchy guard asked me. He had grayish skin but still would have been called white. His eyes were pale with no discernible color. Deciphering his age would have required an algebraic equation that depended upon the variables of *smoking* and *liquor consumption*.

"I'm here to see Rufus Tyler," I said.

Those misty eyes doubted me.

"Name?" he asked.

"Ezekiel Rawlins."

He took a clipboard from the desk in his little booth and read with the help of an unsteady finger.

"No E. Rawlins on the list."

"I was told that you were expecting me," I lied.

"Who said that?"

"His lawyer."

"Hey," the guard said. "Don't I know you?"

"Not that I remember."

"You were an inmate up at Chino five, six years ago."

"Not I," I said, trying to keep the fear from coming out in my words.

I had not been incarcerated at Chino, or any other prison, but I was afraid of what that minimum-wage white man could make out of fancy or spite. In my fears (if not in reality) I believed that he could have me dragged from that car and put me in a cell below-ground for no reason except his faulty or fabricated recollections.

"What's the lawyer's name?" the guard asked, just that quickly losing interest in his own imagination.

"Sweet," I said, "Milo Sweet."

Milo *had* been a lawyer, and his name sounded like some shyster in a storefront promising accident victims that they could retire for life on a broken leg or paper cut.

"I don't have it here," the guard said, "but you could follow this path up to the main building. Maybe they got an update or something in Records."

The asphalt lane leading to the main building was a city block in length. The ways in and out were divided by a row of especially tall lemon bushes. Three prisoners, identified by their pink overalls, were tending the fruit trees.

I could have been driving up to the administration building of a small college.

I parked my car unchallenged and approached the front doors, which were at least locked. Peering through the wire-laced, possibly bulletproof glass, I waved at a tan white man sitting behind a small metal desk. He saw me but didn't respond so I tapped on the glass with a silver quarter.

The guard took this as an affront and jumped to his feet. He raced toward the door I stood at and yanked it open.

"Who the hell are you?" he challenged.

He was a skinny man, what some people might call an ectomorph. The waist of his pants was no more than twenty-eight inches and still loose. His belt was secured by its last eye, and the gun belt he wore over that seemed about to fall around his hips and knees to the floor.

For all his apparent frailty the white man with the tan skin was quite aggressive, jutting at me like a Jack Russell terrier harrying a lion.

"They sent me from the front gate," I said, half answering the question. "I'm here to see Rufus Tyler."

Charcoal Joe's given name had had no impact on the front gate, but the Barney Fife inner guard got a canny look on his mug when I mentioned the name.

"Who are you?" he asked again.

I told him.

"You have some kind of documentation?"

"You mean like a driver's license?"

"Hell no. I mean something telling us that you're here to see the prisoner."

"Mr. Tyler's lawyer didn't tell me that I needed it."

"I don't have any record of you," the angry man said.

"I don't wanna be rude, sir, but you haven't checked."

Easy in Wonderland, that's who I was. I had driven down the rabbit hole and found myself in a world where the rules were cracked and cockeyed. The thin-framed guard took my words as some kind of incantation. His anger disappeared and he shrugged.

"Behind me and down the hall to your left," he said, "second door on the right."

Without further engagement I followed the directions to a dark wood door with an opaque glass window dominating its upper half. Stenciled on the window were the words

DOROTHY STIEGLITZ
ASSISTANT TO THE ADMINISTRATOR

I knocked.

"Come in," a friendly female voice said.

I opened the door onto one of the smallest offices I had ever been in. No more than seven feet deep and a little less than twice that in width, there was only room for the assistant to the administrator, a slender desk constructed from a plank of wood held up by two metal filing cabinets, and a visitor's chair.

She stood up straight, looking quite nice in her gray pantsuit and red-rimmed glasses. Ms. Stieglitz was near my age with a Dorothy Lamour figure and graying black hair that made her look striking rather than old.

I suppose my eyes said what I was thinking, because the hint of an inviting sneer crossed her lips. For a man in my emotional state that smile was a boon.

"Yes?" Ms. Stieglitz said. "May I help you?"

"My name is Ezekiel Rawlins and I'm here to see Rufus Tyler," I replied, instead of giving her the answer on my tongue.

"Have a seat," she said.

I accepted the offer. It was a small, metal, institutional chair not made for form or comfort.

Sitting, I appreciated her again. She sneered nicely.

"Do you have the proper documentation?" she asked.

"The man at the front door asked me that," I said. "I told him that Mr. Tyler's lawyer hadn't apprised me of that necessity."

I thought she'd like fancy words. I was right.

Dorothy gave me a broad grin and said, conspiratorially, "We cannot allow visitation without documentation."

"If that's so, I've come a long way for nothing," I lamented.

"What is your business with Mr. Tyler, Mr. Rawlins?"

"That's between him and his lawyer."

"What's the lawyer's name?"

"Milo Sweet."

"Do you have his number?"

I did.

I waited patiently while the handsome assistant to the administrator dialed, listened, and then said, "Yes, may I speak to Mr. Sweet? . . . Dorothy Stieglitz from the administrator's office at Avett Detainment Facility." A moment passed while, in some distant part of town, Loretta Kuroko called into the open door behind her, and Milo got on the phone.

"Yes, Mr. Sweet, I have an Ezekiel Rawlins here saying that you have directed him to meet with inmate Rufus Tyler. . . . You are Mr. Tyler's lawyer? . . . But we don't have any record of that request. . . . I see. Yes, Central Records is notorious for dropping the ball. You should have contacted us directly. : . . I understand. . . . Yes, yes."

She hung up the phone and smiled at me.

"Everything seems to be in order, Mr. Rawlins," she said. "Mr. Sweet made his request through Central Records, and even though that is perfectly acceptable the people there aren't always running on a cogent time schedule. His request was probably lost between offices. But even though I believe you, I don't have the authority to let you in to see Mr. Tyler. You'll have to talk to the administrator—Mr. Bell."

She stood again and said, "Let me show you."

I shifted to the side, letting her go past. When she drew close I caught a whiff of the perfume *Tabac*. The tight scent fit her look.

Following her into the empty hallway, I felt an urge to ask a question.

"At the end of the hall," she said. "The last door."

I wanted to ask for her home phone number. I thought that she might want to give it to me. But I was on the job and any disruption could cause serious problems.

So instead I shook her hand and said, "It was really very nice meeting you, Ms. Stieglitz."

"You too, Mr. Rawlins," she said with emphasis.

"Who is it?" a masculine voice said to my knock on the glass and wood door of Administrator Desmond Bell.

Instead of answering the question I opened the door, entering the anteroom of the man in charge.

The uniformed male receptionist looked up at me and then stood.

"Yes?" he said.

He was wearing the gold and brown costume that all the guards had. He was white and tall and maybe in shape. He had a sidearm on his hip and a cap set on his desk. The anteroom was exactly the size of Ms. Stieglitz's office. A really big man might feel claustrophobic in such a space.

"I'm here to talk to Bell," I said.

"I don't have any—"

Before the nameless guard could voice his doubts the door behind him opened.

"Mr. Rawlins?" an egg-shaped man in a natty, dark blue uniform said. He had his cap on his head.

"Yes," I replied. "Mr. Bell?"

"Warden Bell," he corrected. "Miss Stieglitz says that a lawyer has caused a snafu for your visitation."

"So it seems."

"Come in, young man," he said, though he was probably younger than I. "Come in."

10

The administrator's office was opulent compared to those of his receptionist and assistant. It was a large room with a dark blue carpet and lavender-colored walls from which hung various diplomas, photographs, and one painting. The painting was a portrait of Administrator Bell in the same dress uniform he was wearing that day.

He settled behind a broad mahogany desk gesturing at three yellow padded chairs that were set out as if for visiting dignitaries.

"What can we do for you at our little prison?" he asked when we were both seated.

The most dangerous people in the world were men like Desmond Bell. They became SS officers and postmasters; church deacons and cops. In their minds there was always a marching band playing the tune that they stepped to.

He was an administrator of a detainment center but called himself the warden of a prison. He was supposed to wear a suit, not a uniform. But I wasn't there to treat the incurable ills of megalomania.

"I was sent to meet with Rufus Tyler," I said.

"Ms. Stieglitz says that paperwork is most likely lost."

"I don't know anything about that."

"What is your business with Inmate Tyler?"

"His lawyer needs me to ask him a series of questions and he's too busy to conduct the deposition himself."

"What questions?"

"Sorry," I said, "but that's client-attorney privilege."

"I don't understand," Administrator Bell said. His skin color tended, ever so slightly, toward yellow and I believed that his head was bald under that hat. "Mr. Tyler pled guilty in court and has already served more than half of an eighty-seven-day sentence. I haven't heard that he's contesting the decision."

"Another case completely," I said, believing that brief was better with Administrator Bell.

His eyes were deep blue and his lips both small and protruding, like a cartoonist's rendering of a personified baby duck.

Pursing those lips further he said, "Is there anything that I should know?"

"I don't get you," I said, affecting an innocent stare.

"Does this visit have anything to do with Avett?"

"Not in the least," I assured him. "Mr. Tyler was married at one time and the ex-wife has taken him to court. That's all."

"And are you a lawyer?"

"No. I'm just a man with a high school diploma and a list of questions."

Bell tapped the long, manicured nails of his pudgy fingers on the desktop.

I was thinking that the whole encounter so far was like a comic interpretation of Franz Kafka, one of Jackson Blue's favorite writers.

Bell pressed a button on a console to the left of his emerald green blotter.

"Stoltzman," he said.

"Yes, Warden Bell," a disembodied voice said.

"Have Willow come to my office."

"Yes, sir."

"Miss Stieglitz said that she spoke to the lawyer in question," Bell then said to me.

"Yes she did."

"She's got quite a body, don't you think?"

"She never stood up," I said.

"That's a shame. You know sometimes she wears those Jayne Mansfield sweaters and soft fabric bras. On cold mornings you can see her nipples from down the hall."

I liked nipples. I liked Miss Stieglitz. Desmond Bell, on the other hand, would be detestable in any color, nationality, or era.

"Willow's here, sir," Stoltzman said over the intercom.

"Send him in."

The door came open and I turned in my yellow chair.

The guard that entered was an affable-looking young white man. He wore the same uniform as the other guards but it had a civilian look on him. Locks of his longish blond hair came out from under the cap at the forehead and over his left ear. He was smiling and moved with almost feline grace. The top button of his tan shirt was undone and the golden trousers seemed to be of a better cut than those of his counterparts. I wondered if he'd had them tailored.

"Tom Willow," Administrator Bell said. "Mr. Rawlins."

I stood to shake the young man's hand.

"Hey," he said.

"Hello."

"Mr. Rawlins has an appointment with Inmate Tyler," Bell said. "The paperwork has been lost but I've assured myself that he's okay."

"You want me to take him back?"

"Yes," the pompous bureaucrat allowed. "But because we don't have the proper forms I want you to stay with him during the interview."

"Yes, sir."

We walked past Dorothy Stieglitz's closed door all the way back to the entrance of the administrator's building. But instead of turning right we went left down twenty-two granite steps to a very institutional-looking metal door that was painted light green.

Guard Tom Willow had a complex-looking key for the lock.

We went down a long hall to another metal door, used another key on it, and then walked down an even longer hall to yet another portal.

Willow's pockets were filled with keys.

The air in the halls was dank and close.

"This is more like it," I said as Tom looked around for the proper key.

"Say what?" he uttered.

"This jail," I said. "Up until now it looked more like a high school campus."

"Avett's one of a kind," he agreed and then jammed a key into the door.

We entered a room that had metal walls, floor, and ceiling—all painted a hideous orange. At the far end from the door we'd come through there was a counter behind which another gold-and-tan-clad guard stood.

"Hey, Maxie," Tom Willow said as we approached the counter. "This is Mr. Rawlins. Bell wants me to take him to Joe."

Maxie was short. Only his head and shoulders made it above the counter's edge. You got the feeling that he was trying to stand tall. His straining stature reminded me of tall women who slouched in an attempt to disguise their height.

"He's in bungalow eight," Maxie said in a surprisingly deep voice.

The short guard hit some kind of device under the counter and a set of double doors to our left opened onto a sunlit and grassy field.

"Come on," Tom Willow said to me.

It was a broad tract with salmon-colored buildings in the distance and fairly high triple-fences beyond them. Here and there inmates, identified by pink jumpsuits marked with random thick black dashes, sat on benches, played softball, or just lounged on the grass reading or napping.

"What kind of jail is this?" I asked aloud.

"Like I said," Tom Willow answered, "one of a kind. Sometimes the courts have to detain special defendants. The public would be up in arms if they weren't put in jail. So if they have to be locked away they send 'em here to wait until the lawyers and judges find a way to set them free. Or, like with Joe, he has to do a little time and so they let him do it here."

"Must be a pretty easy job."

"I hate it," the guard said with real feeling.

"What's to hate? You're down by the beach and the jail's more like a hotel."

"It's just California, man. Sun always shinin'. People say shit they don't mean. And everybody's from somewhere else. All I'm doin' is savin' up my money till I can go back to North Carolina and buy me a little commissary store in tobacco country. You know I miss the dogwood trees and words that sound right on people's tongues."

"So you're going to be a shopkeeper?" I asked.

"Commissary store," he said as a kind of correction. "I'll be out among the Negro tobacco sharecroppers. I'll do great because I'll give 'em a good rate and they'll be able to pay it off instead of goin' into debt to the plantation owners."

"That almost sounds political." We were nearing a large bungalow that had a big black number 8 painted on its door.

The guard stopped and looked at me.

"Don't get me wrong, brother," he said. "I don't believe in inter-marriage or integration or nuthin' like that but black people and whites got equal rights as Americans and everybody should get a equal try. I'll have me a nice white wife and kids but the people I work with will get a fair shake."

"The plantation owners might not like that," I suggested.

"Hell, my own daddy won't like it," Willow agreed. "But you know a man got to stand by his convictions."

No matter how crazy and contradictory they are, I thought to myself.

11

Bungalow 8 was the prison cafeteria. There was no one there eating and it was nearing noon. I figured that Avett Detention Facility had lunch at a decent hour; 1:00 p.m. or maybe even later.

To the right was a long serving station. Behind that cooks and helpers of many races were getting ready for the meal: chopping salads, flipping burgers, moving great kettles of soup and trays of sliced white bread.

To my left, at the far end of a room filled with long lines of pine tables and benches, three men were gathered—two standing and one sitting down.

Tom Willow and I approached the trio walking along an aisle formed by two equal rows of maybe nine sets of tables—the men at the end were all black men in pink jumpsuits. This struck me, I realized, because all of the prisoners I'd seen so far had been white.

"Hello, Mr. Tyler," Tom said to the seated man when we got within earshot.

"Tom," said the small dark man. Before him was a *New York Times* folded open to page two.

Taped up on the windows behind the trio were six newsprint drawings. These were charcoal portraits; mainly of white men in different attitudes and poses. One drawing was from memory, I supposed. It was of a naked Negro woman lying back on a dais, running the fingers of her left hand over her sex.

To Charcoal's left stood a light brown man of medium height with distrustful eyes. His pink jumpsuit didn't seem appropriate to his demeanor but that was the one rule that seemed constant at Avett: the color scheme of prisoners and guards. Only the administrator and his assistant broke these imperatives, and they were exceptions anyway, her being a woman and him an autocrat.

On Joe's right, standing at least six foot eight, was Ox Mason. Bison-brown Ox had broad shoulders, a thick frame, and a protruding belly made mainly from muscle, not fat.

"Ox," I said.

"Easy."

"You two know each other?" Joe asked in a voice so deep that it was disturbing; like the rumble of a wild animal that was considering a roar.

"We've met," I said.

"This is Easy Rawlins, Mr. Tyler," Tom said.

The little man's keen and amicable eyes studied me a moment.

"How do you know Ox?" he asked.

"He was forcing an insurance scheme on some shop owners that needed relief," I said. "I brokered a deal between him and them."

"I always meant to thank you for that, Easy," Ox said in a tone that was anything but grateful.

I shrugged slightly. I had been up against people much larger than I was since the age of eight. Considering my current height and weight, Ox wasn't nearly the largest among them.

"Some other time," Charcoal Joe ruled. "Today Mr. Rawlins and I have business to transact. Have a seat, Mr. Rawlins."

I sat down on the bench across from the artist. Tom took up a position behind and to my right.

"This is private," Joe said to Tom.

"Bell told me I had to stay."

The little boss kept his eyes on Tom and, after a few moments, the guard moved off toward the kitchen workers. When the kindhearted racist was out of earshot the gaze turned back to me.

Rufus Tyler was somewhere between sixty and seventy, not heavy or thin. I imagined that if he stood up he'd be five and a half feet tall. His danger was primarily an intellectual experience—with the exception of his deep voice. He looked like a schoolteacher in pink overalls but you knew, if you had the brain, that his power was something to reckon with.

"What do people call you?" I asked to break the short silence.

"From saint to shithead, take your pick."

"I meant Joe or Rufus."

"CJ'll do just fine."

"Well, CJ, what am I doing here?"

"How long have you known Mouse?" he asked.

"Since we were children scramblin' 'round the streets of Houston."

"He says that when it comes to people and problems that you're the smartest man he's ever known."

"That's kind of how I've made my way," I admitted. "It started out tradin' favors. Now I'm a licensed private investigator."

"I don't deal in certificates," Charcoal Joe said. "Lots of fools got diplomas and degrees on their walls. What I need is a man who could get the job done. Are you that man?"

"I don't know."

"You don't know?" It sounded like a threat.

"I believe that a man should never make promises before he fully understands what it is he's expected to do."

"Mouse didn't tell you?" Joe asked, almost innocently.

"He said something about a killing up the coast from here. But you know, people gettin' killed in Vietnam every day. If you were to ask me to prove guilt or innocence in a war I'd have to decline."

"They gave William Styron the Pulitzer Prize last night," Joe said as if in direct response.

"I heard that. *Confessions of Nat Turner* getting an award like that is really something."

"You read *Ten Black Writers Respond*?"

"You mean *William Styron's Nat Turner: Ten Black Writers Respond*?" I said.

A wisp of a smile passed over the undertaker's face.

I hadn't actually yet read the powerful critiques of Styron's award-winning book. But Jackson Blue had. He reveled in the scathing black critiques written by everyone from Lerone Bennett Jr. to John Oliver Killens to John A. Williams.

"Saul Lynx and Whisper Natly."

"Whisper an' me never got along too well," Joe said, sitting back in his institutional wood chair. "He's smart as you could be but he think he better than most. That's a mistake only fools and brilliant men make.

"Now that Saul Lynx is a mothahfuckah. I still never found out how he traced that kidnapped girl to my ex–business partner. I seriously thought about puttin' him on this job but when I stacked it up it was you had the higher pile."

"What job are we talking about, CJ? Mouse told me a thing or two but I want to hear it from you."

Charcoal Joe leaned forward on the finished wood table, lacing his fingers and planting his elbows so as to form a perfect equilateral triangle.

"Life is hard in the big city," he said. "Poor people don't have no protection, no recourse, and no relief. That's why the young people have started up street gangs. Hell, that's why the Sicilians started the Mafia." The serious man in the pink overalls sneered and shook his head before continuing. "Most'a your poor people is black and brown. Some poor whites too. But even your better class of white people not immune. Peter Boughman for instance. The police fount him and another man on the floor of a Malibu beach house. Dead as mackerels washed up on the beach outside.

"They arrested a young man who had the misfortune of being found leaning over the bodies. That young black man only wanted to help. He didn't wanna hurt nobody. He had gone to Stanford and UCLA, got himself a PhD in physics before his twenty-second birthday, and still they arrested him, charged him, slammed that iron door, and closed the book.

"I want you to prove Seymour innocent. I want you to save my good friend's foster child from the gas chamber or even just one day in prison."

"You know this young man?" I asked.

"I know his former guardian."

"Does he work for you?" I pressed.

"No he does not, nor has he ever. We don't even know each other all that well. But I know the woman who cared for him and I know he wouldn't commit no murder."

"Maybe not first-degree murder," I allowed. "But he might have found an open window somewhere and went in lookin' for loose change and whatever. Two men come in on him and one thing leads to another. . . ."

"The young man is a doctor of science," Rufus Tyler the prodigy intoned. "He's teachin' at UCLA right this semester while he finishes his postgraduate work. Now how's a man like that gonna be some kinda niggah like the people you and me consort with?"

I could think of a dozen ways. The universities in the late sixties were hotbeds of bombers, Liberation bank robbers, and stone-cold killers.

I didn't share these opinions with Mouse's friend.

"Mouse asked me to come here," I said. "He put money down on the table and said that he wanted me to take any case you offered. He also told me that I was in your debt over a piece of information you shared with him."

Charcoal Joe shrugged and held up the palms of both hands.

"Information comes to me," he said. "Knowledge is the only real wealth any man can have; knowledge and the will to power."

I wondered if the gambler/killer/artist was referring to the German philosopher or just heard those words and instinctively understood their authority.

"You tell me what I need to know and I will go out to either prove or disprove Dr. Brathwaite's innocence," I said. "I won't lie or fake evidence but you can be sure that I'll give it my best."

Joe stared at me a moment. I was fully aware that such a look had probably meant the death of some men.

"Okay," he said. "Okay. I mean I say it's all right because I know Seymour is innocent and I believe Raymond when he tells me that you're the best.

"There ain't too much to add. The police know about the murders and you got an in with them I hear. Anything else you need you can get from Jasmine Palmas-Hardy."

"Who's that?"

"She was Seymour's foster mother up until he was eleven or twelve."

"What's her number?"

"She lives behind a house and up a stairway on Hauser." He gave me an address. "Just go there anytime today and she'll be waitin' for ya. Anything she says, treat it like you heard it from me. Anything you need: introductions, information, or cash—you just ask her."

Joe opened his eyes wide. This meant that the meeting was over. I realized that he had not introduced me to the medium-sized guy that stood at his side. I didn't ask because I understood that Rufus Tyler/Charcoal Joe never did, or did not do, anything in error.

12

At the end of Tucker Street, in a far corner of Compton, there was thick barrier of eucalyptus and avocado trees buttressed and interspersed by thorny bushes that might have been colloquially called barbed wire scrubs. Through this jungle there was a path that was barely passable. You were bound to get scratched and there were moments when a man of my height couldn't stand up straight. You definitely needed a long-sleeved jacket, and some boughs were stronger than Ox Mason.

But if you persevered for just three or four minutes you would reach a yellow door that had cracked veins of green lichen branching out here and there.

I had never been to that door without it opening before I could knock. I stood there maybe thirty seconds waiting for the yellow portal to swing inward. When it didn't oblige I rapped with my knuckles and then counted to twelve, breathing in the sharp scent of the leaf-heavy woods.

Even before she answered I knew that something was wrong, but when I saw her my concern made me forget my mission—at least for a while.

As a rule Mama Jo stood six foot three, two inches and a bit taller than I. Her stature had always been erect and unbending. Her skin was kissed by night, and her eyes were dark enough to see evil that poor mortals like me couldn't even imagine. She was nineteen years older than I, but, as a rule, no one would know that by looking at us.

That day Jo sagged and looked every one of her sixty-seven years. Sadness leaked from those barrier eyes; weakness too. She reached out for my shoulder and touched me lightly, showing none of the physical strength I knew she possessed.

"Easy?" she said. "Baby."

She fell forward into my arms, and I held her tightly as she cried and moaned a deep and painful lament that was beyond my ken.

"It was the earth that brought you here," she whispered.

The earth was her Goddess; not a sentient being but rather a concoction of forces that moved in mathematical precision, organizing spiders and grains of sand, human beings and clouds.

Her tears were hot on my neck, and I was reminded of the intimacy we shared twenty-nine years before in the swamplands between Texas and Louisiana.

"Baby," she said over and over.

"Maybe we should go inside," I suggested.

The sigh coming from her was deeper than Charcoal Joe's grumbling. She lifted up from my shoulder and I put an arm around her waist to help her into the medieval abode.

It wasn't until we were inside that I noticed that all she wore was a man's long-sleeved and navy blue dress shirt. It fit her as well as any modest dress; this was because it belonged to her son Domaque Jr. He was a monster of a man, deformed and different, with a soul as deep as his mother's and an innocence that had little use for his nearly impossible strength.

Jo was wearing that shirt because she needed love, and the love for her son was the gravity granted her by the earth spirit she revered.

The dwelling hadn't changed much. The floor was packed ocher earth. The ancient bench and alchemist's table still dominated. Small armadillos wrestled in their corner under the watchful eye of a cat that looked very much like a miniature lynx. A full-grown raven croaked at me from his shoulder-high stand and the bedding was still made from straw bound by thick hemp and coarse material. My regular chair, cobbled together from rough tree branches and animal hide, was there and the fireplace, which never emitted smoke above the forest keep, was crackling low.

The only real difference was the mantle above the hearth. The last time I was there it had been lined with thirteen candles all lit and winking. But now the previous inhabitants had returned: twelve armadillo skulls, six on each side of a man's head that had been cured in a barrel of salt for seven years after his death. Domaque Sr. yowled there. Jo had removed the macabre setting when Helen Ray, called Coco by her friends, moved in. Young, white, collegiate Coco was disturbed by the ex-lover's skull watching her and Jo writhing in passion on the straw mattress.

I moved to sit in my usual chair but Jo took me by the arm and said, "Come sit next to me on the bench, baby."

We held each other for long minutes. She'd stopped crying but the depths of her pain thrummed in our embrace. Her sorrow leached into me. I could read it on the mantelpiece and her nakedness under that beloved shirt. I knew it when she wasn't at the door waiting for me as she always had been, and in the emptiness of the cottage that would have been in style at any time in the last thousand years—somewhere.

"Go sit in your chair, baby," she said after our long embrace.

I did as she bade and our eyes met in the pleasant gloom of her otherworldly hideaway.

"How long she been gone?" I asked.

"Three days."

"What happened?"

"I, I wanted a baby. I guess that was too much for her."

"Some orphan?" I asked, being an orphan myself.

"We agreed that if there was to be a father it would be you."

I frowned and Jo peered into me and then gasped.

"Bonnie done gone," she said as a revelation. "Oh, baby, I'm so sorry. Here I'm such a mess I didn't see what was written on your heart."

I never asked how Jo interpreted the world. I didn't believe in voodoo or black magic, Jesus Christ nor any of his relatives or counterparts. But even though I had my own worldview I couldn't deny that Jo knew things and did things that I could not explain.

"Can I help?" she asked me.

There was no one else in the world that could ask me that question and give me pause. Jo had power in her potions, notions, and hands. I could ask her to help me forget or maybe even how I might get Bonnie back. I could ask her anything, confident that she would never take an action that would hurt me or mine.

"No," I said after stumbling through the corridor of those thoughts. "Bonnie's left me and that's the right thing for her. It's right for me too. I love her but her need is not me."

Tears flowed down Mama Jo's black cheeks. I believe that she saw my truth in her own breast. This feeling was a balm because I had never before felt on equal footing with the backwoods witch.

"Then why are you here?" she whispered.

"Maybe it's that thing about the earth spirit you're always talking about."

"But even then you had to have a reason to come," Jo offered.

I told her the whole story of Joguye Cham and my ex.

"Hard to be angry in the face'a true love," Jo said. "Add to that how generous Bonnie is and your heart could break three times over."

"You know people who could take her and her husband in," I said, "people that could hide him from whatever assassins the governments might shake out the woodwork."

"America might grab him," Jo agreed. "Kill him in his cell or deport him to his enemy. Money could do that in its sleep."

"Do you know a place?"

"I do. I'll call Raymond and have him make the right moves. By Saturday morning nobody'll find them."

"You need to call Jewelle or Jackson," I said. "They put them somewhere safe until I got in touch with you."

"You wanna know where I'm sendin' 'em?" Jo asked.

"No."

She smiled and reached for me even though I was too far away to touch.

"But I need somethin' from you too," she said.

"What's that?"

"I ran Coco outta here 'cause I loved her too much. I could see the mother in her and the changes a baby would bring out. I could feel the strength of her womanhood and the hidden mind that was sleeping inside the mind she knew. I know better than to try and wake a woman up to what she is, what she can be. But you know love's a fool; they tell you that on the radio a thousand times a day. We hear it but that don't matter. We done heard it so often that it's just sounds in the air."

I was surprised that Jo knew anything about a radio.

Jo stopped talking and stared at the dirt floor. The raven vocalized some kind of complaint and the cat pounced on something in a corner.

After maybe three minutes I said, "You wanted me to do something for you, Jo?"

She smiled and then looked up.

"I wrote a letter," she said.

She turned on the bench and rummaged around the jars and bottles, bunches of branches and dried dead things. Finally she came out with a stack of blue-lined school paper, maybe eighteen, twenty sheets. These she handed to me.

She had written on both sides of each sheet. Her tiny script made up two lines for each space provided. I didn't read the words.

"I been writin' it since she walked out the door," Jo said.

"You want me to take it to her?"

"She's at that hippie house above the Sunset Strip."

"No problem." I folded the tome and put it in my jacket pocket.

Jo stared at me for a few long seconds.

"What else happenin' with you, Easy?"

I told her about Charcoal Joe, Mouse, and the boy they wanted me to vindicate.

"I know Rufus," she said. "The poor man done let his soul overrun his heart."

"As long as it doesn't overrun me," I said.

"Would you like some tea, Easy?" she asked then. Her voice sounded as if a great weight had been lifted.

"Lipton or special?"

"It's a little potion help when the heart is all beat up," she said. "You don't get high or nuthin', just look at things in a way that's a little more real."

"Can I drive?"

"Oh yeah. Give you enough time and you could probably fly a jet plane."

I liked Jo's medicines. She brewed the tea in an iron pot on her pink porcelain and black iron woodstove while we talked about little things.

"Your friend Jackson Blue come out to talk to me a week ago," she said while handing me my tea mug.

"Oh yeah?" I said and sipped.

"He was worried that maybe Jewelle's child wasn't his."

"What did he want from you?"

"To know if he should look for the truth."

"And what did you say?"

"That the only truth about chirren is that they're yours if you love them."

I drank my tea. It tasted like lemons and rhubarb steeped in wild-flower honey. I didn't feel high or happy. I was the same as before and that was just fine with me.

13

You could walk down the main street of a tiny little town like New Iberia ten thousand times and every time you do you might see something new to you, my father had said to me forty-one years before. *Sometimes things be different like new paint or a puppy dog in a flower garden. But many times you see things you never noticed before because, even in the smallest place, there's just too much for one man to see and remember all at once, or even in his whole lifetime.*

Hauser Boulevard turns into a hill on the way from Pico up to Wilshire. I'd driven that route more times than I could remember but that day, when I got to the address Charcoal Joe had given me, I saw an orange and blue house that I'd not noticed before. Behind the house was a long staircase that led to another house that was situated between Hauser and South Ridge Drive to the east. The house was painted white, set on forty-foot stilts hoisting it high in the sky.

I had been down that street, driven past that high house a hundred times at least but I had never noticed it. Seeing it and remembering my father preparing me for that experience made his love a palpable thing; like the steering wheel under my palms. I realized then and there that Jo's tea had opened me up in such a way that all things had an equal weight.

―――――

"Who are you?" a man said in a voice that hadn't been friendly to strangers in a very long time.

I was a little surprised, not by the unfriendliness, but by the fact that I'd gotten out of the car and walked to the wire gate without really thinking about it. In my mind I was down home in Louisiana, a boy with two parents and the best food I ever ate.

"I'm here to see Jasmine Palmas-Hardy," I said.

"I'm Uriah Hardy," the smallish black man said.

His physique was thin and knotty; his color like copper that needed a polish.

"Pleased to meet you, Mr. Hardy. Jasmine your wife?"

"What's it to you?" he said. He had on blue jeans faded by time, not design, and a T-shirt that had gone from white to gray.

"I'm just here to speak to the woman," I said.

Mr. Hardy puffed up his chest and shoulders, trying, it seemed, to be taller than his five feet eight.

"What's your name?" he asked in a tone that plainly expressed that he expected a lie.

I reached into the breast pocket of my shirt, producing my PI's license for him to see.

He read the little card closely, looking at the picture and my face, comparing them suspiciously.

Handing the card back, he said, "So?"

"Your words asked me who I was," I said. "Your tone told me that you wanted to know my business. I'm Easy Rawlins, a private detective. I'm on a case and I believe your wife has some information for me."

"Who told you that?" he asked, making no move to open the gate.

"Man named Rufus Tyler."

Bonnie Shay and Joguye Cham were way at the back of my mind. They were there like that house hovering up and to the left of the smaller orange and blue place guarded by Uriah.

The out-of-uniform sentry leered at me with anger and suspicion as his musket and dagger.

"What's Joe want?" Uriah asked.

"You have to ask him that yourself."

This was not an option that the maybe-husband of Jasmine Palmas wanted to entertain.

"Listen, man," I said. "If you're worried about me being on your property—that's okay. I'll wait here and you can go and ask Jasmine if she wants to talk, and if she wants you with her. I got time."

"She not here," he said. It was almost a question.

"Okay. Rufus said that she would be so I'll go back out to Venice and tell him he was wrong." I was enjoying the banter way too much.

Uriah, maybe ten years my senior, was actually sneering, he was so upset. He was like a domestic animal cornered and slowly turning feral.

"Uriah!" a woman shouted.

We both looked to the elevated white house.

There was a black woman in an off-white dress looking down at us.

"Yeah?" the angry man answered.

"Is that Mr. Rawlins?"

He hesitated before shouting, "Yeah!"

"Let him up!"

The look Uriah Hardy gave me was not inviting, and so when he pulled the gate open I felt that I'd won a little victory. There was no pleasure in the triumph however, because I knew that this was only the first skirmish in what promised to be a great war.

There were eighty-seven steps from the street-level house up to Jasmine Palmas-Hardy's aerie. Now that I was down to one cigarette a day the climb hardly left me breathless. She was waiting on the unfinished wooden platform that was three steps down from the front door of the nosebleed house.

Also five-eight, and well formed, Jasmine was dark-skinned and handsome with almond-shaped eyes that could, I believed, say cer-

tain things while her mouth engaged in a completely different conversation. Her summer dress was sleeveless and very, very short. Her
moccasins were cut from white leather.

"Mr. Rawlins?"

"Yes, ma'am."

I presumed that Jasmine and Uriah had been married but were
now separated by eighty-seven stairs instead of some legal notice.
He inherited access to the street while she got the view and all the
charm.

She smiled at my down-home manners and said, "Come on in."

We entered the main room of the small house. It was a little larger
than my office, sporting three doors. I assumed the portals I had not
passed through led to a back exit of some sort and a bathroom. There
was a red sofa and a green sofa chair perpendicular to each other and
facing a glass-topped coffee table. In a far corner there hummed a
squat refrigerator under a wide shelf with two hot plates, a blender,
and a waffle iron. Next to the kitchen area stood a six-tiered book-
case jammed with books in every possible space and nook.

"Sofa turn into a bed?" I asked.

"You want some lemonade?" she said, her eyes smiling about the
bed.

"Sure."

"Vodka in that?"

"No, thank you."

"Too early?"

"I gave it up."

"Religion?"

"Life."

Jasmine took a moment to appreciate my one-word response and
then said, "Take a seat and I'll make your drink."

I sat on the couch and she brought me a green plastic tumbler
filled with frosty lemonade from the fridge. She placed my drink on

78

the coffee table next to a red book-box that contained three full-sized volumes and a smaller book about two-thirds the height of the others. The cover read THE FEYNMAN LECTURES ON PHYSICS. I picked it up. It was heavier than it looked.

"Kid's book?" I asked.

"When I asked Seymour what was it that he did he gave me that book. He said it was everything any layman needed to understand the science. He called it the holy scriptures of physics. I never got past the second page but I keep it there because it reminds me of him."

I put the collection down.

"That's the second one he give me. I loaned the first one to my girlfriend because she wanted a big red book like that on her bookshelf," she said.

"You're a detective?" she then asked, doubt laced through the words.

"Yeah," I said.

"Were you a cop before?"

"No."

"Then how did you even start something like that?"

"That's a long story, Mrs. Hardy."

"Call me Jasmine."

"It's a long story, Jasmine, and I take it we have more important things to talk about."

Sitting down next to me, she let her shoulders sag.

"I don't know what I'd do if they framed my son."

"Your foster son," I said for clarification.

"Yes."

"Did you and Seymour live here in this house?"

"He had the bedroom and I slept out here on the fold-away."

"One of these doors a bedroom?"

"That one," she said, waving her hand at a pink door across from us. "First it's the toilet and on the other side is Seymour's old room."

"Was he a good boy?"

"The best," Jasmine said with emphasis. "I took him in when he was a baby and, and never regretted it for even one minute."

"Then why let him go?" I asked.

The question seemed to hurt. I was thinking that the tea was bringing out something else in me; a callousness, or maybe just simple objectivity.

"I didn't want to, Mr. Rawlins," she said. "I never wanted to be parted from him. But Sy is some kinda genius and there was this science family up north in Walnut Creek. The father, mother, sister, and brother was all scientists or at least science students. They met my son at the state science fair where the mother was a judge, and after a while they decided to take him in and show him how to be what he could be."

I did not doubt her sorrow or sacrifice.

"Have you talked to him?" I asked.

"He called me when he was arrested. He told me that he'd found the bodies and that the police arrested him for murder. That's when I called Joe and asked him to get a lawyer for Seymour."

"Have you gone down to see Seymour?"

Her initial response was to look away, as if there was a courtroom lawyer there to tell her how to answer the question.

"They, they wouldn't let me in because I'm not blood."

"But you were his legal guardian, right?"

Just the question was painful to her. She turned away again, made to stand, and then didn't.

"Seymour was abandoned as a baby," she said. "He was left in a basket in front of a church where a friend of mine's husband was deacon. They didn't want to turn a poor baby over to the state orphanage so they asked me and I took him."

I didn't believe her. But it didn't matter that she was lying. I hadn't been hired to find out where Seymour had come from.

"What about Rufus?" I asked.

"What about 'im?" The feeling in her face shifted from anguish to something ambivalent.

"How does he fit into all this?"

"He don't have nuthin' to do with Sy," she said. "We was friends a long time ago and he knew the boy. Rufus is what you call a rough customer and so, like I said, when Sy got arrested I called him for help."

"He told me that you spoke for him."

"Only because'a Seymour, only because'a him."

As we spoke, Jasmine seemed to become more vulnerable. I was aware that this vulnerability was also dangerous.

"What happened?" I asked.

"When?"

"To get your foster child arrested."

"Um, he said, he said that he knew a woman lived out there some-where," she lied. "He went to the door, saw that it was open, and walked in. He called out but nobody answered. Then he found the bodies and the police came. He was gonna call the cops himself but they got there before he could."

"You believe all that?" I asked because I had to.

"I believe that he didn't know those men or kill them, or have any idea who did."

It was a rehearsed response but there was truth in there.

Jasmine reached behind the arm on her side of the sofa and came up with a shiny black handbag.

She reached inside. There might have been a pistol in there but I figured that I was close enough to wrest it away if I had to; besides, she had no reason to shoot me, not yet.

What she came out with was a very large stack of new bills—hundred-dollar bills.

Handing the stack to me, she said, "Eighteen thousand dollars."

"What's this for?"

"You need it to get Sy out on bail."

"They've given him bail?"

"The lawyer Joe got said it had somethin' to do with there bein' no witness and no weapon."

"Why don't you go do it?"

"Rufus said I should tell you."

I took the money. I almost always do.

Jasmine brought her left leg up on the cushion, revealing the greater part of her thigh. The movement caught my attention; the form held my eyes.

When I looked up Jasmine was staring at me. There was great feeling in her.

She stood up and said, "You like my dress?"

I looked at her shapely legs and nodded.

She turned her back to me and raised her hands high as if surrendering to the police. The hem of the dress rose up almost to her waist; she wasn't wearing anything under that.

I suppose that I have seen more lovely derrieres in my experience but I could not, and cannot, remember when.

There was something almost ceremonial about these gestures. First the money, then the woman; after all that, I could go out somewhere to die.

I rose, put my hands on her hips, and guided her down to her knees on the sofa. A few moments later I entered her. The growl that came from my lips was new to me. A moan rose from her and we started rocking back and forth.

When I pressed forward she slammed back. At some point we tumbled from the sofa to the floor, but the motion never stopped. The whole connection lasted three minutes, maybe four.

When it was over I had to tell myself not to close my eyes.

We both sat up.

"Kiss me," I said.

"Why?"

"Just so I know that you know I'm here."

I expected a peck but Jasmine Palmas-Hardy gave me a passionate tongue that spoke in a language beyond words and maybe even ideas.

"Will you save my son, Mr. Rawlins?" she asked after completing the kiss.

"If I don't," I said, "then he is beyond saving."

14

On the way down the stairs I wondered why I had asked for that kiss. I also speculated about Jasmine; why she sealed our meeting with sex. The late sixties was an uninhibited era where people changed apartments and had sex at the drop of a hat. But there was something else going on with Jasmine. She had to connect with me, not because she was after release or a feeling of power, but because she needed me to want to do what I had promised.

And why did I respond? I was almost half a century old. I had known many women. Usually when there's a jealous husband nearby I demurred when being offered sex. Why put my life on the line?

Maybe Jo's tea really had opened a door in my bruised heart.

"What happened up there?" Uriah Hardy put words to my unspoken questions.

He stood at the gate to the street, this time blocking my egress. There was a tremor throbbing at the back of his neck and his left hand was held at hip-level, balled into a fist. This reminded me of Joguye Cham's paralyzed hand, but with the memory came no anguish.

"I'm looking for reasons to get Seymour Brathwaite off the suspect list for murder," I said. "You know Seymour, don't you?"

"That woman up there is my wife," he said, telling me that he wasn't concerned with my questions. "We were married at city hall with a witness. I got the government certificate to prove it."

I noticed that my breathing got deeper. We might as well have been two dogs snarling at the bait of pheromones on the air.

"Seymour Brathwaite," I said. It was only then that it dawned on me that I should have asked Jasmine for a photograph.

"What about him?" The question wanted to be a curse.

"Do you know him?"

"He used to live in the little side room off the toilet upstairs."

Upstairs; that was the word he used to pretend that Jasmine was still his faithful spouse.

"When was the last time you saw him?"

"Not for a long time."

"Have you spoken to him?"

Uriah resented the question but he said, "I don't know. A couple'a weeks ago I guess. He called looking for Jasmine but she wasn't here."

"Did he own a gun?"

"This is California, man. One thing you could be sure of is everybody got a car and gun."

"So he had one?"

"His mother do."

"You mean Jasmine, his foster mother?"

"Yeah. Right."

"You have a picture of him?" I asked as politely as possible. I was trying to prove that I was there in the role of PI and had no other interest.

But my attempt was off-target. Uriah glared at the question. It was as if I was trying to condemn him.

"She's my wife," he said.

"I asked for a picture of Seymour, not your marriage certificate."

"The foster mother thing was her job. He wasn't none of mines. Why I wanna have his picture?"

I thought of asking for a family photograph or maybe hoofing it back up the stairs to Jasmine's stronghold. But none of that seemed possible. Uriah was not a part of Jasmine's family and he had a car . . . and a gun.

It was time for me to get into my car and drive off.

"Excuse me," I said, looking past his shoulder at the gate.

But Mr. Hardy did not budge.

"I don't want you comin' 'round here no more," he said.

I should have felt threatened. My breathing was that of a worried man but there was cold logic flowing side by side with the hot blood in my veins.

"You realize that the next time Mr. Tyler asks me to come around here I'll have to say, 'Her husband told me to stay away.'"

"You think I'm ascared'a Charcoal Joe?"

"Everybody else I talked to seems to be."

The cuckold gave my words serious consideration. Maybe if other people also were afraid of Joe then he wouldn't be so much of an unmanned coward.

"What she tell you?" Uriah asked, and I felt that the conversation had finally begun.

"That Seymour was her foster son and that Joe hired me because he was a family friend."

"Friend," the little man spat. "That's like sayin' a mosquito is your friend. A stroke is your friend."

"If Tyler's that bad then why did he call me to visit him in jail and ask me to prove Seymour innocent?"

"Her."

"Jasmine?"

"Listen here, brother," Uriah cautioned. "Joe ain't nobody's friend. Even if he shake your hand and slip you a ten-dollar bill, it ain't gonna turn out good. If Seymour's in trouble then you could bet it's on Joe. If that bitch upstairs pulls up her dress, he's behind it. If the ground shakes and that house falls off its poles, then that's him too."

He was saying that if I had sex with his wife while he waited down below that it was Joe doing it. This displacement, I thought, could work for me.

"He hired me to prove Seymour innocent," I said again. "What could be wrong with that?"

"I know you a detective and all," Uriah said. "Your ID card said WRENS-L company. I aksed information for the company numbah.

I talked with a white guy called Lynx. I know you all sure and confident and think you know how things work but believe me, man, you don't."

"How do things work?" I asked. I really wanted to know.

The angry husband suddenly looked frightened. His fist released and I realized that the wrinkles across his forehead were from rage and not age. In a twinkling, the expression on the grumpy old man's face transformed into that of an innocent who harbored a child in his heart.

Uriah licked his lips instead of answering my question.

"Really, brother," I said. "I don't need to be in no deep shit here. I thought I was just tryin' to get an innocent man free."

"Innocent," Uriah said. "You can't even just be in a room with Joe and be innocent."

The anger was coming back.

"Uriah!" Jasmine yelled from the platform above.

Again we both looked up.

"What?" he said in a voice that wanted to be in charge.

"Stand out the way and let Mr. Rawlins get on with his business!"

Uriah uttered a foul word under his breath.

"Fuck you!" he yelled. "Fuck you all!"

He turned abruptly and rushed into the orange and blue house.

I looked up at Jasmine and she down on me. The sex we had had had been no more than the complex handshake of a not-so-secret society.

I nodded and went out through the gate.

On my way to the car I wondered if the husband at the bottom of the stairs would get his gun; if he would shoot himself, Jasmine, me, or any possible combination of the three.

15

If Mama Jo had a phone I would have called her and asked about the tea she gave me. Failing that, I decided to go get a haircut.

On Pico Boulevard, three blocks west of La Brea, on the south side of the street there stood a small barbershop that looked like a big incinerator. The ash gray bunker-shaped building had inset windows that were long and thin. The door had a curved metal handle instead of a knob, making it looked more like a hatch than a portal.

During business hours the front door was always unlocked. At the close of every day Angelo Broadman, the proprietor and head barber, snapped six heavy padlocks into their hinges and went home secure that nobody would break in.

"Hey, Easy," the New Orleanian greeted, rising from the lead barber chair. He wore the standard barber's uniform—a white smock with black trousers and sensible, rubber-soled black shoes.

There were six barbers lined in a row along the eastern wall of the small, sweet cologne–smelling room; five men and one woman. Angelo was the only barber without a customer in his chair.

After thirty years shearing heads Angelo had saved enough to buy a shop, and so now he only worked on his regulars and friends.

Half a dozen men waited along the west wall, sitting in chairs made of green leather cushions with chromium arms and legs.

"Mr. Broadman," I said, shaking his hand.

Angelo was a short, green-eyed Negro with skin lighter than

many white people I've known. His limp hair didn't need to be straightened and his handsome features were closer to Clark Gable than Bill Robinson. As a matter of fact, the only reason we knew Angelo was one of us was that he claimed this ancestry, and in America, who would lie about that?

"Hey, Easy," Lena Arthur, mistress of the number-two chair, said.

Lena had brassy skin with freckles and gold edging on her front teeth. She smiled and winked. Both she and Angelo had passed fifty but they didn't look old.

"Have a seat, Mr. Rawlins," Angelo said.

As I obeyed he took a folded white apron with almost imperceptible blue lines and spread it out over me.

"I was next!"

The speaker was of medium height with dark brown skin and a big belly, dressed in the milk chocolate–colored uniform of a national parcel-delivery service. Though the same in name, the colors of his skin and livery clashed. He had gotten to his feet.

Angelo was tying the apron at the back of my neck.

"You better sit down, brother," the barber rumbled. "Sit down or get out."

"I been sittin' here for forty-five minutes," the delivery man complained.

"You didn't make no appointment," Lena said in a voice that would have harmonized well with a trio of trumpets.

"That's okay, baby," Angelo said to his stylist neighbor. "This man knows that I got a straight razor and a bad temper. He knows that barbers used to be doctors and dentists too, and so we accustomed to the sight'a blood."

The would-be customer's face had generous features. His lips were thick and malleable, so it was easy to see the fearful reaction to the barber's threat. But even though he was somewhat afraid, he didn't want to back down—at least not immediately.

"I'm just sayin' that I been waitin' and this niggah here just waltz in and you sit him right down."

"Niggah? You want me to take this sheet off, Easy?" the barber asked me, "or you gonna kick his ass with it on?"

That made it easier for the angry customer. Two against one meant that he could back down with no shame.

"Fuck this shit!" he yelled. He walked to the hatch and out into the street.

Lena laughed and went back to her head of hair.

Looking after the retreating delivery man, I thought of Uriah and all the black men and women I knew who woke up angry and went to bed in the same state of mind. Life was like a bruise for us back then, and today too. We examine every action for potential threats, insults, and cheats. And if you look hard enough you will find what you're looking for—whether it's there or not.

"What you need, Easy?" Angelo asked.

"Just a razor line."

"You got it."

The barber lowered the back of the chair and raised the whole seat until I was almost prone, with my head at his diaphragm.

I liked the nameless barbershop because it was old-fashioned. They used real barber's chairs and straight razors sharpened on leather strops attached to each station. There was always good company and often a crap game going in a corner. At the barbershop people read the newspapers and discussed racism and politics. The stylists wrapped hot towels around your face and you could close your eyes and relax for that precious few minutes that might be the difference between harsh words and hard blows.

"You want a little color up top, Easy?" Angelo asked while I was drowsing.

"Color?"

"You got a few gray hairs, baby. . . . Don't want the girls thinkin' you a old man."

"What I need is more'a them suckers," I said, in full barbershop mode.

"More? Why?"

"Gray hair is the smart man's bait."

"Bait for what?"

"Female company."

"How you figure?"

I opened my eyes and saw that Lena was glancing at us, listening in.

"When a man looks at a woman, what's he thinkin' about?" I asked Angelo.

"Her butt," he said. "Maybe her face."

"Now what's the woman thinkin' about, lookin' back at him?"

"Hearth and home," he chanted. "Hearth and home."

"That's right. A man is thinkin' about right now tonight, but the woman got her eye on the future. She might like that man. Hell, she might lust after him, but at the same time she could tell you what kinda drapes she wants in the house you haven't even thought about yet. She can tell you what kinda silverware you will eat with at two thousand Sunday suppers."

"What's that got to do with a few gray hairs?" Angelo wanted to know.

"Girl see one or two and she thinks maybe the man done aged enough to calm down, make somethin' outta himself. She willin' to let him look so maybe she could see what his prospects are like. That way a man like me might get a great night or a lifetime of pot roasts, fat babies, and halfhearted regrets."

"Halfhearted regrets!" Lena shouted like a parishioner agreeing with the preacher's words. "That's why Easy Rawlins is a detective. That man knows some shit!"

She laughed so hard that she had to hold the razor away from her client's face.

"Damn!" Lena cried.

Angelo used his razor to even the line around my short hair and then to shave the stubble from my chin. We talked about the Dodgers and the Lakers, the state of Watts and Vietnam. His wife's mother had come up from Louisiana to live with them.

"Wife in the bedroom," he said, "and her mama's in the kitchen. All I got to do is bring home the mortgage payments and my life is perfect."

I liked the community of black barbershops. I liked Angelo and the tough love of his establishment. But I was there for another reason altogether.

Barbers were like telephone poles carrying the intelligence of a whole community at their stations. Los Angeles was once small enough that most black people knew one another, but the population was too large for that by the late sixties. The major players, however, were known in pool halls, barrooms, and barbershops.

And Angelo Broadman knew just about all the names.

When he was almost finished with my face I asked, "What you been hearin' 'bout Charcoal Joe?"

Angelo stood up straight and looked at me with his glassy green eyes. He pondered a moment, wiped the blade with a towel, and then pursed his lips. He leaned closer than he had to to shave my right jawline.

"They sayin' that he wants to move out the country," he whispered.

"Where?"

"Canada," Angelo speculated, "maybe Paris. You know he once played a trumpet and cello duet with Louis Armstrong over there."

"He's that good?"

"He's that good."

"His people know he's leavin'?"

"If I do then they do."

The barber wiped my face with a hot towel and then raised the back of my chair while lowering the seat. He pulled the apron off and snapped it to discard whatever hair might be there.

"How much I owe you?"

"That story about the gray," he said. "That'll keep Lena happy for weeks."

"Thanks, man."

"And, Easy?"

"Yeah."

"Walk softly wherever it is you goin'. You know Charcoal Joe is a tombstone just waitin' for a name."

16

It was late afternoon when I was driving in my car again.

I had already called Jewelle to pick up Feather at her school.

On surface streets I made my way from the west side down to Florence Avenue and San Pedro, there to park in front of a three-story, brown-shingled building that housed a Laundromat on the first floor.

In order to get where I was going I had to walk down the aisle that separated the coin-operated washers from the dryers to a red door that had a sign above that read STAIRS.

The second-floor door opened into a short hallway that had two apartment doors on either side. At the far end of that corridor was a bright blue door with a red glass knob.

I always liked that door. Every time I saw it I was reminded of a fairy tale that my father once read to me before he disappeared. It was a story about a curious young man who investigated every corner of every house he was in. The only details I retained from that story were the blue door and a little witch-girl he found imprisoned on the other side.

With my hand on the faceted knob, I wondered if I had grown up to become that curious young man, opening doors and looking for my father.

On my way up the last tier of stairs I decided, not for the first time, never to take another potion from Jo.

The final door in my private fairy tale was black with an iron knob painted white. I didn't try to open this door because it was always locked.

"Who is it?" a sweet woman's voice asked in answer to my knock.

"Easy Rawlins."

The door came open immediately, revealing a man that was an inch or so taller than I, a shade or two darker, and maybe twenty pounds lighter. He was wearing a cheap, steel-gray suit cut from cotton cloth, designed for some Alabama sodbuster to wear when he went to the bank to ask for yet another extension on his loan payments. The man's shirt was white dress with no tie and had long sleeves that came out of the cuffs of his jacket. His face was angular and well formed. Nobody would have called him handsome, but then again, I knew that there weren't many women who could resist his charm. And Fearless Jones was not a conscious womanizer. He met women and bedded them but he would have paid for the dinner or done the favor they needed without recompense.

"Easy Rawlins," the black Prince Charming hailed.

"Fearless Jones."

We clasped hands and smiled broadly. Fearless was a mighty friend to have. He was one of the three people that Mouse claimed he wouldn't want to tangle with.

"Come on in, man," he invited, as if this was his apartment rather than Milo Sweet's bail-bonds office.

The reception area of the disbarred lawyer's office was smallish but well appointed. There was an ornately carved rosewood desk, and three ash chairs along the wall to the left of the entrance.

From behind the desk Loretta Kuroko was rising to greet me. Tall for a woman, five-ten or so, there was no questioning her beauty. Her dark eyes actually glittered and her long black hair was tied up into a bun, making her extraordinary features seem to jump out at you.

"Loretta," I said and we kissed.

She was wearing a black silk jacket over a yellow satin dress. Her shoes, I noticed, were bright red and the sash around her waist was deep green, dark enough to be mistaken for black in low light.

"Milo's down at the jail," she said.

"I thought that he was usually back by now."

"As a rule," she said as she made it back to her chair, "but they arrested Thaddeus Melford for manslaughter, and Thad's lawyer needed Milo with him when he argued with the judge over him getting bail or not."

Loretta was like that blue door; she made me happy. As a child she spent three years in a detainment camp for Japanese Americans during World War II. This experience caused her to hate white people. That's why she went to work for Milo. It's also why she dressed the way she did and used her own Japanese-made furniture for the front office.

"He'll be back soon," she assured me.

"Come sit with me, Easy," Fearless offered. "I haven't seen you in two, three years. How you doin'?"

I went to the wall and took a seat next to the reluctant Lothario.

"Cain't complain," I lied. "Started a new detective agency. We call it WRENS-L."

"What's that mean?"

"Whisper Natly is one of my new partners."

"Whisper," he said with a smile. "Paris an' me did some work with him some years back. He's a real nice guy."

"Yeah he is," I agreed. "Saul Lynx is the third partner. We were wondering what name we should use, and Whisper just took the initials of our first and last names and made as close to a word as he could."

"I like it," Fearless said, a little uncertain. "It's good to work for yourself. I mean most people who become bosses get all in your face and stuff. Better off without 'em. How's that girl of yours? That Bonnie Shay."

"She's doing very well, thank you. Happy as a clam."

Loretta gave me an inquisitive glance. It's hard to hide a broken heart from a woman.

"What you doin'?" I asked, to change the track of our conversation.

"I been chasin' down fools who buy bail from Milo and then run."

"I thought you did work with Paris Minton?"

"He moved back up to San Francisco."

"Really? He left his bookstore?"

Paris Minton and Fearless Jones were what I called a perfectly mismatched pair. Paris was as well-read and intelligent as Jackson Blue; he was just as much of a coward too. Fearless was not so smart but his will was indomitable, his heart attuned to truth, and physically he was the strongest man I ever met; possibly with the exception of Jo's son—Domaque. Separately, Fearless and Paris were just two more black men destined for ignominy, but together they formed the perfect genius of the American spirit.

"Me and Loretta open it up on weekends," Fearless said, answering my question. "He got about ten thousand books in the upstairs storage area so we won't even make a dent before he move back down."

"He's planning to come back?"

"He says no but Paris got to be down here. He know that between him and me there ain't nuthin' we cain't do."

That was Fearless: He knew for certain things that he didn't understand.

"You want me to make you some tea, Easy?" Loretta asked in the lull of our conversation.

Before I could answer, the black door came open. In strode Milo Sweet wearing a baby blue three-piece suit, brown shirt, mustard tie, and a brown hat that might have been a derby at one time, before the weight of the world came down upon it. If Milo's skeleton was found in some troglodyte cave, the anthropologist's first thought would be Neanderthal, not Cro-Magnon. Five-seven at the height of his youth and one ninety if he was an ounce, he smelled of the cigar between his lips.

"Easy Rawlins," he bellowed. Milo's voice was both gravelly and low. His place would have been in the bass section of the church choir—if he ever joined some congregation. His skin was always the darkest in the room, unless, that is, Fearless Jones was in that room with him.

"You had me goin' this morning," Milo said. "That woman callin' me and sayin' that I in some way represented one of her inmates, and that I had sent Easy Rawlins down to give him some message."

"Sorry about that, Milo. You know they weren't gonna let me in and I had made a promise."

"That's okay," the ex-lawyer proclaimed. "When I heard it was Avett Detention I wasn't worried."

"Why not?"

"In a corrupt barrel, Avett's still a bad apple. So you here to ask for another favor?"

"Since you were so helpful on the phone I thought I'd come by and do you a good turn."

Milo grunted and gestured at the door behind and to the left of Loretta's desk.

The bail bondsman's office was three times that of Loretta's space. He had a black desk the size of a baby grand piano. I often wondered how he moved that piece of furniture around but whenever we met, the business I was on kept me from idle chatter.

There was a brown leather sofa under a row of three windows that looked over the palm tree–lined slum streets of South Central Los Angeles.

He had a dozen metal file cabinets of every color and size set in a row and stacked one on top of another. But what I liked the most about his office was the visitor's chair.

It was a gangly light brown seat that reminded you of a two-year-old doe coming out of the woods after an especially bad winter. The legs didn't look like they could bear the weight of Loretta but I had seen Milo sitting on it, leaning back on the hind legs. That was the only chair I had ever seen that seemed to have a personality.

I sat on the chair and Milo leaned back in his.

"What you need, Mr. Rawlins?"

I took out the stack of cash Jasmine had given me and set it on the tan blotter before him.

The whites of Milo's eyes were bloodshot. He wheezed when just walking. He had a smoker's cough that was a fright, but for all that he seemed immortal.

Those godlike glaring eyes fixed themselves on the pile of cash.

"Eighteen thousand dollars," I said.

Milo had to swallow before asking, "For what? You want me to shoot my mother or somethin'?"

"A man named Seymour Brathwaite has been arrested and charged with double homicide. This will cover his piece of the bail."

"Bail on murder? Is this a black man accused?"

"Yes, sir."

"And is it black men they say he killed?"

"White."

"And they still set bail?"

"Charcoal Joe put his lawyer on it."

"How'd you get mixed up with him?"

"Mouse called in a favor."

"Damn, Easy, you travel in some bad company, man."

"I vouch for the bail, Milo."

A light entered the Cave God's eyes. He cocked his head to the side and said, "Then I will go down tonight. If everything you say is right they'll let him free in the morning."

"There's something else," I said.

"Yeah?"

"The men they say Seymour killed were a guy named Peter Boughman and somebody else they call Ducky. You ever hear of either of them?"

"No."

"I'd like to know what there is to know about Boughman, and Ducky too if it's possible."

Up until then Milo had been talking past the cigar clenched in his teeth. But then he plucked out the stogie and gave me a speculative look.

"I heard you started a new office with Whisper Natly and a Jew," Milo said.

"Yeah?"

"And Whisper done brought that fine young thing Niska Redman to be your secretary."

"He has."

"So why not just ask her?"

"Come on now, Milo. I willin' to pay for this and we both know Loretta is ten or twelve IQ points over you. Just give her the job and bill me what it's worth."

"You ain't no fun, Easy. Don't you know you s'posed to haggle over shit?"

I stood and said, "Eight a.m.?"

"County courthouse, on the dot."

17

In the outer office Loretta rose to kiss me again. I had once done her a favor and she wanted me to know that she remembered.

When Fearless got to his feet and stuck out a hand I had a thought. "Fearless."

"Yeah, Easy?"

"Now that I started WRENS-L I might, or Saul or Whisper might, need some help now and then. You know . . . an extra man, a strong back, maybe some bodyguardin'. That means we can pay in cash under the table but not have a full-time man."

"Okay," Fearless allowed.

"You'd be our first choice. Pays forty dollars a day, that is if you're not too busy here."

"Problem with workin' for Milo is that when people know I'm here they don't jump bail too much. Mr. Sweet only pay me my bonus when I bring somebody in, so I'm usually hungry with nuthin' to do."

"Why don't you meet me down at the county courthouse tomorrow morning at eight? That'll be at least one day's pay."

I called Jackson Blue's office from a phone booth on San Pedro but he was out. I called Jewelle's answering service but they didn't know where she was. When I tried a third number my daughter answered, "Blues' residence."

Blues' residence. It struck me that this would be a good title for a poem or song; maybe even a novel.

"Hey, honey."

"Daddy!" she cried. "Are you okay?"

There are ten thousand perfectly good reasons not to have children but hearing the love in Feather's voice trumped every one.

"Fine," I assured. "Just workin' a job. I was thinking that maybe it would be good for you to stay with Jewelle and Jackson one more night, maybe two. I mean if they could put up with a wild child like you."

She giggled and then laughed. "Cilla York wanted me to stay at her house tonight so I could help her with her French homework."

A feeling akin to despair rose up in my chest. I didn't want to miss a single moment of my daughter's life. I didn't want to be shot down in some alley over another man's troubles. I'd lost Bonnie but I still had Feather.

"Daddy?"

"Yeah?"

"Can I?"

"Can you what?"

"Stay at Cilla's tonight."

"Is she nice?"

"You met her and her parents at the school orientation. Mr. York is the one that knew you because he saw you at P9."

A building that thousands of people walked through every day but Jordan York remembered me, one of two suited black men who ever got past their corporate barricade.

"You can stay if you want, honey, but let Aunt Jewelle take you over."

"Okay."

"And tell Jewelle that I'll be picking you up from school tomorrow."

"Okay."

"Can I talk to her?"

"I love you, Daddy," she said and then banged the phone down on its table.

"Easy?" Jewelle said a few moments later.

"Hey, J, thanks for keeping my girl."

"She's so good with the baby. I think I might want to borrow her some more."

"If you and Jackson ever wanna get away me an' Feather can take the baby. You know I'm good with diapers."

"Maybe after a few months. What can I do for you?"

"Where's your old man?"

"Up in Oxnard with a few of the other senior vice presidents. He'll be back at the office soon."

"Feather wants to go stay at a girlfriend's house tonight. Can you drop her off and maybe go in to see that it's okay?"

"You're a good man, Easy Rawlins."

Rush hour in L.A. in the sixties wasn't too bad. I took surface streets again, wanting to give Jackson the time to get back from whatever company business he was handling. He'd be coming back on the company helicopter but still I wasn't in a hurry.

P9 was on Wilshire Boulevard in the heart of downtown.

I parked on the street because after 6:00 p.m. downtown was almost abandoned. P9 was one of the few corporations that had people working twenty-four hours a day; this because their investment base was international and their president, Jean-Paul Villard, wanted to keep his position on the multinational playing field.

"Can I help you?" a big white man in a private security uniform asked me.

It was a self-negating question because he put his body in the glass doorway to block my passage. My lower brain perceived this action as a threat, so I had to pause a moment to keep my fists from getting me into trouble.

"I said," the guard repeated, "can I help you?"

"No," I replied, cheerfully moving as if I was going to walk around him.

He put a hand on my shoulder and said, "This is private property, soul brother."

Though shorter, the guard had at least fifteen pounds on me. The tan of his skin was natural coloration, not sun-induced, and his hair was both brown and greasy. His breath smelled of the roast beef he'd had for lunch.

I noticed all these things because in the United States you had to fight for your freedom every damn day; and sometimes that struggle was keeping from hurting somebody—no matter how good that hurt might have felt.

"Jim!" someone shouted. "Jim! Jim!"

Each exhortation got louder.

Finally my nemesis-of-the-moment turned his head.

Running toward us was another uniformed white guard. This one was slender. His movements were herky-jerky, reminding me of a marionette.

"Jim," he said again, a little out of breath.

"What?" the larger guard demanded.

The newcomer took a gulp of air and then said, "This man is Ezekiel Porterhouse Rawlins and you do not want to have your hands on him."

I think I must have smiled at that point. There wasn't one person in a hundred that knew me who could recite my full name; but Jackson Blue had put a bulletin downstairs telling the guards and interns to let me by when I came to the door.

The chubby guard regarded me.

"Get out of my way," I said.

He winced and then obliged.

"What is going on 'ere?" a young woman inquired.

Asiette Moulon was five-three in stocking feet with black hair and gray eyes. Her skin identified her white ancestry, millennia in the making. A Frenchwoman from central France, she was quite fetching in her little black dress.

"Not a thing, Miss Moulon. Jim was just showing Mr. Rawlins in."

Mr. Rawlins. Times were changing.

"You are okay, Easy?" she asked me.

"I am lookin' at you."

"You are," she said with a smile.

"Yeah. Jim here didn't know me and was makin' sure I wasn't gonna sneak in the toilets and steal the copper pipes."

She smiled, understanding me better than Jim ever could.

"Come on back to my office," she said, taking me by the arm.

When I'd met Asiette she was just another intern guarding the front desk from salesmen and hustlers. The only difference was that she loved black Americans because, when she was a child, she first met us as soldiers liberating her nation.

I sat in the same green visitor's chair while she perched on top of the same orange desk she'd had the last time I was there.

"Overtime?" I asked her.

"Just putting my papers away," she said. "I am very sad, you know."

"Sad about what?"

"That you 'aven't called."

"Called?"

"The last time I saw you you said that we would 'ave lunch."

"Oh. . . ."

"Don't worry. I am not angry. 'Ow 'ave you been?"

Her gray eyes disarmed me somehow. I tried to say that everything was fine but there was a catch in my throat and I was only able to say, "Okay."

"Can I 'elp?" she asked, hearing the far-off distress in a single word.

"Maybe later," I said.

Asiette's response was a smile on partially pouted lips.

Jackson's office was on the thirty-first floor of the P9 building.

The most difficult time Jewelle and I had making him take the job was the floor number. His superstitions told him that 31 was just 13 backward.

His secretary was gone by then so I walked to his private door, which was open, and called out, "Hey, Jackson."

He was seated nearly forty feet away behind a huge white desk, his back turned toward the entrance as he gazed out of the window that comprised the outer wall.

"Easy?" he called out, his back still turned.

"Yeah."

"Have a seat on the sofas, baby." He turned and sprang up walking toward me, his gait determined to be that of a man.

Jackson was an odd product of the American ghetto. He was a genius and he was small. Impoverished and outcast, he was also afraid of almost everyone and everything. This fear however could not daunt his intelligence and so he was in trouble more times than not. And even though he was now a corporate kingpin with a six-figure salary, he was still haunted by the fears heaped upon him since the first day he could remember.

Toward the entrance of his office Jackson had two long yellow sofas facing each other over a glass coffee table. I took the couch on the left and he took the other.

"Asiette called," he told me. "That girl likes you."

"I need to talk, Jackson."

"Talk about what?" he said, trying to master his natural dread of anything new.

"Rufus Tyler."

"Oh."

"Yeah," I said. "Like that."

I told Jackson the whole story, leaving out nothing. It's not that I'm so honest or anything but Jackson was too smart for me to lie.

"Mouse on one side and Charcoal Joe on the other," Jackson declared. "That's the definition of a rock and a hard place."

"Tomorrow morning I get the young professor out of jail and I was wondering if you knew anything that would help me."

"Like what?"

"Anything about Joe. I know you still make the rounds of the old neighborhood now and then. Maybe you heard something."

"Not about Joe," he said. "But I know that Seymour all right."

"You do?"

"Yeah, man. Black PhD at twenty-one . . . I'm into that shit. I could work in my field a hundred days in a row and not meet a black scientist. They more rare than a Negro violinist in a big city orchestra.

"I had him right here on this couch. You know computers read paper cards today, but soon they be on the phone lines and radio waves. I wanted to come up with somethin' that would let a program stay in the air and we could call it down whenever we want. Seymour's a physicist so I wanted to get his ideas, maybe hire him. But he liked the university too much so we didn't get nowhere."

"You think he could be a murderer?"

"Anybody be a killer, Ease. You know that. Shit, there's grand-mothers poison their own husbands after fifty years in the same bed."

"But did Brathwaite seem bent?"

"No. He was pretty innocent and sheltered. Didn't even talk like a brother."

"And nothing about Joe?" You had to ask Jackson any important question twice.

"Look, Easy, I don't even mention that mothahfuckah's name. I don't want him and me in the same breath, talked about in the same room. Because if he sets his sights on me and P9 there'd be some fireworks for sure."

I could see his argument.

"Thanks, Jackson." I stood to take my leave.

"How's Bonnie?" he asked, before I could take a step.

"Why?"

"Jewelle called and said you two broke up."

I told him the tale.

When I was through he nodded as if this was somehow expected.

"Did you know about it?" I asked him.

"About the boyfriend? No. But it was obvious about you and Bonnie."

"Obvious how?"

"All you got to do is look, Easy. All you got to do is look. She like a granite cliff and you the ocean poundin' away. Seein' you together was beautiful, but you know in the end one's unable to leave and the other always got one foot out the door."

That was the closest I came to crying over losing Bonnie. When he wasn't afraid, Jackson didn't only have a mind, he also had a very smart heart.

"Oh yeah, man," he said. "Here."

He handed me a slip of notepaper that was folded in half. Written on the outside was the word *grandmamma*.

I pocketed the paper, sniffed back a tear, and walked down to the elevator wondering if I would live long enough to forget my pain.

18

"Easy?" she said when I had almost reached the exit door.

Asiette walked up to me and smiled.

The white guard standing at the door, Jim, shifted a bit. I was very much aware of his discomfort because when I was a boy and then a young man down in Texas and Louisiana, Asiette smiling like that could have gotten me killed.

"You still here, girl?" I asked lightly, pushing down the fear.

"I was waiting."

"For what?"

"You said that I could 'elp you later."

We took my car.

She moved close to me and put a hand in my lap. This was another danger. Any policeman that saw us was at liberty to stop the car. In a courtroom that cop would say that he was suspicious of white slavery from just seeing us cruise down Wilshire Boulevard.

I was aware of the risk but not as much as her hand upon my upper thigh.

"I feel that," I said as we crossed Western.

"I do too," she whispered. The pressure of her hand increased ever so slightly.

"Are all French girls so bold as you?"

"You were there," she said.

"That was wartime," I said and then grunted softly.

"I like you."

"Why's that?" I asked.

"You are so patient."

"Patient?"

She squeezed and pressed down. "Yes."

"How do you mean?" I asked, trying to keep a clear mind and both eyes on the road.

"When the white men insult you, you do not lose your tempair. When I tell you I want to see you, you say okay but there is no 'urry and that makes me want you more."

At the house she asked me if I had a shower; she wanted to clean up after a long day at work.

"Upstairs," I said.

"Come with me," she offered. "I will wash you."

That shower was the best part of a mostly nice visit. The physicality seemed particularly familiar; an intimacy far beyond what I usually experienced on the first night of sex with a new friend.

Holding my erection, Asiette guided that intimacy into the bedroom and for quite a while my worries retreated—the spontaneous, if temporary, remission of a broken heart.

There came the single note of a silver chime in the middle of my sleep.

"Easy?"

"Shhh."

I pulled on my boxer shorts, went to the window of the second-floor hall, and looked down. There were three of them standing at my front door.

"Easy." She had come up behind me already wearing her little black dress.

"Back stairs," I said.

One of the deciding factors in buying the new house was the fact that the upstairs had a back way out. It was a little doorway that looked more like it led to a closet than a set of stairs.

Asiette and I went through, locking the door behind us. We got to the back porch where I kept a .45 revolver on the doorsill. Before we made it outside I heard a window break and another silver chime.

Clad in only boxer shorts, I led my barefoot lover toward a dense stand of Texas privet at the northwest end of my yard. The eight-foot-high, twelve-foot-wide hedge stood against a fairly tall redwood fence.

Both hidden and cornered, I cocked my pistol and waited.

Asiette stood by me, silent and still.

For three or four long minutes we stood in the shadow of the hedgerow.

A light came on in one of the upper windows of the house.

After a few more minutes the back door came open.

Three men entered the backyard. Two of them had handguns. The nightlight above the garage illuminated the invaders. They were white men in dark clothes, two large and one not so big. They ambled around awhile, looking for me no doubt.

One came close to our hiding bush. I aimed the hidden muzzle at his head.

The moment passed. The men got together, said words I couldn't make out, and then went back into the house.

"We're gonna wait a quarter hour," I whispered to Asiette.

She nodded her assent.

My breath came cold and clear as I wondered who those men could have been; who might have sent them?

"Asiette."

"Yes?"

"They could still be in the house waiting for me. I'm gonna go in through that back way and see. You stay right here. Don't do nuthin' till I get back. If they kill me they'll think I was alone. If I kill them or they ain't there I'll come back."

She nodded and squeezed my left forearm.

Ever so slowly I moved from the hiding place to the back door that led from the house. It took me two minutes to pull that door open and five to creep up the stairs.

They had broken the lock of the back-exit door.

Though the house was silent and cool, the palm of my gun hand was sweating.

The lights were still on upstairs but the rooms were empty.

I went to the top of the stairs looking down on the first-floor foyer and waited five minutes, ten.

The silence seemed final. My nostrils were open wide. I was thinking that the only way those men would have been this quiet was if they had heard me coming up the back stair. But they outnumbered me. This wasn't a squad of crack commandos, just a bunch of thugs who broke out windows and shook locked front doors. They wouldn't have had the patience to sit in silence in the dark.

Convincing myself that this logic was good only took three minutes, or maybe seven. I came downstairs ready to shoot. But they weren't there. The house was empty and the thugs gone.

"Asiette," I called into the shrubs.

Seeing her emerge from the dark shrubbery in that black dress, barefoot and pale, made me realize that we'd survived. I took her in my arms and hugged her too tightly.

She didn't complain.

She put on her shoes while I dressed in T-shirt and jeans. After gathering my wallet, car keys, and Mama Jo's letter from yesterday's suit, I took a deep breath and said, "We better get to it."

The hardest thing either one of us did that night was walk down to my car. I had parked at the curb because Asiette's restless hand on my thigh made turning into the driveway a little difficult.

There didn't seem to be anyone lying in wait for us in some unfamiliar car, but I had my gun out and to my side when we scurried down the slight incline of my front lawn. I had given Asiette the keys because I wanted to be ready for the firefight if it came.

Three blocks away we changed seats and I drove.

"I 'eard music," Asiette said after a few more blocks. "Before those men broke in, there was a bell."

"That's you," I said.

"What do you mean?"

"Jackson convinced the head of the home insurance department of P9 to give people a break on their rates if they got this new burglar alarm that he read about."

"The bell?"

"Yeah. Then Jean-Paul bought the alarm company and gave Jackson a bonus. It could be a chime like I got or a loud alarm. Jackson convinced me that because of the company I keep I might want a heads-up. I guess he was right. . . . I'm sorry to put you through all that."

"That's okay, I don't mind."

"You don't?"

"Not really. I 'ave seen my father kill German soldiers on the road late at night. I 'ave seen what the Nazis do when they break down a door and drag people into the street."

Just at sunrise we got to her apartment building on Olympic in Santa Monica.

My breathing was almost normal by then.

"Easy?" she said with her fingers on the door handle.

"Uh-huh?"

"I want to see you again."

Our kiss good-bye reiterated that claim.

19

I got to the office a little after five, took my bath from the restroom sink using a red washrag and a bar of Ivory soap. After that I went to my private office to change. There was a brown suit and a pale green shirt in the closet, hanging there just in case.

In the kitchen I made scrambled eggs, pork sausage, and coffee strong enough to open my eyes.

It didn't surprise me that the men who invaded my home didn't know about WRENS-L. It was a new company and my name was nowhere in evidence. The agency name was listed but there was no address given, not even on our business card. Saul, Whisper, and I decided that we didn't want clients picking us out of the yellow pages and walking in from off the street. Enough people knew who we were to keep the boulder rolling downhill.

I had already decided to move houses by the time the second silver chime rang. They could kill me, that was all part of the job, but Feather had to be safe.

Working on my third cup of coffee, I tried to imagine why three white toughs would be after me. I was hired to prove, or disprove, a young man's involvement in murder—but who even knew that?

There was a time that if white muscle came at you then there were white men behind them. But that truth was no longer absolute. Black and white worked together in the new world of integration.

As Mouse often said, "Even crime got a bottom line."

"Mr. Rawlins?" Niska Redman said in a tentative voice from the front of the offices.

"In the kitchen," I called.

She came in wearing a light rose-colored dress that fell in an elegant line from her shoulders to her knees. Her eyes showed some worry.

"What's wrong?" I asked.

"You never get in before me."

"Is it seven already?"

"Six forty-five."

"I better be goin' then."

"Why are you here?"

"This is where I work." I stood up.

"That's a nice suit."

"Tell Whisper and Saul that I'm down in the coal mines."

When I moved to go past the young woman she said, "A man called you yesterday afternoon."

"What'd he say?"

"Nothing."

"He had to say something."

"He asked for you and when I said you were out he said to tell you that Mr. Stapleton had called."

"That's all?"

She nodded.

"Do you know who he is?" I asked.

"No."

The county courthouse was a well-appointed and large white stone building that loomed over a gentle park where retirees and winos stopped to rest on the redwood benches now and then. Homed and homeless, they were all on their various roads to oblivion.

A big brown bus from the county jail pulled up on the side of the structure just as I was about to enter the building.

The door to the bus came open and five uniformed guards assembled to flank the long line of men in gray prisoner garb and street clothes. The captives were chained hand and foot and to one another. They were being led toward some side entrance that I couldn't see.

As I watched the men shuffle out of sight, I wondered if one of them was Seymour Brathwaite; but most were young and black or brown with their heads bowed down. He could have been any one of them.

"Easy."

Fearless Jones was almost always a source of happiness and inexplicable pride. Wearing the same cheap suit he had on the day before, he was bright-eyed and clean-shaven, ready to go to work.

"Fearless."

"Poor guys chained up," he said. "White people don't know that when black folk see a parade like that we thinkin' 'bout a whole different circus."

There was no need for further comment so I said, "You ready, man?"

"Am I black and blue?" he replied with a smile.

"Hey, Dora," Fearless said to a dour white woman who sat behind the only small window cut into a lacquered cedar wall that was forty feet wide and over thirty feet high.

The nameplate on the ledge before her read MRS DUBITSKY. I wondered about the missing period and the fact the Fearless knew her first name.

Dora Dubitsky had at least ten years on me. The flesh of her face was succumbing to the pull of gravity and her glasses had a severe glint to them, mostly obscuring her eyes. The sour turn to her mouth seemed to say that she hadn't smiled in a very long time. But when she looked up and saw Fearless she actually grinned.

"Mr. Jones," she said, leaning forward as if intending to walk right through that wall. "How are you?"

"I woke up this morning," he said. "Them stairs and railin' for your father holdin' up?"

"He loves them," she averred. "Now he can get out of the house with no problem. But he told me that you wouldn't take his money."

"Just a few hours' work for one of my elders. You cain't put a price on somethin' like that."

Fearless couldn't do long division but he could build a house with a hammer, a saw, and a few nails.

"This my friend Easy Rawlins," Fearless said.

Dora's smile diminished but not so far as a frown.

"He's here to get out a client of Mr. Sweet's," he continued.

"Name?" she asked me, not unpleasantly.

Fearless earned his day rate just cutting the red tape at that window. Dora filled out the forms for me and gave me the release card to get Brathwaite out of lockup.

"What did you do for her?" I asked when we were waiting for the prisoner to be brought down to room 1001-B, the prisoner-release room.

"I seen her a lot 'cause Milo send me down to get thems that he's worried about; you know, so they see me and know I'ma be the one be aftah them if they run. One day Dora was on the phone soundin' all worried. I aksed what was wrong and she said it was her father, that he was old and couldn't get out the house. I said did he need a nurse 'cause I had a girlfriend right then did that kinda work. She said what he needed was some steps out the front'a his house. Said the ones he had broke and the landlord was draggin' his feet. By the time I got my prisoner released I had made plans to fix her father's front porch."

"And you didn't take any pay?"

"He's a old man, Easy. You know it's good luck to do somebody his age a favor."

"Rawlins," a man's voice called.

It was one of two courthouse policemen. Standing between him and his partner was a bespectacled and slender brown man wearing green cotton trousers and a once-red T-shirt that had faded almost to pink.

I stood and handed the guard that called my name the card Dora gave us. He studied the three-by-five pass and then nodded.

"See you at trial," he said to the prisoner.

Seymour winced and adjusted his glasses. The lenses were rather thick and bifocal. He rubbed his wrists and then looked at Fearless.

"You got me out?" Seymour asked.

"Mr. Rawlins here," Fearless said.

Seymour then turned to me. He had an angular face and a short Afro that looked like it hadn't been combed since the time of his arrest.

"Who are you?" he asked me.

"First you say thank you," I told the younger man.

"Yes of course," he said, adjusting his glasses again. "I'm just confused. They arrested me and questioned me all night and through the next day. I called Mama Jasmine. I didn't think she'd be there but she was and she told me that she'd get a lawyer. He came later but he didn't say much. Neither did I. I didn't do anything wrong."

Giving up on the thank-you, I asked, "When was the last time you ate?"

"Yesterday."

"Then let's get you fed."

"Who are you?"

"I'm Mr. Rawlins and this is Mr. Jones. We're representing a client that wanted us to get you out of jail and help with the defense."

"Oh," he said; a man who gets an answer but still does not understand.

Across the street from the courthouse and its Park of Lost Souls was an old-fashioned diner named Dolores. I'd already eaten and all Fearless ordered was a fried egg over easy and a glass of grapefruit juice. I knew this was because I was paying but I didn't argue. Seymour, who didn't look to be much older than twenty, ordered strawberry pancakes, scrambled eggs, bacon, and a pot of coffee.

I let him eat about halfway through the meal before starting the interrogation.

"How do you know Charcoal Joe?" was first on the list.

That caught Fearless's attention but Seymour looked bemused.

"Who?" he asked.

"He's the one who asked us to try and prove that you didn't kill Peter Boughman," I said.

"Is that one of the dead men's names?"

"You don't know?"

"The police didn't tell me. They didn't tell me anything. They just kept asking why I broke in and what had I done with the weapon."

"And you don't know Joe?"

"No." The young postgrad student stared at me through those thick lenses.

"What about the name Rufus Tyler?"

"Rufus," he said, pondering. "He's a friend of Mama Jasmine's. He would bring us a turkey on Thanksgiving sometimes. Once, when I was little, we all went to Redondo Beach together."

Something about the topic killed the young physicist's appetite.

"Well," I said. "Mr. Tyler has asked us to prove that you didn't kill Boughman. So I need to ask you a few questions."

"I'm really very tired, Mr. Rawlins."

"So tired that you're willing to spend the rest of your life on a cot in San Quentin?"

That gave him a face as sour as Dora Dubitsky's.

"What can you tell me about the night you were arrested?" I asked.

"I was looking for Mama Jasmine. I had called her but she didn't answer. Then I went to the high house but she wasn't there. I asked her husband about it—"

"Uriah?"

"Yes. He said he didn't know where she was but I didn't believe him."

"Why not?"

"Mr. Hardy never liked me too much. It was like he was jealous that I got to stay up in the high house with Mama Jasmine while he lived down the stairs."

"So how does that get you to the house at the beach?"

"Mama Jasmine has lots of jobs," he said. "She does catering and flower arranging and there's a few clients she has that have her do cleaning. She'd been a housekeeper down at the Malibu house ever since I can remember. Sometimes when the owners were on vacation she'd stay overnight. She'd sleep on the couch and leave the beachside sliding doors cracked so she could listen to the waves. I stayed down there with her a couple'a times when I was little."

"Jasmine was the housekeeper in the house where Peter Boughman was killed," I said, just to be clear.

Seymour nodded.

"Was she there that night?"

"No."

"Okay. Tell me what happened."

"The door was open and I went in. I called out in case there was anyone there and then I saw them on the floor. One guy was on his back in the middle of the floor. There was blood on his face and chest. The other one was on his face on the floor. There was blood all over and his hand was against the sliding glass door that looked out on the ocean." Seymour looked nauseous. "I tried to see if I could help either one but they were dead. I went around the house afraid that I'd find Mama Jasmine too but she wasn't there. I was about to call the police when they came in the front door with their guns out and shouting. They made me lie down on the floor in the blood, and later they said that I had a dead man's blood on me as if that proved I was the killer.

"Excuse me," he then said, "but I have to go to the toilet."

20

"What do you think?" I asked Fearless when the young man was gone.

"He ain't lyin'," Fearless replied, his words just part of a greater answer.

"But?"

"Everything the boy said was true, it's just that he ain't sayin' it all. I think he's just as worried as you is about where his Aunt Jasmine fits into this. And did I hear you say somethin' about Charcoal Joe?"

"He's the one hired me," I said.

"How you get mixed up with him?"

I explained the situation.

"Damn, Easy," the intrepid sideman said. "Trouble got your name tattooed on the inside'a his eyelids. He be studyin' you in his sleep."

Just when I began to worry that he'd ducked out on us, Seymour returned. He looked every bit the frail young man and I believed that Fearless was better than any lie detector, but I had also learned to be suspicious of everyone and it was not a habit I intended to drop.

"I need to get home, Mr. Rawlins," Seymour said, his breakfast forgotten.

"That would be ill-advised," I said to the college man.

"Why?"

I told both him and Fearless the abridged version of my previous night's home invasion.

In conclusion I said, "This is the only case I'm on and there's nothing my partners are into that would bring bloodthirsty chiggers like that out the woodwork."

"But why would they be after me?" Seymour asked reasonably.

"Same reason they broke into my house in the middle of the night," I said. "Something happened in that beach house and the job's not over yet. Rufus Tyler is what you would call a gangster, and I suspect him getting you outta jail has to do more with business than it does with your foster mother."

"Mr. Tyler? He's just a sweet little guy that plays fiddle sometimes."

"That description fits Nero too."

Seymour glanced over in the direction of the toilet.

"Look, son," I said in my most avuncular tone. "You were chained up and jailed for murder. There is no other suspect that I know of. If the police find anything that ties you directly to the crime, like for instance your foster mother was somehow involved with Boughman, then they'll come to your residence and drag you off with no bail offered."

Young Brathwaite ran his palm over the unkempt 'fro. He swallowed and thought over the little speech. Then he shook his head and crinkled his eyes.

"Where should I go then?"

"Where you stayin' at, Fearless?" I asked.

"Got a beautiful garden house behind this big place off'a Highland."

"You got room for Seymour there?"

"Why don't I go with you?" the lifelong student asked.

"Because people already know I'm in this shit. They got men with bad attitudes breakin' down my door. And Fearless? This man might not look it but he's a goddamned force of nature. He put you behind his door and you might as well be in Fort Knox."

Seymour looked at Fearless, trying to imagine my words on his shoulders.

"I don't have a car, Easy," Fearless apologized.

"How'd you get to the courthouse?"

"Bus."

"Bus? What time you get up?"

"I didn't really make it to bed last night. Beulah Tonk had a party and all the old crowd was there."

"Beulah's all the way out in Compton."

"Yeah. It took three buses," Fearless said. "I don't think you want me takin' son here on the RTD and you probably want him near a car."

"Let's go," I said.

Primo's Garage and Car Repair was on Gage near 1st Street at that time. It was a big lot occupied by old junkers, a little shack where the mechanics took their breaks and did business, and a twelve-by-twelve area sheltered by a flat aluminum roof where cars were raised on a hydraulic lift when Primo or one of his men were working on some poor automobile that should have probably been put out of its misery.

Surrounding the lot were two fourteen-foot-high wire fences, one behind the other, haloed with bales of razor wire. In the space between the two fences, four vicious dogs patrolled. The brown and black canines weighed between sixty and eighty pounds each and looked more like hyenas than dogs. They hated everybody in the world except for world-weary Primo and fair-skinned Peter Rhone.

A man I knew named Nino opened the gate for us to drive through.

I parked and told Seymour to wait for us in the backseat.

"Easy," Primo hailed when I got out of the car. "And Fearless Jones. Hector! Hector, *ven acá*!"

Primo was short and stout with a belly that could have been two pillows. His skin was amber and three of his teeth silver. Children loved him and most women saw him as a shield against the hard world. He was a good friend, and the natural expression on his face was a cautious smile.

The ten or twelve men that worked with Primo, including tall blond Peter Rhone, started to come out of the aisles and corners of the car yard.

Primo was barking out commands in Spanish. In short order a squat wooden barrel and two metal chairs were brought to my car.

The man Primo called Hector swaggered toward us. He was maybe five nine but his chest was huge and his arms bulged with muscle. His hands belonged on a man twice his size.

Hector's smile was the anticipation of another man's pain.

Primo and Hector spoke a moment, then the garage owner turned to Fearless.

"My friend Hector here says that he's the strongest man from all Mexico and therefore the strongest man in the world. I told him that he never met Fearless Jones."

Hector said something in guttural Spanish that was almost definitely an insult to my plain-looking slender companion. The other Mexicans laughed and nodded. A few of them were making bets. I was sure that every one of those wagers covered how badly Hector would defeat Fearless, because between the two, no matter the contest, Hector's victory would have to be seen as a foregone conclusion.

I would have been on their side if I didn't know Fearless Jones.

"He look pretty strong," Fearless agreed. A certain hardness undergirded the usually mild expression on Fearless's honest face.

Primo translated for Hector.

"*Cobarde*," the broad-shouldered Mexican said. Coward.

"I'll do it," Fearless said. "But tell my friend here that he only gets one chance. Either he wins the first time or he loses, that's it."

Primo gave Hector the conditions. The strongman spit on the ground.

They sat across from each other and put their elbows in position. They clasped hands and looked each other in the eye.

"Hey, Mr. Rawlins," Peter Rhone said as Primo explained the rules to the contestants.

"Pete. How you doin'?"

"Good."

"You still at EttaMae's?"

"Yeah."

I had cleared Rhone when the LAPD wanted him to go down for the murder of a black woman during the Watts Riots. He hadn't killed her. He had loved her and so when he was exonerated he went to work as a kind of man Friday for Mouse's wife. He was the one white man in America I knew of who was trying to work off his people's sins with humility and service.

Primo raised his hand in the air.

"Go!" he yelled, bringing his hand down like a hammer.

Hector heaved all of his strength into the contest.

If Fearless was merely as strong as he looked, Hector would have probably inflicted a compound fracture on his forearm. But with all of his effort the mechanic couldn't move my friend's arm more than an inch. Fearless looked at the combined clenched fist of their hands and then nodded. Slowly, with no obvious strain, he began to press Hector's arm back into the upright position; he paused a few seconds and then started moving Hector's arm downward.

Hector's eyes opened wide and his amber face became suffused with red. He trembled and redoubled his effort. But Fearless's arm moved slowly forward. The men watching were astonished, murmuring about the slighter man's impossible progress.

Primo was grinning and Peter wandered back toward the little hut.

Three inches from the barrel-top Fearless stopped, allowing Hector to put everything into pushing him back. Half a minute later the affable Mr. Jones shrugged the shoulder of his free arm and then slammed Hector's hand down into defeat.

The beaten mechanic jumped up and spewed a long diatribe in Spanish. Primo raised his hands and said, I supposed, that Hector had accepted the rules.

Hector then rushed at Fearless, yelling and holding his fists up.

If a man that strong and with so much rage had come at me I

would have shot him or at least hit him with something hard and metal. But Fearless just looked at him. He knew people well enough that Hector didn't frighten him.

Primo barked an order and the men went back to work.

"What can I do for you, Easy?" my old friend asked. He reached into a pocket of his workpants and came out with a half-drunk bottle of beer.

It wasn't yet noon.

"Fearless needs a car and I was thinkin' we could rent one."

"Rent? No."

"I gotta buy it?"

"For what Fearless just did you can have a car. Hector's been a, what we call a *matón machista*, a macho bully, on the yard ever since he came. I'd fire him if he wasn't my wife's cousin. But now you beat him in front of everybody. Now he can't say he's so strong. Come."

We summoned Seymour from his backseat and Primo led us to the far corner of the lot. There he pulled a paint-spattered tarp off of a beautifully refurbished 1958 Edsel. It was dark purple with silver piping. It had been waxed and fairly sparkled.

"This is my gift to you," Primo said to Fearless.

"That's too much, man," my temporary employee said.

"Oh, no. For a friend of Easy this is just the right thing," Primo said and killed the bottle. "He is my best friend outside of Mexico and I owe him a thousand thanks."

Primo took a bottle out of another pocket and a bottle opener from a pouch hanging from his belt.

"Well," Fearless said. "If you put it like that . . ."

Primo popped the cap, took a swig, and said, "The keys are in the ignition. Tank's three-quarters full."

"You go on with Fearless," I said to Seymour. "Nobody'll mess with you if he's around. And they won't find where he lives either."

"What are you going to do?" the young man replied.

"Try to find out what the cops have on you and who else would want to kill Ducky and Mr. Boughman."

"Ducky?"

"That's the other dead man."

"What about Mama Jasmine?"

"What about her?"

"Maybe I could stay with her?"

"No. That's too dangerous. You should be someplace where nobody would think to look. Call her but don't go there. I don't trust Uriah either. You got a phone, Fearless?"

"The garden house do." He wrote down the number on a slip of paper that Primo provided.

"All right, gentlemen," I said. "You should be on your way."

After they were gone I went to the little hut where Primo was drinking as Peter made entries in a huge bookkeeping ledger.

"Thanks, Primo," I said.

He saluted me with his bottle.

"Kinda early to be drinkin', isn't it?" I asked.

"Beer is beer every hour of the day."

"Drinkin' too much of it might not be so good though."

Primo looked at me with razor-sharp intelligence in his blood-shot eyes. "The older I get the more I know Death, Easy. Most of my friends from the old days are gone. They have gone with Death. I know him and he sees me. He tells me that there's a place for me in his wagon and I cannot say he's wrong. For all I know I could die tomorrow and who would deny a dying man his last drink?"

21

Behind a high hedge that needed trimming, a couple of blocks north of the Sunset Strip on Ozeta Terrace, stood a four-story house that looked to be constructed by a baker's dozen of warring architects. There were turrets, empty spaces, boxy additions, and curved walls made from wood and plaster, brick and stone. At the highest point there had been added a maroon geodesic dome that wasn't there the last time I visited.

The hodgepodge house was owned by a nineteen-year-old long-haired hippie named Terry Aldrich. Terry's father was a millionaire who gave his son the house and a ten-thousand-dollar-a-month stipend to stay out of his life. Terry turned the place into a commune/crash pad and bought marijuana by the kilo to keep his residents happy.

I tried the front door but it was locked. This was new—Terry's house had always been open to anyone who needed a mattress, a meal, or some marijuana.

I pressed the button, wondering if there was a bell connected to it, and waited.

Standing there looking up at the crazy-quilt structure, I was thinking that L.A. was a lot like that mansion. The city was growing at a pace so fast that no piece of it was designed to fit with the rest. Houses were being built in wildfire basins and on mudslide hills. Ultramodern skyscrapers stood next to squat brick office buildings built before the last three wars. The sun was almost always shining in a sky filled with smog, and people spent their days sitting in automobiles, at office desks, and in front of TVs at night.

It was a crazy life where housekeeper black women lounged by the ocean in million-dollar beach houses and old black men held private meetings in seaside jails.

"Can I help you?" someone said.

He was young and quite beautiful. A shade under five-ten with lustrous black hair down to his nipples, the skinny hippie kid was bare to the waist with no facial hair whatsoever. Despite his movie star appearance the young man seemed wary, even worried.

"Terry in?" I asked. Terry, the door's owner, was much taller with longer, stringy brown hair, and a face that a mother would only love because it was expected of her.

"No. He's up north."

"I'm here looking for Coco," I said.

The hippie Adonis looked at my brown suit and the usual prejudices between hippies and "straights" rose in his sneer.

"My name is Easy Rawlins."

That changed everything. The boy's eyes opened wide and he actually smiled.

"Easy?" he said.

"Yeah."

"Terry left your name on the kitchen wall so anyone who answered the door would let you in." The kid backed away, throwing the door open wide. "My name's Arthur. I been staying here till I can homestead some land back in Wyoming."

I crossed the threshold and he closed the door.

"I never knew this door to be locked," I said.

Arthur hunched his shoulders and said, "These biker dudes came in one day and ripped off Terry's dope. They beat on this one guy so bad we had to take him to the emergency room. So now the door is locked and there's usually a couple'a vets around in case it gets hairy."

I chuckled at the last word but Arthur didn't get the joke.

"Coco here?" I asked.

"Outside the White Rabbit Room," he said.

On the third floor of the inelegant mansion I came to a black door with the crude image of a rabbit hacked out in about a dozen white slashes, topped with two bright red daubs for its condemnatory eyes.

I walked into the long dormitory-like room. There were a dozen or so mattresses along the wall. Only one of these was occupied; this by a copulating couple. He was on top banging away, breathing hard, and she was looking at me as if maybe she were alone and wondering what I was doing there. I half expected her to wave.

I walked past them and to a window that opened out onto a pizza slice–shaped terrace.

As I climbed through I had my only ever filmmaking thought: I wondered what kind of movie would have a naked white couple fucking as a black man in a brown suit walked through and then out of a window.

She was sitting facing the window in the lotus position, upturned hands on her knees and completely naked. Helen "Coco" Ray had brown hair as thick and long as Arthur's, and breasts that defied gravity like those of a woman wading neck-deep in a swimming pool. She wasn't really pretty but she was beautiful and stormy and self-assured as only young beautiful women can be.

Her eyes were closed at first but they opened as I approached her, crunching the terra-cotta sand that littered the balcony.

"Easy," she said, not frowning.

"Hey, Coco." I pulled up an aluminum patio chair, the seat of which was threaded by a hundred or so strips of leather.

Her legs spread wide like that embarrassed me a little.

"What are you doing here?" she asked.

"I brought you a letter from Jo," I said, taking the bundle of pages from my inside pocket and handing it to her.

That brought her knees together and a feeling of relief in my chest.

Immediately she started reading. I waited through about five pages and stood.

"Wait please," she said. It was both a command and a plea.

I sat back down.

Coco read and I used the moments to wonder at the geometric connections between Charcoal Joe and Seymour Brathwaite. I didn't want to get too deep into that labyrinth. Maybe Melvin Suggs could make me a shortcut.

"Did you talk to her?" Coco asked, the letter on her thigh.

"Yeah," I said. "I needed her to do something for me and she asked me to drop this off."

"Do what?" Coco asked.

"Just a job."

"Did she tell you about us?"

"You weren't there," I said. "What's to tell?"

"She wanted a baby."

I smiled.

"You think that's funny?"

"Usually it's the young woman that wants the baby and the old man that just wants her love."

"Every relationship is different," the sun-kissed white girl said. Her certainty was like a fist.

"Yeah," I allowed, "and every one of those is the same."

"Do you wanna fuck?" she asked.

I wondered where this world of women wanting sex had been hiding when all I was thinking about was Bonnie.

"Come again?" I said.

"Jo and I decided that the only man we knew that could be the father of our child would be you."

"So you talked about it," I said to deflect the request.

"Answer my question."

I climbed off the chair and lowered to the sand-covered patio so that I was sitting next to the hippie siren. I held out a hand and she took it.

"I lost a daughter once. Her mother had stopped loving me because I couldn't be honest. They left and I swore I'd never lose another child. Do I wanna fuck you? Hell yeah. But do I want to give you a child to take away? No, honey, I could not do that."

It dawned on me that this was the second time that week someone had asked me to father their child.

She released my hand and then leaned over to kiss my lips.

"I'm sorry, Easy," she said.

Her eyes said other things and I'm sure mine did too. I thought of a dozen homilies I could share but there wasn't anything to say. That was the hippie age, and truth was in movement and bodies and actions. History had been obliterated and the future was just a waste of time.

"Phone's still in the kitchen, right?" I asked.

"Uh-huh. Are you gonna see Jo?"

"Sooner or later."

"Tell her I love her."

I stood up and walked through the window into the White Rabbit Room.

The young man was lying on his back with his eyes closed. The girl was tugging at his erection and looking at me with an expression I can describe only as bored.

22

Two young men with long hair and beards were smoking marijuana through a hookah at the small dining table in the kitchen. One was black and the other white. They weren't talking at all and their only movements were to either refill or relight the bowl of the water pipe.

The white guy had the dope and the brother the matches.

I was dialing a number on the wall phone, thinking that those hippies were a glimpse into a multiracial future in which I might not wish to reside.

"Yeah?" a voice muttered in my ear.

"You got anything for me?"

"Mr. Sugarman," the voice said. "Where are you?"

"Lookin' at two stoned-out hippie freaks on the Sunset Strip."

"Meet me at the China Box in forty-five minutes."

I took Sunset all the way.

It bothered me that Suggs wanted a face-to-face. That meant my investigation had hit either a live wire or a hornets' nest. Melvin and I were friends but he represented law and order in a city where the police often crossed that line.

The China Box was an old-fashioned establishment where each table was in a private room down a long aisle of closed doors. A gawky waiter in black cotton trousers and a pristine white jacket led me to station 22. He opened the door for me. Melvin was already in there eating fried wonton noodles and drinking a glass of ice water.

"Easy," he said. It might have been a greeting or a warning.

I settled in across from him and the waiter closed the door. The dining cubicle was big enough to seat eight but I still felt crowded.

"I ordered for both of us," he told me.

"Okay."

"You like the hot ribs, right?"

"Why am I here, Melvin?"

The cop was maybe a few years older than I, shorter by four inches and stocky but not fat. His hands were the size of baseball mitts and his eyes the color of a fawn's soft fur. He had two modes of dress. When he was in love his suits were clean and pressed; when she was gone he was a mess.

He was looking pretty good that day in a snappy blue suit and a white dress shirt. The blood-colored tie was loose at the collar, denoting the gravity of our meeting.

"What do you have to do with Peter Boughman?" he asked.

The door opened and another Chinese waiter, this one short and swarthy, placed a platter of at least a dozen glazed pork ribs between us.

When he was gone I said, "Never met the man."

"So why you on the case?"

"Seymour Brathwaite's foster mother asked me to help him out. She doesn't think he's done the crime."

"Mothers never do."

"And they hire me to make their beliefs into truth."

Melvin took a rib and denuded it in five bites.

"Boughman was one tough customer," he said. "He did it all— from extortion to murder for hire."

"So whoever killed him did some widows a favor."

"And made a pain in my ass."

"Why's that?" I asked.

The door opened again. The shorter waiter brought in a broad cork-lined platter with plates of fried shrimp, peanut noodles, and a dose of sweet and sour pork. He set these down between us and backed out of the room.

"Boughman was slowing down in his elder years. He didn't do the rough stuff anymore."

"Somebody should have told the killer that."

Suggs ignored the comment and said, "He was into money laundering. It was goin' around that he was in the middle of a multimillion-dollar transaction when he was killed."

"When I bailed Seymour outta jail he didn't have enough to buy breakfast."

Rough-edged Suggs studied me with his beautiful eyes.

"The guy with Boughman," Melvin said, "was a man known as John 'Ducky' Brown. No one in my department knows a thing about him except that everybody was afraid of him and no one cares that he's dead. Not the kind of guy you take to a sit-down business meeting."

"Maybe he was on the other side," I speculated.

"Doesn't look like it. Him and Boughman were shot with the same gun, and that weapon has not been recovered."

"Well," I said. "I don't know either one."

"And what about Charcoal Joe?" he asked.

Being white and poor or black and poor on the streets of America trained you to hide feelings of guilt. If you were in one of those categories you always felt guilty whether you'd done anything or not. So when a policeman asked you what you knew, you had to remain cool-headed, mastering everything from your furtive eyes to the quaver wanting to come out on your words.

"Never met him either," I lied.

"But you know who he is," Suggs suggested.

"I know his name. I've heard a bad man or two say it with respect."

Suggs eyed me a little longer. Then he turned his attention back to the food.

"They could give your client the gas chamber with the help of the prosecutor," he said while heaping sweet and sour flesh onto a bed of noodles.

"Why you say that?"

"They got a call from a phone booth saying that a black man had broken into a house on the beach and that shots were fired. Bough-man and Brown had been dead at least an hour when the call came in and there was no gun on the kid, in the house, or out in the sand. But medical records can be lost and your friend's foster child was standing over the dead men when the cops busted in. The report said that he had their blood on his clothes."

"But you could save Seymour," I surmised.

"Aren't you going to eat?" he asked.

"Taking my daughter for pizza after I pick her up from school."

"You once told me," Suggs said, "that you trade in favors."

"I did and I do."

"I need to know where the money that Boughman was handling has disappeared to."

"Like the money we took off those kidnappers?" I said, referring to the windfall that we had shared not a year past.

"I'm after the bad guys, Easy."

"I find the money and you take the weight off Seymour?"

He nodded and chewed.

The job I had set for myself had already been done. Seymour was innocent; but innocence was rarely the deciding factor for a black man on trial for his life.

"Okay," I said. "What else can you tell me?"

"There are two people that know about Boughman's current business dealings," Suggs said, pouring tea into a cup from a ceramic teapot. "Want some?"

"What two people?"

"The first, and most important, is Tony Gambol, a regular fixture at Santa Anita racetrack. Gambol has deep connections in the gambling worlds—both legal and not. Boughman went out to see him on the lunch court a dozen times in the last six weeks."

Reaching down at his side, Melvin came up with two manila files. He handed me one of these.

It was a rap sheet on the gambler Tony Gambol. He hadn't been convicted of any major crime but he'd been arrested for everything from assault to fraud. His unusually thin face was dark from the sun.

"The second," Melvin said, "is Willomena Avery. She's a saleswoman at Précieux Blanc on Rodeo Drive in Beverly Hills. She was at two of the meetings at the racetrack, and two other times she met with Boughman alone."

Her file was not official. It was a picture with the address of her workplace. In the photo her hair was pulled back and she wore unflattering glasses.

"No home address on Miss Avery?" I asked after perusing the makeshift file.

"Can't find one. She's not listed and her driver's license address is no longer valid."

"Why not ask her where she lives?"

"We don't want her to know that she's on our radar."

There was a question I had to ask for two reasons: the first was because I needed an answer; the second was to make sure Mel didn't know where my orders were coming from.

"Why'd you mention Charcoal Joe?"

"That beach house belongs to Tyler."

"Who?"

"Rufus Tyler, that's Joe's real name."

"And where was he when Boughman and Brown were being slaughtered?"

"In jail."

"So he's not a suspect?"

"No. He's a small-time gambler and we suspect that he rents out the house from time to time to people who need to do their business in secret."

"So what is it that you want from me exactly, Melvin?"

"If you find out who the killer is then you probably have found the money too. You give that information to me and I'll set your boy loose."

23

I had an hour or so before I had to head out to pick up Feather, so I went into the Chinatown branch of the Bank of America and changed a five-dollar bill into quarters. From there I went down the block to a small hotel called the Red Pagoda. I'd been there before, they had a nice bar and, I remembered, a fairly posh phone booth.

No one molested me when I shuttered myself into the scarlet stall.

The operator asked how she could help and I read the number from the slip of paper Jackson Blue had given me; the one that had the word *grandmamma* scribbled on it. The operator told me that it would be a dollar twenty-five for the first three minutes and I dropped five quarters. Each coin was accompanied by a deep bonging tone as it traveled downward. Five bongs and the operator thanked me.

The phone rang seven times and the connection was made.

A mature man's voice said, "Hello."

"May I speak to Sarah Garnett please?" I asked in the neutral accent of a white Californian.

"She's not in."

"How about her son?"

"He's away at college. Who is this?"

"Ezekiel Rawlins."

"What do you want with my wife, Mr. Rawlins?"

She was married. Of course she was. Sarah Garnett was not the kind of woman to feel that life was worth living without a man to live it with; a man to love and to hold, a man who would honor and provide.

"I'm calling about her granddaughter," I said.

"There must be some kind of mistake. My wife doesn't have a granddaughter. Her son isn't even engaged."

"Milo, right?" Remembering the young man's name, I thought about the other Milo; the darker, cigar-smoking bail bondsman.

"Excuse me?" the man's voice asked.

"Her son is named Milo," I said. "Milo Garnett."

"Is there anything else?" he asked.

I wanted to argue with the man. I wanted to tell him that he had no idea what he was talking about in spite of his assured and confident tone. I wanted to take that receiver and slam it against the glass window of the booth. But I didn't do any of those things. It wasn't my heart on the line in that conversation. I was doing a job.

"Can you give your wife my message and a phone number where she can reach me?"

"I've already told you that my wife has no granddaughter."

"I heard you. I'm not arguing either. All I want is for you to give her my name, message, and phone number. If she thinks that it's some kind of mistake then she won't call back and that will be my answer."

There was something authoritative in the way I strung that sentence. The man on the other end of the line hesitated. My voice on the telephone line was an unexpected threat that his posturing tone could not deflect.

"What did you say your name was again?" he asked.

I told him.

"And what is this about?"

"Her granddaughter."

"And what is her name?"

"Feather."

"That's not a name."

"If that doesn't ring a bell, tell her that it's Robin the younger. She'll know what I mean."

"I'm a lawyer, Mr. Rawlins. We will not submit to any scam or intimidation."

"I'm not asking for anything, sir, whatever your name is. I'm calling to talk to your wife about her granddaughter, Milo's niece. I couldn't care less what you think or what you do for a living."

"Please deposit seventy-five cents," the operator said.

I obliged.

When the bongs were over, Mr. Sarah Garnett said, "What was that number?"

I told him and thanked him and then hung up the phone.

As I walked out of the Red Pagoda I noted that my heart was beating fast. That reminded me about Bonnie, which brought to mind the tea Jo gave me; the potion that made every moment into an absolute present where my feelings were thrusting forward—not, for the most part, dwelling on the past.

Parked down the way from the entrance to Ivy Prep, I considered going into Marvin's Eats to see if Inez would call the cops on me again. But there was enough trouble in my trough; I'd save the reeducation of the white race for sometime later in the week.

With no windmill to tilt at, Bonnie entered my elixir-induced present. Her sudden betrayal had worked its way into my consciousness. I realized, sitting there, that there was no leisure time for me to wait for life to work itself out.

"Hi, Daddy."

Her voice surprised but did not frighten me.

Feather had opened the passenger-side door and flopped almost elegantly into the seat next to me. Her calico dress was printed with red and yellow tulips and cut in a French provincial design. When I kissed her cheek she leaned into the touch.

"How was school?" I asked.

"Okay. Are we going home tonight?"

I pulled away from the parking space and drove out of the compound.

"I need you to stay someplace else for a few more days. That's why I'm picking you up. I don't want you to forget what I look like."

"I'll stay with Uncle Jackson and Aunt Jewelle," Feather allowed, "but I won't stay at Bonnie's house."

"Just because Bonnie and I have a problem doesn't mean that you should be mad at her."

"Uh-uh," Feather said, shaking her head for emphasis. "She's on one side and you're on the other one. And I'm with you."

"But Bonnie's been like a mother to you, honey."

"I know. And I love her too. But she's just *like* my mother. You're the only father I'm ever gonna have."

We were headed for the canyon drive that led from Studio City to L.A. I pulled off onto the side of the road and engaged the parking brake.

Feather gave me a worried look, thinking that she had said something wrong. I saw her fear. I wanted to assure her but I needed a moment to put my thoughts in a line.

"What, Daddy?"

"I was," I said and paused. "I was wondering how a child your age ever got so wise."

She smiled, leaning forward into the grin like she had for my kiss.

"When I was little," she said, "and you were out working, Juice would take care of me. He was really nice and he let me eat ice cream *and* cookies in the same desert. And if you were gone too long he'd put me to bed and tell me a story."

I was a sucker for Feather's stories. She'd tell me tales that I already knew but her point of view would make it all sound somehow different.

"Most of the time he'd tell me fairy tales about giants and princesses and knights in shining black armor. But every once in a while he'd tell me a *very* tale instead of a *fairy* tale."

"Very tale?" I said. "What's that?"

"Those were stories too but they were more real."

"And that's what Juice called them?"

"No. I did. But can I finish what I'm saying?"

"Sorry."

"His very tales were always about us; about how we were lost children and you found us and took us home and took care of us even though nobody told you to and nobody made you. Jesus would say that that was what made you a hero, and whenever he'd say that it would make me cry. And when I'd cry he'd tell me I didn't have to be sad because we could take care of you just like you did with us. And that would make me so happy that I'd close my eyes and go to sleep."

24

I offered to go for pizza but Feather was looking forward to making dinner with Jewelle.

At that time Jewelle and Jackson lived in a marble and wood two-story home on Charleville Boulevard just west of Doheny. Adele Morgan answered the door. She was a top-heavy beauty with skin the color of maple syrup, a Diana Ross flip hairdo, and a look in her eye that was all business. She would have been the perfect mate for either a sharecropper or a captain of industry.

"Mr. Rawlins," she said in a neutral tone that had no invitation to it. But when she turned to my daughter she smiled. "Hi, sugar."

"May I use the phone, Miss Morgan?" I asked.

The young doyenne considered my question, going through all the rules that came down from her bosses. After a brief assessment Adele decided that I could indeed make a call on the house phone of her employer; further, I was not limited to the local area code.

Feather ran past Adele into the house shouting, "Aunt Jewelle!"

"Do you need privacy?" the assistant asked.

In Jackson's library I dialed a number I had only just learned. Listening to the ring, I sat in Jackson's padded office chair. The ashtray to my left was filled with filterless butts, and the greater part of the desk was covered with books open and lying facedown; maybe a dozen of them. There were biographies, technical texts, a novel or two, and one book written in German. Before I could figure out what the foreign-language title said, he answered the phone.

"Hello?"

"Fearless."

"Hey, Easy. How you doin'?"

"Every hour feels like another day."

"Don't I know it, brother. I try an' tell my rich friends that if they wanna live longer all they gotta do is give they money away, because a poor man's day is a whole week longer than somebody got all the edges sanded down."

"How's Seymour?"

"He called his mama. She told him to stick with you so he relaxed and fell asleep on the sofa. You want me to wake him up?"

"No," I said, and then I explained my needs.

The Santa Anita Park racetrack parking lots must have had spaces for five thousand cars; and almost every one of them was occupied. I had to go all the way to the far end of Lot 5. There, next to a fence loomed over by a stand of eucalyptus trees, I finally found a space between a blue Volkswagen Bug and a wood-paneled Dodge station wagon.

It was after six when I got to the food court next to the betting windows. Evening races were scheduled for people who had to work before they threw away their money, and so I felt safe in the anonymity of numbers.

There were maybe a couple of hundred tables out on the asphalt eating yard. The daylight was waning but not yet gone, and the mists of desperation and hope rose up off of the thousand or so diners like vapors from an agitated sea.

People were eating, drinking beers, smoking the next in a never-ending convoy of cigarettes, and studying tickets and racing forms. One middle-aged white woman I saw was reading what looked like a Bible. I moved up behind her and saw that not only was it a Bible but it was written in French. Wondering what use a Bible was at a race-track, I looked up and saw my quarry. On a raised dais that could probably look down on the track were maybe a dozen smaller tables. At one of these sat a small man in a lavender-colored ensemble. He was flanked by two suited bruisers who, despite their business attire, looked like professional wrestlers about to climb in the ring.

I glanced left and right, saw nothing familiar and no one that I recognized, considered a moment, and then approached the dais.

There was a uniformed guard who stood at the base of the few steps up. He was a bronze man who probably called himself white, with broad shoulders and light brown eyes. I couldn't discern his hair color because he was clean-shaven and wore a military-like cap.

This man held up a hand and said, "Private."

"Here to see Mr. Gambol," I said.

The security guard studied me a moment, two. I read in his scrutiny the thoughts as they occurred. He wondered if he should send me on my way, let me pass, or if he was required to go ask the gangster-gambler if he expected me.

I waited patiently. His momentary conundrum was my lifelong struggle. I wasn't worried about the way being blocked because I knew that I would get what I needed in the end. It was, I believe, this certainty in my demeanor that made the bronze man move out of my way.

A race had just started and so the special people on the raised hot-dog court were mostly looking at the track. The announcer was calling the race, and a clamor raised among the throngs of hopefuls.

As I approached the table where the man in the lavender suit sat, I wondered if Charles Darwin or any of his acolytes had ever applied the theory of evolution to the obsessive behavior of gamblers; was gambling a survival technique and did success in that selection process change our relationship with luck?

That's as far as I got in my intellectual pondering because the two wrestlers had moved forward to impede my access to their meal ticket.

These men were a bit larger and more threatening than their bronze brother below. Their suits might be described as *the wrong green* and *a blue too light for its tailoring.*

"Can I help you?" the pink-skinned green-suited muscleman asked.

I waited a moment longer than one would expect and the men listed forward.

"Charcoal Joe wanted me to ask Mr. Gambol a question," I said, both telling the truth and testing the power of my employer.

The olive-skinned bodyguard in the blue suit took a backward step, lowered into the seat next to Gambol, and whispered into the man's ear.

The race ended and the clamor turned into more of a murmuring hubbub. Tony studied me and then said something to his underling who, in turn, motioned for me to come forward.

The man in the light blue suit stood up and held the chair for me to sit in.

Up close I realized that Gambol must have been a jockey in his youth. He had a tough wiry frame on a body not much larger than a chimpanzee's. His skin had been so much in the sun that the tan was permanent, and his pecan eyes had seen things that I wouldn't want to know.

"Joe sent you?" he asked.

"In a roundabout way."

"Say again?"

"Seems like a young friend of Joe's has been arrested for the shooting death of a man named Boughman. Joe's trying to get the kid off and so asked me to help, seeing that he's in jail at the moment. I asked some friends who this Boughman knew and they pointed me at you."

Gambol gave away nothing in his expression. I hoped that my own plans were equal to his stoic reaction.

"Who said that about me?" he asked.

"I kiss and tell," I admitted, "but I never say who I've been talking to."

"Talk," Tony Gambol said speculatively. "Talk is a freedom; the freedom of speech. And, as every blond-haired, blue-eyed American child can tell you, freedom is our most precious possession. And, as any businessman worth his salt will say, that which has value also has a cost."

It was possibly the most elegantly worded threat I'd ever received.

"I take it you can't help me with Boughman?" I asked.

"Never even heard of the man. I mean, I may have seen him. I'm here every day with fifteen thousand other men. Maybe I stood next to him in the urinal, but I don't know him. And if he's dead I guess I never will."

"What about a woman named Willomena Avery?"

Believe me when I tell you that Tony Gambol was the type of man that you do not want to squint at you. He tightened his eyes at the mention of the woman's name and I knew that there was a toll somewhere on the road not too far ahead.

He forced a smile and said, "Never heard of her either."

That was the end of the conversation.

"Thank you, Mr. Gambol," I said, hoping that civility might in some way assuage his ire.

I stood up and walked off the dais, out of the food court, down a path past the bleachers, and out of the gates.

As I walked through the twilight at the far end of the parking lot, the words of a gospel song came to me: *Walk on, walk on with hope in your heart and you'll never walk alone. . . .*

I was hoping that those words were true when a man called out, "Hey!"

I turned quickly but they were on me just that fast. Three guys related in physical appearance to the bodyguards Gambol had with him. They were big and brutal-looking, wearing work clothes, not suits. The work, I assumed, was my demolition.

There was pistol in my pocket but they were too close, and though I might have wounded one or even two of them, the end of that conflict would have almost certainly been my death.

"Excuse me," a voice I knew said.

There came a grunt and a sudden movement behind the men crowding me. One of them fell to the ground. The two left turned quickly, giving me a chance to reach for my pistol. I did this, but before I had a chance to take it out, one more man hit the asphalt. The last standing attacker was able to hit Fearless on the jaw. A lesser man, me for instance, would have been felled by that blow but Fearless didn't even take a backward step. He brought to bear an uppercut that made me wince and even feel sorry for the man who would have most certainly broken a few of my bones.

Fearless let out a hearty breath and smiled.

"Damn, Easy, you got to learn how to make friends, man."

"I didn't even see you, Fearless. I thought I was out here alone."

I clasped his outstretched hand with both of mine.

"When I was a boy my Uncle Bob used to take me out in the South Texas swamps to hunt wild boar. All we could use was a Bowie knife. That made the problem twofold. First you had to be quiet enough to sneak up without that hog hearin' you, and second, you had to sink that blade in the jugular before he stomped you to death."

25

I gave Fearless a hundred dollars for expenses, an address, and a time to meet me the next morning. Then I jumped into my Dodge.

As I was driving off I could see, in my rearview mirror, the men who almost attacked me. They were gathering themselves up from the ground, leaning on each other and dusting off their clothes. I remember thinking that if I were another class and color, maybe in another nation too, I'd be planning on retirement rather than engineering close calls while concentrating on the safety of others.

Then I thought of all the friends I had who shared my race and poverty, my nationality too. Most of them, even Jackson Blue, had everyday jobs and houses and cars without all the trouble I had. Mouse had once told me, "I couldn't live like you, Brother Easy, uniform bangin' on the front do' and a cougar lurkin' out back."

I went to the office instead of my home. I had a glass of ice water in the kitchen and then went to my private office, locked the door, checked the barrel of my favorite .45, and lay down on the old blue sofa that was almost as comfortable as John the Bartender's couch.

As I lay there I contemplated disparate facts.

Feather could not sleep in her own bed because of the mess I'd made. Bonnie had married another man as I prepared to ask her to marry me. Seymour Brathwaite could not have committed the murder he was charged with, and the police knew it; but still he was facing the gas chamber. I was lying on my back in an empty office suite, a .45 on the table next to me, wanting to sleep and worrying about predators coming in through the window or breaking down the door.

Somewhere in the middle of all that I remembered that I hadn't had my one cigarette yet that day. This simple thought brought a smile to my lips and pulled me off that couch. I sat behind my fancy desk putting the pistol within reach, took a Lucky Strike from its pack in my pocket, and lit the tobacco stick.

Ah! That first inhalation dispelled all my dark factualizing. My muscles relaxed and I was safe.

The phone began ringing on the third drag. I didn't answer. I didn't want anybody to think I was there. After the eighth ring the tape recorder/answering machine interrupted the call.

"You have reached the WRENS-L Detective Agency," Niska Redman's sweet voice said. "No one is here right now but we'll be happy to call you back. Leave a message and a number after the tone."

A gong sounded. It was not unlike the sound of coins being taken by a pay phone.

"Easy . . ." was the only word I had to hear before grabbing the receiver.

"Jo?" I said.

"You're there?"

"You're on a phone after nine at night?" I replied in kind.

"I was just gonna leave you a message . . . about Bonnie."

"What you got?"

"All she has to do is go to this address in Ventura. The people there will send them on their way."

"Give it to me," I said.

"No, baby. You said you didn't want to know so I told Raymond to call Jackson and go get them. They're probably already gone."

The last few words hit me pretty hard. It was like hearing about the death of a loved one; a death that was expected but you thought that there was still time to say good-bye. Luckily I had a few drags left.

"Easy?"

"Yeah?"

"You okay?"

"I will be."

"I called your house first but nobody answered. What you doin' in your office at this time'a night?"

"Hiding from shadows. What phone are you using?"

"Neighbor down the street named Morris. He got told he only had a little while left to live and the doctors wanted to experiment with that new heart transplant business. I told his wife that I could probably get him up and out with a few herbs. He's fine now and I can use the phone whenever I need to."

"What about that tea you gave me?"

"What about it?"

"It's like the things botherin' me are there but if a fly passes before my eyes I forget about them."

"So you know what it does."

"How long does it last?"

"Long enough, baby. Did you talk to Coco?"

"She read the letter and said that she loved you."

That information settled for a while.

"Good-bye, Easy," she said.

"Thanks, Jo."

When the cigarette was gone I took my pistol back over to the blue sofa and fell into a dreamless sleep. I woke up with an almost clean slate in my mind.

For breakfast I took a slice of sourdough bread, an egg, a dash of vanilla, a tablespoon of sour cream, and a pinch each of sugar and salt and pureed them in an Oster blender. I poured that concoction into a griddle of sizzling butter, then sprinkled diced strawberries on the wet side. Three minutes on one side and two on the other and I had a first-rate griddle cake without all the fuss.

Later I drove past my house to make sure things looked copacetic; at least from the outside. Then I was on my way to Beverly Hills.

At the top of a pedestrian knoll on Rodeo Drive, eighteen minutes after eleven o'clock, Fearless Jones was waiting for me, standing out in front of a store that sold expensive Italian suits. He was drinking coffee from a paper cup and wearing a dark blue suit that was exactly the same cut and material as the steel-gray one from the days before.

"That's it, right?" he said when I walked up to him.

He gestured with his head at a storefront up the block that had a rusted iron and white enamel facade. The storefront window had the ivory words PRÉCIEUX BLANC stenciled upon it. Below that, in smaller black lettering, it read *The finest jewels set in silver, palladium, white gold, and platinum.*

The day was warm and the sign said OPEN. Fearless and I couldn't stand on a fancy street like that too long before the police were called, so we made our way toward the second name on Melvin Suggs's list.

Fearless pushed the glass door but it was locked. This struck us both as odd because there were salespeople and customers inside.

Then a black man in a security uniform approached the door. He looked at me and I made a gesture clearly showing that we wanted in. He held up the palm of a hand, pushing it forward to indicate that we had to step back. Not until we'd given him a yard and half of space did he unlock the glass door, pull it open, and then step out to meet us.

The guard's uniform was leaf green with black buttons and gun belt. He was shorter than either of us and physically fit in military fashion. Maybe forty; I figured that he had been a cop but retired right at twenty years. Now he worked in white stores so that black customers who were followed and rousted could not complain about racism.

"Can I help you?" he asked the space between me and Fearless.

"I'd like to buy a brilliant-cut half-carat diamond set in platinum," I said.

My request was unexpected. The apple butter–colored guard's eyebrows knitted.

"Don't mess with me, man," he said.

"I'm shopping for an engagement ring and I hear the Précieux Blanc's the way to go," I countered.

"Who told you that?" he asked after thinking a few moments.

"A cop named Anatole McCourt." I couldn't help but smile behind that name.

"Bullshit."

"I got his number right here in my pocket, Mr. Ex-policeman. You wanna call him? Or should me and Fearless here paint us some protest signs and march up and down sayin' that you don't serve blacks up in here?"

The guard took a beat and then backed toward the door, opened it, and ushered us in.

The showroom was a perfect square with each wall twenty-five feet or so in length. Inside the larger square there was a second pen with a black-tile floor and waist-high glass cases displaying jewelry of white metal and red, green, yellow, and white jewels.

Three saleswomen stood behind the cases. Three women and two men were being attended by the staff—that is, until Fearless and I stepped in. At that point every white face in the room turned to us.

The security guard watched us too; his back was to the door.

One saleswoman brought a pale hand to her yellow silk blouse, just below the throat. Her fear was palpable. And so our gestures became small and slow. We didn't want anyone calling the police. I mean, I wasn't armed and neither was Fearless, I was sure, but just a pocketknife on a black man's person in Beverly Hills might be cause for an arrest.

"Excuse me," I said to the frightened redhead. "We were hoping to speak to Willomena Avery."

"What?" she said fearfully.

"Willomena Avery."

"I, I, I," she said.

"I'm Miss Avery," a voice off to my left said.

Tall, beautiful, and white like some cured woods, she was forty, twice the age of the stammering redhead. She might have been the younger sister of the woman in Melvin's photograph.

Willomena's hair was long and brown and tied into a bun. Her figure was a throwback to the fifties. The dress she wore might have been conservative on a lesser body; it was royal blue.

While I was looking at her, she was regarding Fearless. Her smile showed no fear and her stance told me that she was the person in charge.

"I'd like to ask you a few questions, Miss Avery," I said.

"About jewelry?"

"No, ma'am."

"And your name is?"

"Ezekiel Rawlins. This is Mr. Jones."

"Mr. Jones," she said, with the slightest movement of her left shoulder.

"Ma'am."

Then Willomena Avery turned to me. "I'm the store manager. They pay me to sell jewelry, not to answer questions from men off the street."

A silver bell rang, indicating that two of the patrons were departing. The sales staff looked as if they'd like to follow suit.

Seeing the lay of the land, the guard moved closer to us.

"I'm sorry to hear that," I said. "Me and Mr. Jones are trying to find out a few things about Peter Boughman."

The store manager was living proof that beauty is as much an attitude as it is a physical thing. Only her eyes registered the impact of my words; they might have been looking at an unexpected hummingbird hovering overhead.

"Come with me to my office," she said. And then to the guard, "Um, excuse me, what was your name again?"

"Vincent, ma'am."

"Yes. Vincent, you may return to your post at the door."

"Are you sure?"

Avery did not answer the question. Instead turning her attention to us, she said, "Follow me," and led us between two of the glass cabinets, through a green doorway, and up an especially narrow flight of stairs. At the top of the stairs there was a closed door, also green. This door opened onto a small office.

"Have a seat, gentlemen," Miss Avery said.

She went behind a blond desk and lowered onto the straight-back wooden chair there. Fearless and I took the padded maroon seats that faced her.

Lacing her fingers together, reminding me of Charcoal Joe, she smiled at us.

"How can I help you?" she asked.

I told her the story about Seymour and Charcoal Joe (whom I called Rufus Tyler), about the murder and the evidence.

"A man I know on the LAPD told me that you were an acquaintance of Boughman's" was the end of my little spiel.

For a full minute after I was done talking Willomena peered at us, wondering, I believed, what she should and should not say. I fully expected her to deny any knowledge and ask us to leave.

"Peter," she said, as if the name was conjecture. "Peter was involved in some kind of double-cross. He got hold of a great sum of money and instead of moving it down the line he took a sidetrack—a detour which happened to be a dead end."

"Wow," I said.

"Have I surprised you, Mr. Rawlins?"

"Your candor is stunning."

That was the only moment that she seemed surprised. My use of language was as unexpected as a flock of sudden hummingbirds.

"Don't people usually tell you the truth?" she asked with a faint smile.

"I don't know about people but I said the same thing to Tony Gambol and he sent three of his men to beat me senseless."

"You don't look any the worse for wear."

"Mr. Jones here was in the background. And you don't mess with Fearless if you want to stay upright and conscious."

"They call you Fearless?" she asked my associate.

"Just another word for fool."

Her nostrils flared but I didn't feel jealous. I had met Avery's kind before. In the end I'd have fared better with Gambol's men.

"Tony is closer to the fire," she said to me. "The only work I ever do, did, with Peter was to turn currency into diamonds now and then."

"You admit that?"

"In this room with the door shut," she confessed. "Your testimony wouldn't hold up in court and the people Peter dealt with know what work I do."

"Do you know who might have killed him?" I asked.

"No. But even if I did I wouldn't say. You know there is no protection for people who cross that line. Is there anything else?"

"I guess not."

I made to rise and Fearless did too.

"Mr. Rawlins," the bombshell store manager said.

"Yes, ma'am."

"Do you have a card?"

"I do."

I took my wallet from my pocket, then bent down and grabbed a pencil from her desk. I wrote my name across the bottom of the new WRENS-L business card that Niska had ordered for us all.

"Here you go," I said, handing the card to her.

"If I think of something I'll call you," she told me.

I wouldn't be holding my breath.

26

I followed Fearless in his new-old Edsel down Wilshire, then 6th Street, until we got to a huge house made of stone on Highland.

I tailed him into the driveway through to the warrens behind the mansion. There we passed through a green yard that was big enough to be a small Parisian park. At the farthest reach of the property, behind a huge oak tree, we came to a concrete apron that separated the six-car garage from a smaller structure that was probably designed to be the servants' quarters.

Fearless and I parked side by side next to the house.

"How you rate this place?" I asked Fearless.

"Owner is a man named Diggs," my primal friend said. "He had some trouble with a guy. I stayed up in the big house for a while, you know, answerin' doors and makin' sure he was safe. He knew a lawyer and the lawyer knew Milo. Anyway, when the trouble was over Mrs. Diggs offered to let me stay back here till I save enough for my own place."

Fearless rapped twice on the oversized front door, then three times fast. After that he used his key to let us in. The house was larger than it looked from the outside. The room we entered was big enough to be a living room and a dining room too.

There was a large square table with eight chairs on the left, and two sofas and a padded reclining chair on the right.

Seymour was sitting in half-lotus on the mechanical chair reading a large tome. When we walked in he peered at us through his spectacles and then performed a weedy rocking motion to get himself up and out of the chair. If I had seen him do only that, I would have known that he was not a killer.

"Hey, Sy," Fearless said.

"Hello, Mr. Jones, Mr. Rawlins."

He approached us toting the heavy book.

We all settled at the dining table, which looked to be made from teak.

"What you reading?" I asked the gawky young man.

"It was in the den in the back," he answered.

"And what is it?" I insisted.

"Oh . . . yes, sorry, *The Descent of Man*."

"Darwin," I commented, remembering the racetrack and my speculations about evolution.

"You've read it?" Seymour asked. The surprise in his voice irked me.

"In a book club," I said. "There's only three members: me, a downtown librarian, and a man I think you know—Jackson Blue."

"From P9?"

"The same."

"You *know* Mr. Blue?"

"How is Jackson?" Fearless asked.

"Got a shadow a mile long and scared of every inch of it."

Fearless chuckled and asked, "You guys wanna drink?"

I asked for ice water and Seymour demurred.

When Fearless was gone he asked, "You really know Mr. Blue?"

"Why wouldn't I?"

"He's an important man."

I was looking at the slender, four-eyed murder suspect, trying not to let my anger get the better of me. I wanted to ask if what they taught him in college was to hate himself or did he just get that way on his own?

Fearless came back with my water glass and the anger seeped away.

"I need to talk to you about a few things," I said.

He pressed the point of a finger of his left hand against the bridge of his glasses, pushing them up on his nose and, with the same gesture, pushing his head back an inch or so. The movement reminded me of a puppy seeing something that might be a threat.

"Okay," he said.

"Your onetime foster mother gave me eighteen thousand dollars to get you outta hock," I began. "Where does a woman you say is a part-time housekeeper get that kind of money?"

"I, I don't know."

"But you know that some street-talkin' men like me and Fearless shouldn't be acquainted with an important man like Jackson Blue," I pointed out.

"She . . . she borrowed it, I guess."

"From Rufus Tyler?"

"I don't know."

"How long you live with her?"

"Till I was about twelve. Then the Burton family up in Walnut Creek, in the Bay Area, took me in. There was a better high school up there and it was a whole family of scientists. I finished high school when I was fifteen, then went to Stanford for six years."

"Why would Jasmine still be so involved with you if you haven't lived with her in a decade or more?"

"I always thought of her as my mother," he said, pressing on his glasses again. "I spent holidays with her, and she, and she trusts me."

"Trusts you with what?"

"She loves me, okay?"

"Why were you down in Malibu looking for her?"

That stopped the boy for a few moments or more.

"A woman came to see me," he said at last.

"What woman?"

"I never saw her before. She was white but she had on a red scarf and wore dark glasses. She spoke with some kind of accent . . . Eastern European or something. She wouldn't give me her name but she said that she was a friend of Mama Jasmine's and that she *had something* for her."

"What was that?" I asked.

"I asked her why not go to Jasmine," Seymour said instead of answering my question. "She said that Mama Jasmine was missing, that she hadn't been home and nobody knew where she was.

"I hadn't called her since a few days," Seymour added.

"What did the white woman give you?"

"I didn't say she gave me anything," he argued. "I said she said she had something for Mama Jasmine."

"This is not high school debate club, son," I said.

"I talked to Mama Jasmine today." There was great consternation on the young man's face. He looked as if he was about to cry.

"And what did she say?" I asked, even though what I wanted to know was the nature of the gift from the unknown white woman.

"She said that she was leaving town for a while and that I should, I should listen to you."

I took a moment then to order the clues that passed through the young man. Jasmine Palmas worked cleaning a house owned by Rufus Tyler; a house that Jasmine's son went to, finding Peter Boughman and John "Ducky" Brown. Something a mysterious white woman said led Seymour to that house; a woman who maybe knew Jasmine and had something for her.

"How old was the white woman?" I asked.

"Old like Mama Jasmine."

"Did you ask Jasmine about her when you talked today?"

"No," he said, but that surely wasn't true. "I meant to but I was so happy to hear her and she wanted to know about what happened in jail and at the beach house."

"Uh-huh. And what did the white woman give you?"

I could see behind his spectacles that he wanted to change the subject yet again.

"A little red diary," he said instead.

"Did you look inside?"

"No." He pressed his glasses.

"Not at all?"

"It fell open one time when I was hiding it. It was written by hand in blue ink but I can't tell you what it said."

"Why?"

"Because I didn't even know what language it was in. Most of the letters were out of the alphabet but the punctuation was weird and the words didn't even make any sense."

"Does Jasmine speak another language?"

"No."

"What did you do with it?" I asked.

"First I called Mama Jasmine but she didn't answer. Then I called Uriah."

"What'd he say?"

"That Mama J had been gone for a few days. I could have called her or gone over there but . . ."

"What'd you do with the diary?"

"I sewed it into the curtains behind my desk."

"You sewed it?"

"Yeah. Mama Jasmine always said that men should know how to sew and cook and women should be able to shoot and run fast."

"Why would you feel that you had to hide something like that?"

"I don't know," Seymour said, honestly confused. "She, the woman, told me that I shouldn't give it to anybody but Mama J. She said that no one else should know about it."

"So you played James Bond and sewed it into the curtains."

Seymour didn't answer that.

"Where'd Jasmine say she was going when you talked to her today?"

"She wouldn't tell me. She just said to do what you told me to."

"Okay," I said. "Let's forget about the book and Jasmine for a minute. What about Uriah?"

"What about him?"

"Do you wanna go to the gas chamber, Seymour?"

"Of course not."

"Do you wanna run and hide with every policeman in this country lookin' at your mug shot with a warning that you're armed and dangerous?"

"I don't even own a gun."

"You think that PhD you got makes you immune from your skin?"

That question actually stumped him for ten seconds or more.

"Uriah is married to Jasmine but they don't share the same bed," he finally said. "As long as I've known her he's lived in the low house and we were on high. He came to Easter and Christmas dinner most years and he fixed things that broke. If he ever saw me coming down the stairs or coming back from school he'd stop me and ask about Jasmine."

"Ask what?"

"Who she was talking to? If she had any men friends up in the house. Things like that."

"You say he lived in the bottom house as long as you can remember," I said.

"Uh-huh."

"How old were you when you came to her?"

"Um . . . I don't really know. Mama Jasmine says that I came to her when I was just a baby. My parents were killed in a train wreck in Illinois on their way home."

"What else about Uriah?"

"He used to have prostitutes come on the weekends sometimes. Mama Jasmine didn't like it but Uriah used to say that he wouldn't be with those whores if she'd let him up in her bed."

The college man enjoyed the rebelliousness his de facto foster father had shown.

"How did you know they were prostitutes?" I asked.

"One of the nice ones told me. She gave me a card and said men called that number when they wanted a girlfriend for the night."

"What did the card say?"

"It was a real red lipstick kiss with the letters JB and a phone number."

"What else?"

"It didn't say anything else."

"I mean about Uriah."

"He drinks a lot too," Seymour added.

"Did you ever see him with Rufus?"

"I hardly ever saw Mr. Tyler. And, no, I never saw him with Uriah. The two Thanksgivings he came to dinner Uriah wasn't there."

"So the diary is still in the drapes?" I asked then.

"What does it matter? You can't read it."

"I can't know Jackson Blue either." The young man hesitated so I added, "Didn't Jasmine tell you to trust me?"

He nodded, reluctantly.

"Then what's the problem?"

"I don't know. It feels private."

"That might be so but your execution will be on the six o'clock news."

"Why do you keep trying to scare me, Mr. Rawlins?"

"Because you're not scared enough for your own good."

"I already told you that I didn't kill anybody. They can't find me guilty of something I didn't do."

"Did they arrest you?"

He nodded.

"Did they make you lie down in blood?"

He looked away.

"Did they book you for murder and set your bail?"

"But I didn't do it," Seymour insisted.

"You're the only suspect," I said. "The police don't have any other potential defendants they're looking at. The only person looking for somebody else is me."

This time Seymour took off his glasses and rubbed his right eye with the heel of his free hand.

"My apartment is on Weyburn a little west of Westwood Boulevard."

He gave me the numbers, directions, and a key to the door.

"Is there anything else you can tell me?" I asked. "I mean did you see anything or hear anything at the beach house?"

He put the spectacles back on and pressed them hard—but to no avail.

I sighed and shook my head.

"Well," I said at last, "I guess I better go over to your place and get that diary I can't read."

"Want me to come with you?" Fearless offered.

"No. I want to think."

"I could be quiet, brother. You know you got thugs comin' up out the ground. You might need me."

I knew he was right but my frame of mind was askew since he'd saved me in the parking lot.

I wanted to feel like a man.

"Mr. Rawlins?"

"Yeah, Seymour."

"There's a red box containing a three-volume set called *The Feynman Lectures on Physics*. Could you bring that back too? I'm supposed to start teaching over the summer and those lectures are considered the bible of physics."

"I saw it at Jasmine's house."

"I gave her a copy when she wanted to know what physicists did. Actually I gave her two. She lent the first one to a friend. But there's one at my apartment too."

"I'll look around for it," I promised.

27

In those cases where there's a black man on the hot seat I usually spend most of the investigation in the black part of town. His family and friends, loved ones, and those that hate him are usually there. The crime he is suspected of has almost always been committed in the hood. Since the days of slavery black folk have been crammed into slave quarters and ghettos, same-race marriages and schools segregated by neighborhood. In prison our cellmates were black, and in death it was almost always a congregation of black faces that laid us to rest.

But Seymour Brathwaite did not fit the profile. His IQ along with an indecipherable series of events had put him smack-dab in the middle of white America. He had not sought to be there. He had not been trying to escape the harsh realities of racism. And so he felt that he belonged there as well as in the "high house" with Mama Jasmine. And because he didn't feel privileged or even aware of his unique status, Seymour had also accepted the unconscious prejudice of the world he passed through so ignorantly. He expected to receive a fair trial from color-blind justice, and he just supposed that people like me would not consort with important men like Jackson Blue.

Weyburn was a street that was almost pure white in 1968. The address was to an unimpressive lime-and-pink ranch-style house in the middle of the block.

I parked directly in front of the house and got out feeling like a man with a purpose. There was a pistol in the trunk. I considered for a moment but then decided against retrieving it. Somebody might see me, and all I was doing was going into an empty apartment in a part of town where the crime rate was nearly nonexistent.

I walked to the front door of the front house and pressed the button. I didn't want the landlord to think I was invading his castle grounds. After a minute had passed I knocked and pressed the button again. I went through this two-tiered process three times before going down the driveway and into the backyard.

Like Fearless, Seymour lived in a bungalow behind the white man's house, only on a smaller scale. This backyard was somewhat ramshackle and there was no green except for the overhang from trees in the neighbors' yards.

Seymour's place was up a tier of seventeen stairs, because it was situated on top of the garage rather than across the way from it.

I had the key from Seymour but knocked anyway. I'd known too many men that had been shot opening strange doors unannounced.

The apartment was a solitary room, about half the size of Fearless's living/dining room. There was a bed and a couch, a table and a desk. The kitchen was an electric coffee percolator and two hot plates set on a solitary shelf that jutted out from the wall. The bed was unmade and there were clothes, shoes, and underwear on the floor. The big cabinet he used for a closet was open and most of its contents were piled at the bottom, overflowing onto the pine floor.

The messiness of the apartment made me like the postgrad student more. He was just another hapless young man bumbling through a life on a path that he was absolutely sure of.

I noticed these details as I was looking around for a back door. Men in my trade (and black men in general) usually like to know where the exit is before they get down to the business at hand. Whether it was a new lover or an old friend, in a new house it was always good practice to have an escape map in your mind.

Seymour's house had no second door. The windows were too small and the jump too high for a man my age.

I decided to stay anyway.

I located *The Feynman Lectures* first; this because it was out on top of the desk.

There were also textbooks, notebooks, notes scribbled on at least a hundred slips of paper, and dozens of pens and pencils all under a cover of rubber dust from hundreds, maybe thousands, of erasures. There was a coffee cup with the dregs dried into a cracked cake at the bottom and a single-slice pizza box with the contents long gone.

A small black ant was inspecting the edges and corners of the inside of the pizza box; I felt a close kinship to that little emmet.

On a white ceramic plate behind the desk there was a banana that had turned black and a red apple gone soft. There were a few more little black insect detectives at work there.

I looked at the muslin curtains drawn over the window behind the desk. My goal, the foreign-tongue journal, was somewhere up near the top. I would pull it down but first I decided to look through the desk.

The five drawers were all filled to the brim, jumbled with everything from crossword puzzle books to articles cut out of newspapers and magazines. There were a few tennis balls, a stapler, a small tape recorder, and paper files of various colors. There was a box of three Trojan condoms, unopened, and a magazine of naked white women that left nothing to the scientist's imagination.

And there was a letter.

Dear Seymour,

I know that you're very busy with college and that physics paper you want to get published. You're a man now and men have to work hard to make it in this world. But you don't live that far from here and I miss you dearly. You are the son of my heart and the most important person in my life.

I'm writing to tell you that soon I'll be leaving Los Angeles. I'm going to South America where I can get a house for little money and live off my savings. I won't be moving for a while yet but I want to see you many times before I leave.

I've only stayed in America so long because of you, because I wanted to be sure that you had everything that I never did.

I love you,
Mama Jasmine

Seymour had already mentioned Jasmine's leaving the country, but he didn't say South America. I might have thought more about it but just then the only door burst open.

I recognized the two big white men in their dark clothes. I had last seen them through the hedgerow in my backyard in the wee hours of the morning.

I lamented my decision not to pop the trunk while scanning the desktop for another weapon. There wasn't even a letter opener. Maybe there was something on the kitchen shelf but that was one step too far away. Seymour didn't have a baseball bat or even a baseball. The only defense at hand was piles and piles of paper.

I grabbed a great stack of handwritten notes and threw them at the intruders. The momentary flurry of wispy paper gave me time to pick up the straight-back pine chair from behind me. I threw it in the general direction of the men and then vaulted over the desk using my left hand as the spring and my left hip as the slide. I landed more or less steady and moved forward with no thought in my mind except the annihilation of my enemies.

I did pretty good hitting the bald one with a left hook and his nearly bald partner with a right cross. The second man had taken the brunt of the flying chair so I turned to the first, bringing up a knee intent on hitting him anywhere between the groin and the nose.

I don't remember if my knee connected because of the sharp blow to the back of my head. The pain brought to my mind the odor of a ripe cheese. The autopilot that had driven me through the worst slums in Houston, Texas, and all the way through World War II made me pivot and hit the man who'd used a sap on the back of my skull. He fell back a step and a half. I remember thinking that if he went all the way down to the floor I had a chance at survival.

But he didn't fall and his friend, who had somehow come up beside me, laid a haymaker fist against the left side of my jaw.

28

Coming awake was a revelation; an event equal to sitting on my Big Mama's lap while hearing the minister say, "And God said, 'Let there be light, and the light was good.'"

I was hurting, bound hand and foot, bleeding, and a little dizzy. Even though I was lying on my side on the floor, I had the feeling that I might fall.

But none of that mattered. I was alive when I should have been dead. I had expected to give up the ghost and I was still breathing, still able to feel pain. This afforded me a shred of hope.

My hands were tied at the tailbone and my ankles were bound so tightly that it felt like I had but one leg. There was no electric light on in the room but the window let in ample sun. The floor was carpeted with thin green material and there was one wood chair that I could see. Not only did my head and jaw ache but there were pains in my hip and right side. I imagined that I'd earned these extra bruises with the chair I'd thrown.

I was a little queasy but not actually nauseous. I would have liked to urinate but I could put that on hold.

They must have staked out the house, I thought, the two bald men. They were waiting for Seymour. When I came along, one of them made a call. That gave me the time to search the house. The boss, whoever he was, told them to grab me. That meant they were going to press me to give up the college student. And that was the small window through which I might escape.

The door to the small room came open and three men's trousered legs walked in. The door closed.

"Get him up," a voice barked.

Unceremoniously I was lifted and thrown in the chair. Once upright I could see that the two bald men had been joined by the third home invader. He had been the boss in my backyard and he held the same position in this small, sparsely furnished cell. I wasn't so worried about my captors because I was trying not to throw up. My thoughts of escape were orbiting the sharp pains in my head and side.

"Look at me," the leader ordered.

I obeyed as well as I could. The boss was the smallest of the three. He had brown hair and a boxy face with evenly spaced features. His mustache was uncalled for. His breath stank.

"Where's Seymour Brathwaite?"

"I don't know," I said. "I was looking for him when your friends showed up."

He hit me with a backhanded slap. A blow like that would have probably made Seymour cower and cry. But after a life like mine it was a simple declaration. I had to concentrate on not smiling at my torturer.

"Where's Brathwaite?"

"I told you I don't know," I said to the floor with an emphasis I did not feel. "I was at his place looking for him."

"Look at me," the leader commanded.

Gazing upward, I saw him and the bald men at his sides.

"If you don't know, that's too bad because you broke Arnold here's finger with that chair and he will surely kill you if you don't have what we want."

It's an odd feeling to be bound hand and foot and yet involved in a dance. I had to believe that the three men were going to kill me anyway. The question was when. I couldn't just blurt out my answers; they wouldn't have trusted that. But the guy the short boss indicated did have a finger on his right hand trussed up like it might have been broken.

If I pushed them too far they might kill me before I got the chance to craft my survival.

"What's your name, man?" I asked the boss.

He hesitated and then said, "Gregory."

"Listen, Greg, I told you the truth. I was hired by Charcoal Joe to get Seymour outta hock. I turned him over to a guy Joe pointed me at and he took him somewhere I don't know."

"What's this guy's name?"

"They told me to call him Mary Donovan."

"It's a woman?"

"That's what I thought but when he showed up I saw it was a man." I opened my eyes wide, making an insincere plea for sympathy.

"That's not enough, Mr. Rawlins," Gregory said. "Not nearly enough."

"I made a call to the guy," I offered. "I remember the number."

"What is it?"

"Look, man," I said. "All I got between me and Arnold here is that number. You know I cain't go to the police over this. You guys are safe from me. And you already kicked my ass. I'll give you what you need but you got to let me loose."

"Can't do that, blood," Gregory said with manufactured sympathy. "At least not until I have Seymour."

"But once you got him you don't need me."

"I won't need to kill you either. I could tell Arnold to kick your ass a little more and then you could walk home from here. I might even give you bus fare."

For a moment I assumed the role in which I was cast. I felt that maybe if I really gave Gregory what he wanted I could walk away with my life.

"All right," I said. "All right. But you can't call. I got to."

"Why?"

"I already done business with Mary. He don't know you."

"If he wants to save your life he'll do what I say."

"Mary work for Charcoal Joe," I explained. "He don't know me from a hole in the ground."

"What's the number?" Gregory insisted.

"I'll give it to you," I said. "But if you call it and he hears your voice that'll mean your last chance to get at Seymour is gone and my d-death."

The stutter was not part of my plan.

Gregory studied me then. He'd come into the room the man in charge but our interchange had the unexpected result of making me an active element in the equation. The information I had made me a part of the action; even an unwanted partner.

"Untie him," Gregory said to the thug-not-Arnold.

My feet were fine but my hands prickled and felt swollen like a bunch of sausages. For a full minute I couldn't even bend my fingers.

They led me from the small cell to a bright living room with eight windows covered by gossamer yellow curtains. Sunlight blossomed at these windows but no one from the street could see inside.

"Make the call," Gregory commanded.

"Two-one-three area code?"

"Make the call."

Even though my fingers felt like logs I was able to dial the seven digits. On the first ring Gregory picked up a second receiver and Arnold pointed his pistol at my forehead.

The phone rang six times before he answered.

"Hello?"

"Mary Donovan," I said.

"What?"

"I'm calling Mary about that job we did."

There was a brief pause that felt like a year and then he said, "What about it?"

"I talked to Joe," I said. Gregory was jotting something on the front page of a newspaper. "He needs me to see Seymour."

"No one told me about that."

"I'm telling you now," I said, trying to put some authority in my voice.

Gregory handed me the newspaper. Scrawled over the headline was a Culver City address on Red Maple Lane.

"So you want me to take you to see him?" the voice on the phone asked.

"I need you to bring him to me."

"Why not just talk to him on the phone?"

"He needs to talk to him face-to-face."

"Why not—"

"Listen, man, whatever your name is, Joe wants me to see Seymour. You got to bring him to me now." I gave him the address.

"That's in Culver City."

"Yes it is."

"I don't like the way this sounds. What's up?"

"Nuthin's up, man. I just need you to bring Seymour out here to me."

There was another long pause. Arnold pushed the gun forward so that the muzzle was touching the center of my forehead.

The last time I felt so hopeless I was in an automobile plummeting off the side of a Malibu cliff.

"All right," the phone voice said. "He's sleeping. I'll wake him up and we'll come on out."

"'Bout a hour?" I asked.

"Or less."

"Mary" hung up the phone and Arnold put his gun down.

If I was Mouse I would have grabbed that gun and killed those men or died trying. Fearless Jones would have won the fight in Seymour's apartment. But I was a man of strategy wishing it was me on a backwoods journey with Bonnie while the king's corpse lay in state.

"Should we kill him now?" Arnold asked Gregory.

The short boss-man considered the question.

"When we have the kid," he said at last. "First we got to be sure we have him."

I chuckled a bit at the relief I felt for the one-hour reprieve the thugs had allowed me.

"What are you laughin' at?" the thug-not-Arnold asked.

"Just thankful for the few breaths I got left, brother."

The bald bruiser frowned. I believed that he was in agreement about the brevity and the value of life.

29

I was tied up again. This time my legs and arms were lashed to the chair, which had been dragged in from the smaller room. Gagged with a washcloth shoved in my mouth, held in place by black electrical tape wrapped around my head; the only useful powers I had left were sight and hearing.

The man with the broken finger, Arnold, pulled an armless chair to my side and sat astride it, backward.

"Don't worry, son," Arnold said. "After we get your friend I'm going to shoot you right here." He touched my right temple with the tip of a single finger. "It'll be fast, like turnin' out a light."

Knowing the time, place, and method of your death is a deeply existential moment. It was too immediate, too absolute for me to actually feel fear. Instead I concentrated on my instincts for survival.

I closed my eyes.

"You prayin'?" Arnold asked.

I couldn't reply.

"Mayhew!" the man named Gregory barked.

"What?" Arnold complained.

"Let that man alone."

Arnold Mayhew grumbled and got up, leaving me to contemplate his boss's words. *Let that man alone.* I was helpless and under a death sentence. There was almost no chance for me to survive. But what struck me, what caught my attention, was the fact that the boss had called me a man. I tried to remember if at any time I had been called a nigger by Gregory or his cohorts. Arnold had called me "son" but that didn't feel racial.

A virtual mute quadriplegic, I had nevertheless transcended racism because they were going to kill me for the danger I posed, not the color of my skin.

Some victories are so hard-won that they might not be worth the exertion.

I wanted more time and I wanted it to be all over. I worried about Feather hearing I had died. I wondered if Mouse would find out who'd shot me and deal with them in the near future.

The man-not-Arnold pulled the drapes over the windows, cut a small hole in one of them next to the door, and took upon himself the job of sentry. All three of the men had pistols in their hands. That's how I realized that Gregory was left-handed.

During the first half hour they spoke very little but as the time came for "Mary" to bring Seymour, the talk dried up completely.

I was nervous but not scared. I'd been near death many times over the years but rarely did the Reaper move so slowly. It was almost like I had a disease that was killing me. I could still see the world moving on as I stayed behind—dying by inches.

There came a sound. It was the softest of thuds.

Arnold heard it too. He turned his head toward the back of the bungalow. . . .

"Somebody's coming up the path," not-Arnold said. "He's black but too old to be our guy."

"Alone?" Gregory asked.

"Yeah."

I smiled underneath the tape-gag because Gregory was now as worried as I.

He looked at me and then down at his gun hand.

I actually felt the sweat sprouting from my brow.

"Drop your weapons!" a man shouted.

Six cops had somehow entered the space. They were armed with rifles and shotguns, clad in bulletproof gear and Plexiglas-visored helmets.

Gregory, the only man who might have shot me, dropped the pistol and fell to his knees on the floor, placing his hands behind his head.

Arnold, moving by reflex instead of intelligence, turned his gun at the voice and was cut down by a dozen or more shots.

The only mistake not-Arnold made was not dropping his gun fast enough and staying on his feet. He was shot twice and fell to the floor hollering in pain.

The front door was broken in and another six cops in military gear entered. The last of these was Melvin Suggs. Melvin Suggs who lived not six blocks away with his grifter girlfriend, sometimes known as Mary Donovan.

When I opened my eyes (though I didn't remember closing them) I was no longer trussed up or gagged. I was lying on my back in a hospital bed feeling no pain. I took in a deep breath and felt an ever-so-slight ache in my left side.

Looking around the white room I noted the late-day sunlight in the window and the empty bed next to me. When I turned my attention toward the door, a white man in a dark suit saw me and went away.

I thought about sitting up but decided against it. When I closed my eyes it felt like just a few seconds passed, but it might have been more.

"You are a fucking lucky bastard," Melvin Suggs said.

I opened my eyes again and winced at him.

"What happened?"

"You fainted."

"I what?"

"Fainted . . . like a young girl in the hot sun." He was grinning and I was alive.

"That was a close call, Melvin."

"You can say that again. I know butchers can't cut that close to the bone."

"I'm in a hospital?"

"Brotman," he said, nodding sagely. "You were pretty banged up and unconscious too. They wrapped your ribs. Doctor says they probably aren't broken. But he gave you a shot for the pain. What happened?"

"I was lookin' for something for Seymour and the two big guys attacked me. I tried to fight, lost, and then the little one, Gregory . . ."

"Chalmers," Suggs added.

"Him. He told me that if I didn't produce Seymour that he'd ventilate my skull. So I made up a story about a man code-named Mary and hoped that you'd get the idea."

"Chalmers works for a man named Eugene 'the Cinch' Stapleton," Melvin said. "You ever heard of him?"

"No." It wasn't such a big lie. "Who is he?"

"Troubleshooter for the eastern mobs. He settles disputes and tells who to do what. He's big-time, Easy. Much too much for a guy like you."

"Aw, come on, Mel, the Constitution says that every man bleeds the same."

It was nice to wring another grin out of that ugly mug.

"You want to tell me what's going on?" the special assistant to the chief of police asked.

"Like I told you, I'm working for Seymour Brathwaite's foster mother, trying to get her son out from under a murder charge. A murder we both know he didn't do."

"What's she paying you?"

"In kind."

"What kind?"

"Sex with a view."

Talking gave me the strength to sit up and then stand. My clothes were neatly folded on a white metal table next to the bed. I had to concentrate to get my feet in the pant legs without falling. The buttons on my shirt gave me some difficulty too.

"Doctor said he wanted to keep you for the night," Melvin told me as I tied the lace on my left shoe.

"I got girlfriends can't get that kind'a commitment outta me."

"We need you to press charges against the two that lived."

"That other guy didn't die?"

"Shattered femur," Melvin said. "Lost some blood."

"Huh." I tied the other lace.

"So how about a statement?" Melvin asked.

"How about you give me a ride to my car up on Weyburn?"

"With that morphine in your system you shouldn't be driving."

"I'll take it slow, Melvin."

"What about that statement?"

"I'll come by day after tomorrow. You could hold them till then."

He dropped me at my car and I got in. He drove off and I got out again. There was a light on in the lime-and-pink front house, so I rang the bell and knocked on the door.

A small white woman with short blond hair answered. She was maybe fifty and cute.

"Yes?" she asked with no fear or apparent suspicion.

"Hello, ma'am. My name is Ezekiel Rawlins and I'm a friend of Seymour's."

"Oh," she said sadly. "He's in jail I'm afraid."

"He's out now and staying with a friend of his foster mother's down Watts."

"How is Jasmine holding up?" the lady asked.

"Pretty good, considering. Anyway, Seymour gave me the key to his place and asked me to pick up a couple of books. I didn't want to scare you so I thought I'd introduce myself before going back there."

"I'll turn on the back porch light for you, Mr. Rawlins."

I didn't waste any time on my second visit to Seymour's pied-à-terre. I climbed up on his desk, ripped down the curtain, and cut the seam with my pocketknife.

It was a small book bound in soft red leather, maybe eighty sheets. Twenty pages or so were filled with tiny writing in a language more foreign than any I had encountered in my travels through Europe during World War II.

I took the journal and *The Feynman Lectures*, turned off the light, and walked out like a free man in a free country.

"Say hello to Seymour," the little woman said from her front porch just before I opened the door to my car. "Tell him that we know that he didn't do anything wrong."

I waved at her and got behind the wheel.

It had been a long day.

30

Whisper worked late most nights. You always knew when he was there past five because of the music coming from his office. Piano concertos, flute sonatas, now and then he played a symphony from the eighteenth century on his stereo record player.

He was sitting at his desk holding up a single sheet of paper, daring it to try and hide its secrets.

I knocked on the open door.

"Come on in, Easy," he said without looking up.

I took a seat feeling in turns deep exhaustion and stabbing pains. Whisper was taking his time with the sheet of paper but I was in no hurry either. I was supposed to be a dead man, and so sitting there exercising the minor miracle of breath was just fine.

Whisper's suit was as dark a yellow as you can get before turning brown. His nut-colored hat was the only thing hanging from the coatrack in the corner. Whisper didn't have a bookshelf or an in-box. He only worked one case at a time and, by his own admission, rarely used more than one drawer in his desk.

There was a woodwind quartet playing on his stereo, beckoning me to close my eyes and use my ears.

"So what can I do for you, Easy?" Whisper asked, jogging me back to consciousness.

The solitary sheet of paper was lying on the desk without even the company of a pencil.

I dipped my hand into the left pocket of my jacket and placed the little red journal next to the paper.

He picked up the book and began turning pages slowly.

"How's the case going?" I asked him.

"If she's still alive I'll have her within the week. How's yours?"

"Solved but not settled."

He looked up then and smiled as well as he could manage. Whisper liked simple truths.

He placed the book on the desktop and shoved it in my direction.

"You need to go see Mania Blackman," he said.

"Who's that?"

"I'll call her to make you an afternoon appointment and leave the address and time on Niska's desk."

"Mania?"

"Polish," my partner said. "I think she was named after her mother."

"You know the language?"

"Polish too," he said, "heavily influenced by Yiddish. There's probably a hundred different dialects extant and Mania knows a hundred and one."

Whisper was a mystery that defied logic. He knew more single facts than any person I'd ever met. I once asked him how he knew so much. "Proximity osmosis" was his deadpan answer.

I was ready for bed. I don't remember ever being that tired, even after the Battle of the Bulge. I was so exhausted that getting up from the chair seemed like an impossible task.

"You need help, Easy?" Whisper asked.

"Why you say that?"

"Because you staggerin' in that chair."

I woke up on the sofa in my office with the sun in my eyes. I didn't remember if I'd made it there under my own steam or if Whisper had helped me. The room wasn't actually spinning but only shaking at the edges. My ribs hurt. The back of my head and the left side of my jaw were both sensitive to the touch.

My tongue was dry and my stomach felt like a week-old stew had gone bad in there.

The sun told me that it was late morning. My mind told me it was time to test my legs.

I spent the next two hours in the bathroom. Between showering and shaving, brushing my teeth and hair and using the facilities, I was feeling pretty good. My jaw was a little puffy and my eyes somewhat bloodshot but the corners stayed still and I had survived where most men would have perished.

Niska was sitting at her desk in a bright-colored flower-pattern muu-muu dress. Her hair was teased out in the natural hairdo made popular by Angela Davis.

"Good morning, Mr. Rawlins," the lovely young woman greeted.

"Hey, Niska. Anybody but you and me here?"

"Saul had to take his son to the doctor and Tinsford was working late." I was the only one of the partners that she called mister. "There's a note for you."

The pink slip of paper gave an address on 23rd Street in Santa Monica; a time, 2:00 p.m.; and the name *Mania Blackman*.

I read the note over and stood there a moment gathering the forces of my body and mind.

"Feather called at eight and I told her that you were sound asleep. She said to kiss you good morning so consider yourself kissed."

"Thank you. Anything else?"

"Detective Suggs called and wanted you to make an appointment with a Detective Davis Bethune. Mr. Jones called—"

"Fearless?"

"Uh-huh. He's nice."

"What'd he want?"

"Nothing. He just told me to tell you that everything was fine."

My watch said 12:17. A little voice in my head was whining that we should go back to the office and sleep until that night.

"I won't be back till tomorrow," I said.

"Tell Mania that Niska says hey."

The address Whisper left me was for the Star-Hobard Motel a block north of Pico on 23rd. There was a diner across the street where I had two eggs over easy with white toast, strawberry jam, and a single slice of reheated baked ham. The coffee was weak, which was probably for the best, and I was able to hold it all down.

Mania's unit number at the motel was 3F. That was on the top floor.

All the units of the Star-Hobard were accessible to external walkways. I climbed the stairs, feeling each step in my ribs, then followed the numbers down to 3F, knocked on the door, and waited. The food was having the desired effect on my metabolism. The door opened inward, revealing a short and stout woman with stiff, hardly brushed hair that was equally gray and blond. She wore a shapeless navy blue dress and her bare feet were callused.

"Ooo blat gump?" she asked.

"What did you say?" I replied.

I worried that my experiences from the previous day had somehow impaired my ability to understand simple language.

"Tapala lu vem," she said with a yellowish grin that was missing a few teeth.

"Um," I replied.

"Oakla, oakla," she said, nodding and grinning and stepping back.

I walked in and asked, "Are you—Mania?"

"Sure, sure Mania."

The room was dark; drapes were pulled over the windows. It smelled of yeast and potatoes, and the furniture seemed to be turned around—relatives that had stopped talking to one another.

"Whisper Natly sent me."

"Ah compo felika," she said with indecipherable emphasis.

I was lost.

"You're Mr. Rawlins?" a younger woman's voice asked.

She was standing in the doorway that connected unit 3F to 3G. The same height as the older woman, the newcomer was not yet thirty and with light brown skin and hair that was brushed but still could not make up its mind whether to be straight, wavy, or coiled. Her dress was also blue but short, form-fitting, hinting at the hue of peacock feathers. Her eyes were in turn aqua and gold, and the lines of her face were strong and angular while her features contained the soft roundness of the Negro race.

"Mania?" I said.

"You're Mr. Rawlins?" she asked again.

"Whisper sent me to see if you could translate a journal for me."

"Ooo taka," the older woman chimed.

"My mother likes you," Mania the younger said.

"That's nice."

"She likes black men," the young woman said, making a gesture with her hands that said, *That's why I'm here.*

"Asti mo von luppa tin ono," mother said to daughter.

The beautiful young woman answered in the same incomprehensible tongue.

"Oh," the old woman said with a nod. "Tutu."

"Come with me, Mr. Rawlins," young Mania said.

I followed her into unit 3G. She shut the door behind us.

The adjoining room was filled with light. The open drapes revealed a pair of sliding glass doors leading out onto a small patio that had two baby blue chairs made from some kind of synthetic plaster.

"Let's sit outside," she suggested. "It's such a nice day. Can I get you something?"

"No. I ate across the street because I was early."

The only comment I could make on the Polish-and-black woman

was that her features seemed nearly feral. Her eyes were bold and shameless. Her body seemed like it wanted to dance.

"Sit," she commanded.

Seated there across from each other, our view was of a big backyard where a middle-aged white woman in tan khaki shorts and a white blouse was working in a garden large enough to keep a family of three in salads year-round.

"What was that language you and your mother were speaking?" I asked.

"Made up."

"Come again?"

"My mother was born in a shtetl in central Poland. There she mostly spoke Yiddish. In 1933 her parents sent her to Warsaw where she passed as a Christian. When the war broke out she joined the Resistance. The Christian Polish freedom fighters were as anti-Semitic as the Nazis, so she forced all things Yiddish from her mind. But her comrades found out and she fled to France. She was afraid to use Yiddish again and communicated in a kind of broken French. She was able to get to England by 1940. There she met Barney Blackman, an aide to General Monroe Moorland. Barney was a kind man and he didn't mind that Mania had pretty much stopped talking. He was my father, killed in the early air raids on London.

"I was four when we moved to America. Barney Blackman's family wasn't as kind as he was, and by that time my mother's mind was going. She could no longer remember Yiddish, Polish, or French. The only language she had was the gibberish she and I spoke when I was still a very young child."

"Wow," I said. "And that's why you know so many languages?"

She smiled at me, radiating an optimism combined with a confidence that I had not felt in a while.

"How can I help you, Mr. Rawlins?"

I gave her the red journal and explained that I was mostly interested in the last few pages.

She thumbed through the book much the way Whisper had

done, nodded, and said, "Come back tomorrow afternoon. I'll have what you want by then."

"How much?"

"I'll read the whole thing," she said, not understanding the question.

"I mean what's this translation gonna cost me."

"Nothing."

"Nothing?"

"I owe Tinsford and he asked me to do this for you."

"How do you know Whisper?"

"I used to babysit for his children."

"Oh," I said. "Niska says hi."

31

Feather was waiting for me at the entrance to Ivy Prep. I bought us both cold sodas at a hot-dog stand and we talked about her day at school. After that I brought her to Jewelle and Jackson's house.

"When can I come home, Daddy?" she asked when I pulled into the driveway.

"Just a few days, honey. I want to make sure everything's okay first."

She kissed me and hugged me around the neck.

I felt safe going home, because the men that had invaded my house were either dead or in jail.

I boarded up the window that they'd broken to get in and reset the alarm system.

After placing loaded pistols at various easily accessible points throughout the house, I set about making dinner.

Cooking relaxes me. From chopping onions to washing plates, I feel productive and pampered in the kitchen.

That night I sautéed hot Italian sausage with brown mushrooms, minced garlic, stewed tomatoes, fresh basil leaves, dried oregano, and scallion greens. I added cayenne and red wine at the end and let the sauce simmer down into a gravy while I boiled water and then cooked the vermicelli pasta.

I should have used Parmesan but all I had was sharp cheddar, so that had to do.

I was finished eating at seven, considered having my one cigarette, but decided to put it off till later.

"Hello," Fearless said, answering his phone on the second ring.

"Fearless. How's it goin'?"

"Okay. What you been up to?"

I told him of my adventures in detail.

"Damn, brother, you got to slow down. You know we ain't young men in the Fifth Ward no more."

"How's Seymour?"

"He okay. Wants his book'a lectures but he knows that you doin' more important work."

"Tell him that I'm on the case and somewhat optimistic. I should have some answers in a day or two."

"Try not to get killed before that," Fearless said.

When I put down the phone it rang immediately.

"Hello?"

"Easy."

The breath I was taking got stuck, but finally I said, "Hey, Bonnie. How you doin'?"

"I miss you," she said with forthright sincerity. "When I look ahead the only thing I regret is leaving you and Feather behind."

A sound escaped my throat. I tried to think of something intimate and caring to say but failed.

"Mouse got you and Joguye someplace safe?"

"Mama Jo said that you don't want to know where we are."

"I think that's best."

"You're a good man and I love you," she said.

I considered asking her to come back but that milestone was behind us, in the distance.

"Take care of yourself," I said instead.

"Good-bye, Easy," she replied, and we both hung up.

My throat was tight after that conversation. I wanted some whiskey but knew better. Drinking and broken hearts were okay as long as there was no car key in your pocket and no loaded .45 on the shelf.

The phone rang again and I almost didn't answer. If it was Bonnie I wouldn't be able to resist. This thought reverberated until finally I picked up the receiver.

"Hello," I said in a strangled voice.

"Are you okay, Easy?" Asiette Moulon asked.

I cleared my throat and said, "Yes. Yes I am. Especially with you on the phone."

"I wanted to know if you called the police."

"I sure did. They caught them men too." There couldn't have been a better antidote for a broken heart. "I'm sorry about what happened."

"I want to see you again," she said in answer.

"That would be . . . um, magnificent."

"I 'ad a wonderful time," she said. "I like the way you make love to me."

"I could have stayed in that shower all night long."

We went on like that for a while, enumerating each other's charms and talents. It was pretty exciting and so she finally said, "Should I come ovair?"

"I got to wrap up some business first, Asiette. But by early next week I should be free."

After talking to Asiette for over an hour I needed that cigarette.

In the sixties full-grown adults didn't spend all that much time on the telephone. So I didn't expect any more calls. But one came in near nine.

"Hello?"

"Is this Ezekiel Rawlins?" a mature woman asked.

"Yes?"

"This is Sarah Sanderson. You left a message here under my previous name—Garnett."

"Oh," I said, calculating the time back east. I supposed that she waited until her new husband was in a deep sleep before calling. Maybe she put a sleeping powder in his warm milk.

"Where did you get my number?"

"I got a friend has access to a service. He could hook me up with Mao Tse-tung's digits if I wanted. We met once quite a few years ago."

"I remember you," she admitted. "What do you want?"

"Before your first husband, Vernor, murdered your daughter, she put her baby with Sylvia Bride, whose real name was Phyllis Weinstein. Before Vernor killed Sylvia she put the baby with someone else. After it was all over I took the girl and brought her home to live with me and my son. Your daughter christened her Feather and I stayed with that name. It's all she has left from her blood relations."

While I spoke the mother made various unintelligible sounds, reminding me of Mania the elder.

"And do you want money?" she asked after I was finished.

"No, ma'am."

"Then why did you call?"

"Didn't you hear what I just told you? You have a granddaughter in the world that you have never met."

"So?"

"So? Little Feather wants to know her grandmother and her uncle. She's a great kid and deserves to at least meet her real family."

"I'm sorry but that would be impossible."

"Why?" I wanted to know.

"She's . . . You understand, Mr. Rawlins. She's not, not white and I could not include her in my life. I'm very sorry but there's nothing I can do for the child."

"She is of your blood, Mrs. Sanderson. She's your dead daughter's child."

"I thought that she was dead," she said as if in answer.

"You hoped she was dead, you mean."

"I am not a monster, Mr. Rawlins. I'm just a woman trying to survive."

"Your husband was a monster. He murdered Robin. And now you're killing the memory of her by turning your back on Feather. You're just as evil, just as much a demon."

She made another few noises and then hung up.

I sat there for a few minutes, holding the phone. I loved Feather. She was my child and I could not understand how her own blood could turn on her because of pigments in the skin.

When the tone of the receiver turned into a louder beep I pressed the button and then dialed another number. I hadn't dialed it in a very long time but I remembered it because it spelled out a sexual epithet.

"Top Shelf," a woman said brightly.

"Hey, Doris."

"Who is this please?"

"Easy Rawlins."

"The Prodigal Son," she declared. "I thought you were dead."

"Lotta that goin' around. Augusta Tryman still with you?"

"And more beautiful every day too."

"Ask her to drop by," I said, and then gave her my new address.

"Yes, sir."

32

An hour later the silver chime of my alarm system sounded.

I was at the front door with a gun in my hand before the doorbell rang.

Through the peephole, under the porch light, I saw a hale white man in an eggplant-colored double-breasted suit; no hat, oiled and combed wavy hair, clean-shaven, and with empty hands in evidence at his side.

He stood there alone and assured, as American as redwoods and Manifest Destiny.

Pocketing the piece, I opened the door, my mind a blank slate in preparation for whatever this fancy stranger brought with him.

"Yes?" I said, taking inventory of his broad shoulders, thick neck, and big if empty hands.

"Mr. Rawlins?"

"Uh-huh."

"My name is Eugene Stapleton. My friends call me Gene."

"And people in the know call you the Cinch."

He accepted my knowledge with equanimity the general public does not usually associate with gangsters.

"May I come in?" he asked.

My once sparse living room now had three stuffed chairs, a sofa, and a small round mahogany table with three straight-back chairs of the same wood and style. Even though Feather and I lived alone, she had friends come over now and again.

I sometimes entertained also.

The Cinch took the couch and I pulled out a hard chair just in case I had to jump up shooting at a moment's notice.

"Nice house," the bad man commented.

"It's late, Mr. Stapleton, and I've had a long couple'a days—very long."

"You're right," he said. "I'm sorry for coming over at this hour but our kind of business is demanding and it doesn't run by a clock."

"What business is that?" I asked.

"I have an apology and a question for you," he said instead of answering the question.

"Apology for what?"

"I sent three men to break into your house and question you. You weren't at home but the same men grabbed you out of Seymour Brathwaite's apartment and tried to force you to play our game. I apologize for underestimating you. And I'd like to add that I won't make that mistake again."

His words were an offering of respect and a threat rolled up into one; in short—it was poetry.

"How did you even know to be looking at me?"

"I know many things, Mr. Rawlins."

"And what is the question?" I asked.

"Where's the money?"

One thing you learn when dealing with bad men and bloodletters is that money is a very touchy subject, whether a dispute over a thin dime or the disposition of a bag full of gold doubloons.

"I haven't had anything to do with any money," I said.

"But the people you're around have," he rejoined.

"Not to my knowledge."

"Then why are you involved in the Boughman murder?"

"I'm only involved as far as it has to do with Seymour being cleared of the crime."

Stapleton's eyes were a jaunty brown but when those orbs drilled into me I felt anything but cheerful.

"Boughman had a great deal of my friends' money," the Cinch said. "Now he's dead and no one knows where it is."

"Seymour was arrested at the scene," I said, trying to sound logical. "He didn't shoot Boughman and he certainly didn't have any money on him when they dragged him off to jail. I'm not trying to say that somebody else didn't steal it. But he was at that house looking for the housekeeper who was once his foster mother."

"Maybe I'm not making myself clear, Mr. Rawlins. There's a great deal of money missing; more money than three generations of a dozen Catholic union men could make in their lifetimes. If somebody just saw the back of the thief's head as he turned the corner I would want to know the color of his hair. I'd kill for that information alone."

"Killing doesn't provide answers," I said, giving up hypothetical reasoning for blunt fact.

"But it is a great motivator."

"I don't have your money and I have no idea where it might be. If I had stolen from your friends I'd be in Mexico City at this very moment with a new name on four senoritas' lips."

Stapleton smiled and pursed his own lips in appreciation of my lyrical turn.

"You mind if I have a drink?" he asked.

"I been off the stuff for a while now. Nuthin' stronger than orange juice in the box."

When my guest reached into the left breast of his many-buttoned suit, my hand drifted down toward my gun pocket. And I wasn't embarrassed when he came out with a tarnished silver flask.

He unscrewed the top, took a quick swig, then recapped it and put it away.

He looked at me very closely and said, "I want my money."

"The closest I've gotten to it is asking Seymour what happened at the beach house. He said that he went there looking for the housekeeper, found your man Boughman and some other guy, both dead. Before he could call the police they busted down the door."

"I don't care about any of that," the gangster uttered. "What I want to hear is where has the money gone."

"Help me out, Gene. What can I possibly know that would get you what you want?"

"Who hired you to get the kid out of trouble?"

I answered immediately but the matrix of thought behind that answer was convoluted and complex.

I considered the truth, telling Stapleton that Rufus "Charcoal Joe" Tyler had hired me to help a friend of his clear her foster son of unfounded charges. But I didn't know if Joe would like his name mixed up with a powerful mobster's business. Then I thought of Jasmine; she was the reason that Joe even cared and so, in a way, she was the one that caused me to be hired. But it had been grilled into me since childhood never to put a woman in harm's way unless there was no other choice.

For a moment I thought of saying that Melvin Suggs was the source of my work. He had as much as told me that finding the money would be the fastest way to get Seymour cleared of the crime. But I had already used Melvin against Stapleton's minions, and getting the police involved was never the preferred option. And, anyway, I didn't want the Cinch to know that I had been aware of the missing money or what Boughman was doing with the cash.

Those thoughts passed through my mind as quickly as the striking of a match. With the fire came a light.

"Raymond Alexander asked me to do it," I said.

"The colored man they call Mouse?"

"Me and Ray are old friends and he knows the kid from the neighborhood. When Ray asks a favor it's hard to decline."

A new light of respect came into my well-dressed guest's eyes. Mouse's name carried weight from coast to coast for those in the know.

"How is Mr. Alexander involved with Boughman?"

"He's not. Ray was clear that he wanted me to talk to the cops about Seymour. He knows that I have connections and he believed Seymour was innocent. He never said anything to me about suit-cases full of money. But let me ask *you* a question."

"What's that?" he allowed.

"How did you know to send your men to my house just hours after I took the case on?"

"Can't tell you everything, Mr. Rawlins. If I did I'd have to kill you."

"Your men already tried that."

"You called the cops on them," Stapleton said.

"Look, man, your people had me tied hand and foot with a wash-rag taped over my mouth. Your boy Arnold Mayhew touched my temple with his finger and told me that he was going to shoot me there."

Recalling the experience unexpectedly ignited a rage in my breast. That's how I knew that Mama Jo's tea was still doing something.

"Arnold's wife is a widow," the gangster said.

"I'm sorry for her but happy about him. Those motherfuckers didn't give me any choice but to fool 'em. Tie a man up and hold a gun to his head—fuck that."

I can't say my anger intimidated the Cinch but he took it into account.

"Did you ask your cop connection about the kid?" he asked; the dead men floating on waters that had already passed under the bridge.

The question quelled my anger because I realized that I did have information for the mob man.

"Yeah," I said. "Boughman and the other guy had been dead a couple of hours before the cops grabbed Seymour, and there was no gun to be found."

"So they cleared him?"

"Nobody cares about a dead gangster, man. And if they could blame some brother why not do it? You know that's two birds right there."

"So you're still trying to clear Mr. Alexander's friend?"

I nodded.

"And Alexander's not looking for any money?"

"And I'm not talkin' to him about it. All I want is charges dropped and young Seymour back at college where he belongs."

It was time for Stapleton to consider his options. I was sure one of these possibilities was my death.

"So you might still come across some information about who killed Peter," he speculated.

"That's a far cry from proof."

"I don't need proof, Mr. Rawlins. I'm not the law. If you get a good idea of who might have done this I would like to know and I would certainly pay for that knowledge."

"How much?"

"Fifteen thousand sounds right. That is if your information leads me to our money."

"What if you're sure the man I point you at is the one that stole from you but the money is not there?"

"I don't know. Maybe a five-thousand-dollar kill fee could be arranged."

33

I walked the Cinch to the front door at around eleven. I'd promised to tell him anything I found out about Peter Boughman's murder and anyone who might have seen him in the days before his demise. He gave me three telephone numbers, saying that I'd find him at the end of one line or another.

He stepped across the threshold and stopped, made a half turn, and regarded me.

"Why haven't you asked me for money up front, Mr. Rawlins?"

"Same reason I wouldn't steal from you, Mr. Stapleton. I don't want you to think that I'd take your money without giving something in return."

He considered my answer, nodded, and said, "I'll be waiting for your call."

He strolled down the walkway, past the sidewalk, and all the way to the curb. He stopped there and the headlights of a dark Lincoln Continental came on four houses down, across the street. The car pulled up to where Stapleton was standing. He opened the door to the backseat and climbed in.

The Lincoln didn't take off immediately. Maybe they were just discussing the next stop on their late-night rounds. Maybe. But I knew that if he didn't like my answers the entire carload of killers would be at my door.

As the car pulled off I realized that I had my hand on the gun in its pocket.

"Mr. Rawlins?"

The most courageous act I performed on the whole Charcoal Joe job was not shooting myself in the leg when petite Augusta Tryman called my name from behind the poinsettia bushes next to my front porch.

She emerged from the dark boughs in a shimmery silver micromini dress; the darkness of her skin was equal to the blackness behind her. Stepping into the yellow electrical light of the porch, she was both smiling and scared.

"Was that Eugene Stapleton?" she asked.

"What would a sweet young thing like you know about a bad man like him?"

Augusta had thick lips and a protruding rear end. The rest of her was quite thin.

Her fear turned into a sneer. "Every man needs a woman sometimes. Prince or pauper, they all get down to that."

"How long have you been out here?"

"I was comin' ovah when I seen him. You didn't tell Big D 'bout no party so I thought you had some business to take care of before."

"It's nice to see you, Augie. Come on in and have a seat."

I took her to the dinette off the kitchen. The small octangular room was surrounded by windows on four of its eight sides. The table was the same shape.

I sat down and she sidled up next to me.

"You want a soda or something?" I asked.

"Tap water be fine."

I got her modest request from the kitchen and sat down to join her again.

"Thank you," she said.

Augusta had intelligent eyes. She was at least thirty but most bartenders would have asked her for ID.

She took a drink from the tumbler then sat back and exhaled. In that sigh was all the pain and exhaustion of a whore's life.

"You sound like the weight of the world is on you, girl."

"You bettah believe it," she agreed. "He weigh three hundred and fi'ty pounds and his name is Oscar. He like me so much that he always sees me the first or second Friday of every mont'."

"Well," I said. "You can rest here."

"People don't pay me to rest," she observed.

"It's good to think that way," I said. "Because then somebody might surprise you."

"Surprise me how?"

"If you could go home right now what would you do?"

"Kiss my baby asleep in her crib, make a plate'a eggs scrambled in butter with some ketchup, an' take a bath so hot the mirror be steamed."

"Go on upstairs and run the bath," I said. "I'll make the eggs while the water's rising."

When the butter was melting in the pan I dialed the kitchen phone.

"Who is this?" EttaMae Harris challenged, answering on the third ring.

"Easy, honey."

"Oh." The anger dissipated. "Anything wrong, baby?"

"I hope not."

"I'll get him up."

I beat three eggs with a fork while she coaxed her bedmate to consciousness.

"Easy?" he said.

I was pouring the eggs into the skillet.

"Hey, Ray. Sorry to wake you up but a guy named Eugene Stapleton was just here."

"The Cinch?"

"That's him."

"What he want?"

"The name of the man hired me to help Seymour."

"You didn't say our friend's name, did you?"

"I told him that it was you."

Using a rubber spatula I slowly shifted the eggs so that they cooked evenly and in layers.

Mouse was quiet for fifteen seconds, no more.

"All right," he said. "All right. Yeah. What else you gonna say? He probably had a gunman or two somewhere close, so you had to."

"I just wanted to give you a heads-up."

"I appreciate that, Easy, but the Cinch ain't gonna fuck with me. He got to get the okay to come after me."

"He does?"

"Oh yeah, baby. People I know put the people he know to shame. But that don't mean he won't hurt you. So you did the right thing."

"What's his thing?"

"He used to have real power but the old heads and young guns have been pushin' him out. He strugglin'."

Augie was standing next to the deep tub when I came upstairs with her eggs and ketchup. The mirror was fogged up and she had only taken off her bright blue high-high heels.

"I thought you'd be in the tub by now," I said.

"I didn't know if you wanted to watch me take off my dress," she said. "A lotta men get mad if you just naked. They wanna show."

"I get my excitement making eggs in butter."

She shrugged and then pulled off the flimsy dress like it was a T-shirt.

Augie's body was like a teenager's too. I was sure that Doris, Big D, would sell her as underage-and-willing to any new client.

"You want to get in with me, Easy?"

"No thanks."

"That's not what your eyes is tellin' me."

"Get on in there."

Augusta moaned as she lowered into the hot water. I was absolutely sure that no client ever made her cry out like that. I handed her a fork and the plate of eggs.

"Oh my God this is delicious," she said after three fast forkfuls. "You could cook too? Damn, Mr. Rawlins, you should take me outta this life and make me your wife."

I put the lid down and sat on the commode, there next to the bathtub. She finished her eggs in quick order. I took the dish and set it in the sink.

"This is perfect," Augusta said, luxuriating. "If you wanna call me and go out on a real date I will definitely say yes. But you can't tell Big D."

"I won't. You look better than you did the last time I saw you, girl," I said.

"That was two years, right?"

I nodded.

"I was still doin' aitch back then. Got pregnant, kicked the habit, and now I go to beauty school in the daytime and work three nights for Doris."

"I guess I was lucky that you were on the job tonight."

"I was workin' but you know I would'a come in anyway if they told me it was you. We all like you down at the office."

She closed her eyes and lay back.

That was a very peaceful moment. Augusta had dumped her flimsy dress on top of her blue high heels. The water from the bath faucet was dripping. Somewhere there was a distraught woman grieving over the violent death of Arnold Mayhew.

"Are we gonna fuck?" Augie asked. I looked up to see her intelligent eyes focused on me.

"Not tonight."

"You don't like me?"

"No," I said. "I mean . . . I like you fine but I called for you because I had a few questions."

"Questions about what?"

"They used to call you Jailbait, didn't they?"

"Still do sometimes."

"And they used to just say JB sometimes too, right?"

"Uh-huh."

"Then I wanted to ask you about Uriah Hardy."

"That nasty old man? Why you wanna know about him?"

"His wife's foster son, Seymour, got into some trouble and I'm trying to get him out. I tried talking to Uriah but he just stubborn."

"Stubborn? Uriah Hardy is livin' proof that some people cain't win for losin'. Here he got everything an' all he is is mad at Jasmine Palmas. She give him a house, a allowance, freedom to see any woman he want, and a new car every three years. Niggah don't know what side his ass is buttered on. That's why she introduced him to Big D an' paid half what we cost so he keep usin' us. Jasmine wanted to hear if he was schemin' against her."

"Jasmine paid for Uriah's prostitutes?"

"Half herself and the other half came outta the allowance she give him."

"I was told that Jasmine was a housekeeper," I said. "How's a cleaning woman get all that money?"

"The only kinda cleaning woman Jasmine Palmas is is the kind that clean up."

"What kind of business she in?" I asked.

"I don't know and I don't ask."

"And what did she get out of you?"

"She just wanted to know if Uriah said anything about her."

"Did he?"

"Did he? The second time I was with him, after he made me do all kindsa disgustin' stuff, he wanted me to rob Jasmine. Told me he had the key to her place and that he would tell me when him and her and her foster son would go out for dinner. I was supposed to use the key and take a albino-crocodile-skin bag she use. He said he'd gimme fi'e thousand dollars for that bag. I was usin' pretty heavy back then but I wasn't so out of it that I wanted to cross Doris and Jasmine too."

"Doris knows Jasmine?"

"Jasmine was her number one girl way back. One day she went to a job with Charcoal Joe Tyler—after that she never worked again."

"Why would Uriah need you to steal the bag if he already had the key?"

"That way he could say that he was with Jasmine when the house got robbed."

"Did he tell you what was in the bag?"

"Naw. He said that it'd be locked and if the lock was broken he'd kill me. But I didn't care 'cause I wasn't gonna steal it in the first place. I told Doris and she told Jasmine. Jasmine had the lock changed and Uriah never talked about it again."

"Was he suspicious?"

"I was strung out back then and so I did whatever nasty thing a client wanted; and Uriah wanted a lot. I think he suspected but you know nine men outta ten think with they dick. I was half price and on time. He never talked about Jasmine no mo'."

"What about Jasmine's foster son?"

"What about him?"

"He told me that you gave him your card."

"That's why you called, huh?" she said. "Damn."

"Seymour?"

"He was just a child, Easy. You know, havin' a crush one minute, watchin' *Mighty Mouse* the next. I give him my little card to make him feel important."

"Did he ever call you?"

"One time he did. It was pretty late and I was watchin' TV or sumpin'. He said that his mother wasn't home and he was scared and was wonderin' if he should call the police. I told him that I'd call her friends and see where she was but before we got off the phone she come in. She was mad that Seymour had my number, and Big D told me the next day that I wasn't gonna see Uriah no mo'. Cain't say that I cried."

34

The phone rang a few minutes before one in the morning. Augusta and I were sitting in the living room drinking chamomile tea and laughing about our assorted misadventures. She was curled up in my big yellow bathrobe on one of the stuffed chairs.

If I sat very still my ribs hardly ached.

Lifting the receiver, I thought of Eugene Stapleton saying, *Our kind of business is demanding and it doesn't run by a clock.*

He was right about that.

"Hello?"

"Are you finished with my girl, Mr. Rawlins?" Doris asked.

"It'd take me a few weeks to be finished but I guess I'm done for the moment."

"Then pay her one-fifty and tell her to put on some clothes. Stuart Short is in a car in front of your house."

I definitely had to move.

I walked her out to the black Caddy parked directly in front of my house. Stuart Short—who was six-three, two hundred fifty pounds at least, and the color of an overcooked bran muffin—was standing next to the passenger's door. He wore a black suit and even sported a chauffeur's cap.

"Mr. Short," I said, extending a hand.

"Mr. Rawlins," he countered, taking the offer.

When I opened the door for Augusta, Stuart headed for the driver's side.

She kissed my lips and said, "Thanks for the surprises, Easy. And watch out about Uriah. He the kind'a coward wouldn't think twice about shootin' you in the back."

I believe that it is my psychological makeup that makes me a good detective. I'm 90 percent pragmatist and the rest superstition. Augie's warning about being shot in the back felt to me like a portent. I didn't necessarily think that it would be Uriah to shoot me or even that I'd be shot; the fear was that there was a trap I wouldn't see waiting to be sprung. Maybe the danger was in my past, not my future; it could have been the men grabbing me at Seymour's. But whatever it was, the trepidation left me wide awake like some leaf-eating forest creature who just heard a branch snap outside his lair.

I washed the dishes and then put a load of laundry in the machine on the back porch. While waiting for the cycle to finish I read the newspaper. I put the clothes in the dryer, decided on the suit I'd wear the next day, folded the dried clothes, and then went to the living room and picked up Styron's *The Confessions of Nat Turner*. Jackson Blue had already read it and told me, "Ole Willie Styron made the mistake of gettin' into a public debate with Ossie Davis. They had Jimmy Baldwin moderate. I guess Styron thought that he was too smart for some black actor but old Ossie tore him a new one. He made Styron understand that the plantation days is ovah an' there's black men out here know they own stories."

I only read the first paragraph. I remember that it was a lovely and peaceful meditation of a man floating in a boat. . . .

I was that man drifting down a tributary of the Mississippi in southern Louisiana in the spring. It was near the Gulf I knew because there were gulls and pelicans everywhere. Huge fish moved slowly just below the surface of the water, and lazy alligators lounged on the banks. I was wearing the horizontal black-and-white stripes of a convict and there was a manacle, cut loose from its ball and chain, attached to my ankle.

I was an escaped prisoner headed for Mexico, the Caribbean, or maybe even South America. I tried to recall what my crime had been, what the circumstances were surrounding my escape. A little voice was telling me that I had to get cracking on my getaway, but the day was so beautiful and sleep beckoned me.

The Americas were not my home. Maybe nowhere was. It came to me that I was free for a brief moment on that peaceful watercourse; that if I couldn't enjoy such a lovely respite then life was not worth living.

This sober thought brought me awake on the raft and then on the couch in my living room. I was a free man on a dangerous path. What more could anyone ask?

I showered and shaved, thought about my reflection in the glass and Bonnie, wherever she might be. I put on the medium-gray two-piece suit over a dusky orange T-shirt. The shoes I chose were made from black leather and had rubber soles; this because Augie's warning might still come to pass.

I drank strong black coffee at the eight-sided dinette table while loading fresh cartridges into my .45. I got the short, wide-bladed pocketknife from the tool chest in the garage just to feel like I had an extra edge.

I took the car down to the Safeway at Fairfax and Pico, did the shopping for the week, then came home to put away the larder.

At 11:59, I walked out the front door just as Fearless Jones's Edsel pulled to the curb.

Many of my black friends complain about our brethren always being late for appointments; they call it CP time. But the black men

I knew were never late. Mouse was a career criminal and you can't make it long in that profession without shaving time down to the microsecond. Jackson called his watch a chronometer because he saw time as an exact, if variable, mechanism by which all phenomena were judged. And Fearless Jones was simply a man of his word; whatever he promised, that's what came to pass.

Fearless drove us to the Star-Hobard. He went to the diner to have some tea while I made my way up to the third floor of the low-rent motel.

I went down to the door of 3G, seeking to avoid Mania the elder, but she answered that door too.

"Ook del ta doe mon," she said, looking me in the eye.

"Your daughter," I said slowly.

"I'm here, Mr. Rawlins."

The older white woman's brown daughter came up next to her. She put her arm around Mania the elder's waist, gently pulling the confused lady away.

"Aspell pea-no taspin," the younger woman said.

"Tappa is papa?" The old woman seemed confused. I thought that even her grasp of the nonsense language was fading.

"Aspell, aspell," my translator said while guiding her mother toward the inner door to 3F.

Once the woman was gone, Mania the younger said, "Come in, Mr. Rawlins. Come sit on the sofa."

The settee was turquoise-colored vinyl, hardly more than a padded bench. Mania plopped down in half lotus on a chair that hailed from the same family. She wore a mottled green housedress that was loose on her but still quite fetching. There was something about the young woman that was both down-home and alien.

She was considering me in the way that bomb squad cops look over a cardboard box that might contain an explosive device. While she pondered I noted the beauty underneath her exotic looks.

"Did you get to that journal?" I asked, just to pretend that there was something normal about our meeting.

"I called Mr. Natly," she replied.

"About me?"

"What are your intentions about Julia?"

"Who is Julia?"

"The woman that wrote the journal you gave me."

"You see?" I said. "I know a hundred percent more than when I brought it to you."

This answer confounded the young translator. She was expecting something more . . . devious.

"You haven't answered my question," she demanded.

"Because I don't know," I admitted. "I didn't even know who wrote it. A young man I'm trying to help says that a woman he didn't know gave this to him to give to his mother. He didn't and she didn't say that she wrote the journal, so just the fact that it was a woman who wrote it is a revelation."

I like reading and I like words. When speaking with people I have come to understand that what I say is informed by the tone I use. So I can say anything and make myself understood by the context and the placement of the words. But during this case I found that the fact I spoke a language that educated people understood made them look at me differently. That's how it was with Miss Mania Blackman. The use of the word *revelation* seemed to tip the balance in my favor at the courtroom bench in her mind.

"A woman named Julia wrote the diary over a three-month period," she said. "The last three months. She started it when she met a man that she called John. I don't think that was his real name. Anyway, John was a bad boy but she loved the way he talked to her and the innocence of his smile. John was in trouble and he was trying to find a way out. He wanted to run off with Julia but didn't have the money.

"Julia never trusted John. It was just that he made her happier than any man ever had and so she stayed with him even though her head told her to leave. And after a while she knew that even if he was using her, even if he was going to make her do bad things, that she would do them because there might never be a love like that again in her life. . . ."

There was great feeling in Mania Blackman's rendition of the personal memoir. I remember thinking that it would take a woman to convince another woman about the possible depths of love.

"He made her do something that was very dangerous," Mania continued. "She was frightened and afraid that she would die."

"And she did what he asked?"

"The second-to-the-last entry says that she was going to meet a man on John's behalf," Mania replied. "That was ten days ago. Then there was no more until seven days ago."

"What did that say?"

" 'No one knew that the green-eyed serpent could climb trees,' " Mania recited, " 'but the little owl hid her crystal eggs because she had a dream that the moon had green eyes and a pointy tongue. And where could she hide the eggs where a snake would not look? Inside the red apple of wisdom.' "

"Ummmm, that's all?" I said.

"She was using the fable to tell someone she knew where to look for something."

"What?"

"Whatever it was that John made her steal."

"Is there anything in there that says what John looks like?"

"She says that he's tall and fair and from someplace other than Los Angeles."

"That's fifty thousand surfers right there," I said. "And I only know one full-grown man that was born out here. How about his eyes? Women like men's eyes."

"She says that they were beautiful."

"Blue or brown?"

The young translator shrugged and shifted in the seat.

"Where were they gonna run to?"

"I could only say that it was out of California."

"That could be anywhere."

Mania's smile, through Jo's tea, made me forget for a moment why I was there. I think she saw this shift in my gaze.

She smiled and said, "The one thing I got from her writing was that she was no longer young."

"That's something."

"Can you tell me what your intentions are now?" she asked.

"Without knowing who the men were and what was being stolen or whatever—I can't say. My only concern is with my client, and he's the young man that gave me the journal and said that he didn't know the woman who gave it to him."

"Your eyes are both kind and hard," she said out of nowhere.

"You sure I can't pay you for this?" was my reply.

She thought for a moment and then said, "Kiss me once, lightly on my lips."

I stood up, leaned over, felt a stitch in my side, and did as she requested. She arched her body upward to meet me. After the first kiss I leaned over a little farther but she put her hand softly against my throat and said, "Not yet."

35

I called Melvin Suggs from an outside phone booth on the first floor of the motel. I didn't mention his name and he called me Mr. Sugarman; then we set a meeting at a popular hot-dog stand halfway between us.

But before meeting the cop I had other duties. There was the little red diary in my pocket and pertinent information only partly translated from a foreign language in my head. And then there was Fearless.

"How's it goin', Easy?" he said when I came to light on the stool next to him at the counter.

"I really don't know," I answered.

"This here is Marybeth Reno and she's from Reno too."

"Hi." Skinny, freckled, and redheaded, the young waitress smiled and did a little shoulder dance to show me how happy she was to be not only seen but noticed.

I said hello and even shook her hand, ordered coffee black, and watched her go to perform my wish.

"You came in yesterday," the young woman said when she returned. "Tina served you."

"How'd it go?" Fearless asked me.

Marybeth took this as a cue to move off.

"I think I might be in trouble if I don't move just right," I said.

"I knew that when you said 'Charcoal Joe.'"

I sighed and then asked, "How's Seymour?"

"He's gettin' kinda restless. Can't say I blame him."

"Tell him to keep his head down and if we're lucky he won't even see the inside of a jail again."

"Okay. Marybeth wants to go see that space odyssey movie, that *2001*. I told her that me an' Seymour would take her there when she got off. Maybe he'll relax a little goin' out."

"Maybe he likes redheads," I added.

Fearless dropped me off at my house and I drove to Pink's to meet Melvin. He was sitting out front at a wooden picnic table with two chili dogs and a paper tub of cheese-and-chili fries. Melvin was always early if the meeting place offered liquor or food, earlier still if they served both.

"You hungry, Easy?" he asked when I settled across from him.

"Not really, Melvin. Every time I think about eating I wonder if this is gonna be my last meal and then I lose my appetite."

The top cop grinned and bit into a chili dog.

"That other guy we shot died," he said. "Doctor said it was shock that killed him. Can you imagine that? Here you can take the bullet but you can't survive the scare."

"Two dead men," I said, "four if you count Boughman and Brown. It's a regular Roarin' Twenties out here."

"The prosecutor told Gregory Chalmers, the brain of the three, that he could try him for the murder of his partners; said that the fact that they were in the act of the commission of a felony, a kidnapping at that, meant first-degree murder and a death sentence. Greg asked for witness protection so we knew we got ahold of something."

"Has he said anything yet?"

Melvin put down the nub of his dog and gave me a hard stare.

"You and me are friends," he said. "You've done me a good turn here and there and I respect you. I do. And I know that people in my department plow black men like you into the dirt every day. I often wonder how you can even stand it. But even with all that, why should I share sensitive internal department intelligence with you?"

"Because, Melvin, I will open doors that you don't even know are there. Because I'm better at what I do than anybody you got on your team."

He popped the nub in his mouth and picked up the second dog before he was through chewing.

"Chalmers says that Stapleton was in charge of taking mob money and moving it out the country," Melvin said. "But the Cinch was losing power with the men he worked for, and so instead of moving the money he decided to rob Boughman and run. Boughman was setting up a meeting to trade the cash for diamonds. Boughman was worried about Eugene so he hired muscle, John Brown, for protection. The Cinch said he had an in and so he brought Chalmers and his men in on the deal. They'd kill both Boughman and Brown."

"So then what happened?"

"The four of them were waiting for Boughman at the meeting place but he never showed up and then, the next morning, Boughman and the bodyguard turned up dead and there was no money anywhere. The eastern mob puts out a notice on the Cinch and so, instead of retiring to Rio, he's running around looking to save his ass. That's why his men were on you. Because he thought he could get a line through Seymour."

"So Stapleton's still in Los Angeles," I said as if I didn't already know.

"He was when he sent Chalmers after you."

"Who gave Stapleton the wrong address?"

"That's not clear."

"But it's enough to get my boy off the hook," I concluded.

"It might could be," Suggs half-agreed.

"It is," I countered.

"It would be if we could lay our hands on Stapleton and he corroborated Chalmers's testimony. But you know that man is in the wind searching for the mob's millions, and we still don't know what part the kid might have played."

"He's just a college kid," I said. "There's no connection between him and mob money."

"The prosecutor needs a man to pin the charges on. They wouldn't even call Chalmers to the stand unless they were sure it was going to pay off."

I weighed the benefit of telling Melvin that I had a line on the Cinch; that I'd met with the man and had his phone numbers. I could set him up for a fall, free my client, and move to a new house with numbers the bad men couldn't calculate.

But from what he was saying there was no solid proof on Stapleton. As a matter of fact Gregory Chalmers's account gave the man an alibi. And even if he could get something on the Cinch, Melvin couldn't promise that he'd put him out of commission; he couldn't keep that man from plotting my demise from his prison cell. Suggs would make me all kinds of promises—and believe them too. But in the end Stapleton could make a deal and Seymour might still find himself the only defendant accused of murder.

"So what can I do, Melvin?" I asked. "You know that Seymour is innocent. You know that because this shit is way beyond some burglar killing another burglar."

"That's why I'm eating this chili dog," he said. "I came out here to tell you what's what because of the work you've done. I came out here to see you face-to-face, to tell you that your boy's got an uphill climb in his future."

Melvin was my friend but the world we moved in didn't rate friendship very high. The difference between friends and enemies in our neck of the woods was that a friend said that he was sorry when he had to slip the knife between your ribs.

I picked up Feather from Saturday afternoon softball practice at Ivy Prep and took her out for pizza. We talked about how bored she felt waiting for somebody to hit the ball her way and about her coach, the algebra teacher Miss Simon. She loved taking care of Jewelle's baby and was getting homesick for her own bed.

"Are you okay, Daddy?" she asked me when I pulled into Jackson's driveway.

"Sure. Why do you ask?"

"I called Juice and he said that when you need to be alone that you might be in trouble and want to protect me."

"It's just that I'm keeping really late hours, baby, and I don't want you home alone or waking up in the middle of the night with nobody there."

"It's not about Bonnie and Joguye?"

"They left Los Angeles already," I said. "Uncle Raymond and Mama Jo took care of that."

"Joguye's gonna be safe from those men that want to kill him?"

"Yes he will, but you got to do me a favor, baby."

"What?"

"You can't ever mention him or Bonnie to anybody. Okay?"

"Okay. And, Daddy?"

"What?"

"I love you."

The office was empty by the time I got there. It was Saturday but because all three of us were working, Niska did her semi-regular Saturday morning hours. She'd left three pink slips of paper on my desk.

I might need you and Saul's help in a day or two, Easy, Whisper wrote. From anyone else that might have sounded like a request for a hand moving some boxes. But from Mr. Natly this was a serious business.

Harry got the pictures to the consortium. They want a formal meeting with us next week, Saul said.

Miss Kuroko called, Niska wrote, *she said to call her anytime before 8:00 at the office.*

"Three two nine eight," she answered. Milo and Loretta had decided that on weekends she'd answer his phone with the last four digits of the number. I'm not really sure why but it didn't matter to me.

"Hey, Loretta."

"Easy. How are you?"

"I think you might know better than me."

"The man called Ducky, John Brown, was, plain and simple, a killer for hire. He went to prison for beating his mother's boyfriend to death when he was fifteen. He spent six years for manslaughter and came out west. The rest of his life has been spent killing and hurting people for money. He's never planned any other kind of crime and he doesn't, or didn't, ever hurt anyone for personal reasons other than his mother's boyfriend."

"What about Boughman?"

"He's a very bad man," she said. "I spoke to Adolpho Venturino about him. He once defended Mr. Boughman on a manslaughter charge."

"Successfully I imagine."

"The main witness for the prosecution went missing. The others lost their memory. After that, Boughman used Adolpho for everything."

"Damn."

"Is that all you needed?" she asked.

"No," I lamented. "I need addresses, names of friends and business associates, and anything he might be into."

"You know that he's dead, right?"

"I do. But often our actions in life go on beyond the grave."

"I don't have much. Venturino owes Milo a favor so I asked if he knew an address for Mr. Boughman. He said that his residence was listed as the Hotel Leonardo in Santa Monica but that he also had a wife that no one knew about who has a house in Coldwater Canyon. Her name is Denise Devine."

"Kids?"

"I don't know. Boughman only told Adolpho about her because he wanted her taken care of in case he died unexpectedly."

"Has he gotten in touch with her?"

"He's gathering the information first. He won't call before Monday."

"Give me the address," I said. "Do you have a phone number too?"

"Yes . . . but, Easy?"

"Yeah, Lore?"

"These are serious men. They kill people."

"I'll be careful."

"Sometimes careful is staying away."

"If you took that advice to heart you'd have quit Milo years ago."

I wasn't sleeping much. That night I didn't even go home. I smoked my one cigarette and wondered if it was worth it trying to quit when the odds of my survival were so low.

At midnight I called Fearless.

"Hello?" he said.

"How was the movie?"

"Crazy, man. Ape-men and astronauts. Spaceships flyin' all over and a computer wanna kill ya. And then, at the end, there was this big unborn baby floatin' out in the stars. Marybeth came home with Seymour. They out back right now tearin' up the sheets."

"I appreciate all that you're doing for me, Fearless. I don't think I'll need you tomorrow but Monday morning at eleven we have to go see Joe out at Avett Detention."

"You the boss, Easy."

"Thanks, man. You can't believe how much I appreciate it."

36

"Hello?" she said with the sleep still in her voice. It was 7:36 in the morning.

"Miss Devine?"

"Yes?" The sleepiness was laced with fear.

I almost hung up the phone. I almost did because I read the story behind Denise's tones. Her man had not been home for days. He hadn't called or told her where he was going. She probably had bags packed and ready for a journey he'd promised. Now all she could do was wait for that call telling her that the life she had been living was over.

"Ma'am, I have to talk with you about Mr. Boughman."

"What is it?" she cried, her voice doubling in volume.

"I have to see you in person."

"Peter told me never to tell anyone where we lived."

"I already have the address, ma'am. I just wanted to call first. I didn't want to show up at your door unannounced."

"What's happened to him?"

"I can be to you in forty-five minutes. I promise that I'll answer every question you have."

"I don't know."

"I can come there now," I said. "I'm involved in a difficult, um, negotiation and later I can't promise that I'll be available."

"What's your name?"

"Ted Waters."

"Where is Peter, Mr. Waters?"

"I can come to your house or not. I can tell you the things you need to know or you can figure them out on your own. Those are your choices, Denise."

I didn't exactly feel like a dog on the ride from my office into the canyon. Peter Boughman was one of the bad guys, like the men that bound and gagged me and promised a quick death. I didn't know his woman; maybe he didn't either. Maybe he thought she was all ignorant when really she chose him because she knew what he was and wanted to share his dirty money while feigning innocence.

Maybe.

The Coldwater Canyon address was just a mailbox surrounded by bushes and sapling trees. I pulled off the road as well as I could and picked my way along the slender trail that led from the mailbox up a steep, wooded incline.

I was breathing pretty hard when I came to the clearing maybe a hundred yards up from the road. The right cuff of my green-gray jacket was folded in at just the right angle to keep the snub-nosed .22 from falling out. All I had to do was curve my hand toward the wrist and the pistol would fall into it.

Not the best defense but probably unexpected.

The house was nothing to speak of, boxy and gray with few windows. It would have been a good starter home for a working-class family six or seven blocks deep on the wrong side of the tracks.

I reached for the buzzer but she opened the dull brown door first. Her dress was blood orange in color, loose with two big white pockets over the thighs. Her blond hair was stiff and brittle from too much washing and application of the dye. Maybe her natural color was black and so she had to double bleach before dyeing. But the face was lovely. White skin like some rose petals with red lips that were never far from a kiss. Her eyes were gray like Mouse's eyes.

The grimace on that fair apparition was something you'd expect to encounter on a mourner coming from the grave.

"You're black," she said.

"I can't deny it."

"Who are you?"

"Ted Waters."

"What are you doing here?" She looked around as if she expected my confederates to descend upon her.

"I told you. I came to ask a few questions about Peter Boughman."

"How did you find this address?" She was not going to let me past the front door.

"I found a note in his room at the Hotel Leonardo."

The fact and fiction caused a quite lovely knitting mostly above her left eye.

"You're lying," she said.

"If you say so. But here I am. Can I come in?"

Denise Devine produced a .25-caliber chrome-plated pistol from the right pocket and pointed it in the general direction of my diaphragm. I could have fallen to my left, grabbed my own gun, and killed her but I'm not the kind of guy who kills lovely young women in the deep woods.

"The gun isn't necessary," I said. "I can just leave."

"Where is Peter?"

"He's dead."

Her own diaphragm wanted to genuflect, and when she wavered I snatched the gun from her hand. She grunted and reached for the piece but I held it away—out of her reach.

"We can stand out here and I'll answer your questions, Denise. And maybe you can answer one or two of mine."

"Tell me what happened?" She accepted defeat with dignity. I liked her.

"He was found in a house down in Malibu," I said. "Someone had shot him in the heart and the eye. Only good thing about it is that he couldn't have suffered much with either wound."

"Why? Why would somebody kill Petey? He wouldn't hurt anybody." I believed that she believed these words.

"You know what he did for a living, right?"

"He worked for a gambler named Rigby in Gardena. He was a floor manager in a poker parlor."

That was the story Boughman told.

"Gamblers can be serious people," I opined, using his lie to soften the blow. "Were you and Peter planning a vacation?"

I got the feeling that she got the feeling that I could read her thoughts.

"Why?"

"Where were you going?"

"He wouldn't say. He just told me to get a passport and pack, and pack my bags."

"Doesn't that sound like he was expecting a windfall?"

"He might have saved the money."

"You don't believe that."

"Is that why you're here? Are you looking for some money? Is that why you want to come in my house?"

All very good questions. Maybe there was a fortune on the top shelf of the closet or buried under the flagstone before the dull brown door.

"Found money can be good," I said. "Getting dealt blackjack at a card table or an uncle you never knew about who leaves you a coffee can filled with gold doubloons. But the kinda money Peter was after belonged to some very bad men. And those men are on the warpath."

The bottle blonde sneered at me. She was trying to make sense of what I was doing at her door, why her man was dead, and if his death meant that she was now in danger.

"I don't have any money," she said.

"Well I hope you have some family somewhere because you know you are no longer safe in this house or this city."

"Why not?"

"Because your man was plotting against people that will kill anyone that gets in their way. Because the money he was after is missing from their pockets and they will not rest until it's found."

"I don't have any money," she said again.

"Listen, honey, the man looking for this money told me that he'd kill somebody if he even thought that they might know one thing that could get him closer to getting it."

The lady farted. She was so scared that this bodily function didn't even embarrass her. Tears were coming from her eyes, and tremors traveled up and down her limbs. In the days alone in the house in the woods she had worked out that Peter wasn't coming back, that the trouble he was in might come back on her.

My information just proved her suspicions.

"I don't know what to do," she admitted.

"Do you have a car?"

"No."

"You just stay up here and wait for Peter to come?"

"The market at the bottom of the hill makes deliveries."

"Do you have a friend?"

"Peter and I live pretty much separated from our old lives. He does business and goes to work but we don't socialize. I used to have friends."

"Anybody you still talk to?"

"There's one man I used to know. I call him now and then when Peter's gone for a long time."

"Can you trust this guy?"

"He doesn't know anything about Peter, not even his name. We had a thing before and, and I think he still wants something."

"Call him now. Tell him to pick you up at the art museum parking lot and I'll drop you off there. Go through your suitcases and take only what's necessary. This will not be a vacation."

I waited outside while she did as I asked. She might have had another gun in there. She might have called the police. But I wasn't worried. Women in her position knew when they were looking at their last chance.

———

"Why are you helping me?" she asked as we crossed Sunset Boulevard.

"Why do you believe that what I'm telling you is true?"

"Because Peter promised me that he'd be home last Sunday night. Because if he didn't come he would have at least called."

"I'm helping you because it's the right thing to do and if you feel like I'm okay you might tell me something."

"What?"

"Is there anywhere other than your house and the hotel that you could get in touch with Peter?"

"I'm just wondering why a black man would go out of his way to help a white woman," she said.

I had all kinds of answers for that question but they didn't seem worth voicing. So we drove on in silence.

When I pulled into the parking lot of the Los Angeles County Museum of Art, she reached into the backseat to take her small suitcase. I pulled into an empty space and waited for her to garner her resources.

She opened the door and put one foot on the asphalt.

"What happened to Peter, Mr. Waters?"

"He tried to rob his bosses but before he could get away with it another thief killed him," I said. It was as close to the truth as I had come.

A sob escaped her throat.

I put a hand on her shoulder.

"And what do you care about it?" she asked.

"The police have blamed a young man for the killing. I'm trying to get him off."

"Did this, this young man kill my Peter?"

"Not a chance."

"I met him when I was waiting for standby tickets for *The Magic Flute*," she said, one foot in the car and the other on the tarmac.

"The opera?"

"He loved opera. He had a box. He offered to, to let me sit with him. I had come to L.A. from Omaha with a boyfriend. He left for work one day and didn't come back. I was really lost and Peter was a perfect gentleman."

"What about the guy you're meeting?"

"He's a good guy but he doesn't make any money. He wanted me to live with him so I could help pay three months' back rent. Peter paid my rent and took me to the opera four weeks in a row. One time we flew up to San Francisco. He was good to me."

I stayed silent.

"I didn't have any other way of getting in touch with him," she said. "But one time, maybe eight months ago, he left a package with me and said that I should wait a few days and then have the people at the market put it in the mail."

"Big package?"

"No. Small, but it was heavy."

"Do you remember the address?" I was hoping that it was something simple that stuck in her head.

"No, but I remember that it was addressed to Beulah Edwards. I remember because I wondered if she was a lover. He told me that I didn't have anything to worry about so I didn't."

"Beulah Edwards."

She nodded and climbed out of the car.

37

Miss Edwards was in the West L.A. directory. She lived on Cushdon, near Westwood Boulevard.

It was Sunday and I could have taken Feather to Marineland, Knott's Berry Farm, or even Disneyland. I wanted to relax and see my daughter but Denise Devine might have the same thoughts I did, or maybe her on-again boyfriend would help her with the white pages. I drove to the address, then around the block, and parked. I walked up the street and to the front door, which, like many L.A. homes, had the doorway secluded by a trellis grown over by a few dozen sweet pea vines.

The flowering creepers reminded me of Bonnie's abandoned home, and of the crippled hero Joguye Cham.

No one answered my knocks or the buzzer. The mailbox was overflowing with junk mail. Local newspapers, menus, and various flyers littered the welcome mat.

I considered lighting a cigarette but decided against it; that was my optimism operating.

I had brought with me two detective and/or burglar tools: the loaded .22 and a twelve-inch gooseneck crowbar that fit uncomfortably under my jacket.

The crowbar could be used as a defensive tool if Beulah turned out to be a big bruiser instead of a fat grandma. But if, as I suspected, the house was abandoned, then I could pry my way through the front or back door and see what evidence I might find.

The windows all had pink-painted iron bars over them, and the doorjamb was reinforced with two long metal slats.

But I persisted.

It took longer than it might have because I was trying to keep the racket down.

Half an hour and I'd made it inside.

It was a house but not a home. There was very little furniture anywhere, and the only light came through shaded windows and from electric lamps set here and there on the floors of the small empty rooms.

No tables, one straight-back chair, a few empty cartons of Chinese and Mexican food, and six very big sack-like leather bags sitting on the otherwise empty bedroom floor.

The denominations were twenties, fifties, and hundreds neatly wrapped for easy counting. The smallest bag contained $175,000. I didn't count the rest. The total was probably more than one million; less than one-point-five. It was enough so that I felt a trickle of sweat run down my cheek.

If Feather wasn't in my life I would have been out of L.A. that night.

But she loved her Ivy Prep and had had enough pain in her thirteen years.

I was doing okay; and starting up a new life at the age of forty-eight, like Bonnie and Joguye were doing, didn't have the appeal it might have in the younger years.

The telephone had been disconnected. There was no radio or TV, no book or even a magazine. The house was so barren that not even a black ant was bumbling around. I went to the front door, tried to make it look unmolested, and then picked up a copy of a local paper, the *Pico Post*.

There were various notices and ads, the local police blotter, and an article about some oil wells that had been drilled up and down Pico. The derricks were camouflaged by big aluminum structures made to look like windowless buildings. A neighborhood artist,

Pepe Hernandez, had offered to paint giant murals on them but the four town councils concerned had turned him down.

Again I was like the little ant at Seymour's apartment. I had found a morsel so large that I couldn't move it and there were no fellow colonists around to help me out.

And so I waited. I read the paper, four menus, and flyers about everything from fortune-telling to department store sales.

At one point I lay down on the floor, placing my head on a hundred-thousand-dollar pillow.

My sleep was unsettled but it was a way to kill time.

When I woke up the sun was going down.

I walked around the gangster's hideaway wondering what mischief beyond the stolen cash had gone on there.

I considered going out back to see what might be hidden in his garage but decided that I had enough to keep me occupied. So I sat in the straight-back chair with all the electric lamps turned off and waited—for hours. That was the real discipline of the private detective.

When my watch said that it was 10:17 I went around the block, picked up my car, and backed into Miss Beulah Edwards's driveway.

On the eastward drive I tried to think of someone who might keep the cash while I finished my job.

I couldn't think of a soul who would be able to resist the temptation of a million dollars that would never be reported stolen. Not Mouse or Jackson, not John the Bartender, and certainly not Milo Sweet. Jean-Paul of P9 wouldn't be impressed, but getting to him would take time. Loretta might have taken it but I saw no reason to put her in harm's way. Fearless alone would have been trustworthy, but he had Seymour in tow and I know nothing about him.

So I drove home, parking my Dodge in the garage. The trunk of that car would be my bank vault.

I stayed awake all night long with a .45 on my lap.

It occurred to me at 3:07 a.m. that this was how all wealth had to be treated: with fear of loss and eternal vigilance. It was the first time that I understood that being rich was not necessarily an enriching experience.

I reached the Avett Detainment Facility at 11:13. The same flush-faced and blowsy guard sat sentry.

"Your friend's already in there," he said, waving me on.

Once again the ectomorph guard sat at the small table on the other side of the locked doors. As before, he ignored me until I knocked, and once again he advanced on the door angrily.

But this time he recognized me and said, "Your friend's down in Stieglitz's office."

Fearless was facing the handsome assistant and she was taking him in. That day Fearless was wearing a dark red suit that was a cut above his sodbuster ensembles but still not equal to my dark green outfit. Dorothy looked up at me and smiled. That was a gift, considering she had Fearless to grin at.

"Mr. Rawlins," she said, rising from the chair.

"Easy," Fearless said.

"Administrator Bell has given me permission to allow you to see Mr. Tyler at any time during visiting hours," she said.

"Fearless," I said. "Give us a minute here."

My friend and temporary employee stepped from the broom closet of an office out into the spacious hall.

"You don't call Mr. Bell 'warden,'" I said.

She smiled and touched my right forearm.

"What did you want?" she asked.

"I know this isn't the time or place but could I have a phone number for you?"

"Avett's listed," she said with a challenging smile on her lips.

"Not here."

"I live in Santa Monica. That number's in the book too. All you have to do is remember how to spell my name."

We were met in the hall by a tall brown man in the uniform that all Avett guards wore.

"This is Frederick Smith-Hall," Dorothy Stieglitz said. "He'll see you to the visitors' hut."

"Where's Tom Willow?" I asked.

Fred Hall's chest and biceps bulged under the gold and brown costume. I thought that he must have been a football player wherever he went to high school—two or three years before. His frown wondered how I knew a guard at Avett by name but he said, "He didn't come in today. They called me to take his shift."

The accent in his voice had some high notes in it, like people I'd known from St. Louis.

Fred led us down the dank halls and through the metal doors, past the midget guard Maxie, and out into the huge exercise park.

"Do I know you?" Fred asked when we were away from walls, corners, and doors.

"I don't know your face," I said.

"I graduated the LAPD police academy two months ago. They put a freeze on hiring but I start in January."

"Hard job," I said.

"You say your name is Easy?"

"Yeah."

"I heard about you. You friends with the motherfucker Mouse, right?"

"Raymond and I came up together in South Texas," I said.

"And now you comin' in to see Charcoal Joe," he said, more as a pronouncement than an inquiry.

I didn't say anything and Fearless gave the linebacker a glance that should have scared him.

"I'm just sayin'," Fred continued, "that you a crook too, huh?"

I stopped walking and turned to face my inquisitor.

"You got the job and the uniform, man," I said. "You got some knowledge and opinions too. That's cool. But believe me, brother, when you start passin' judgment on your own people because'a somethin' you heard, you might as well be stabbin' your own self in the back. Because believe me these white people here will not save you if anything goes wrong. And whether you from Bogalusa or East St. Louis, you better fuckin' believe that somethin' will go wrong."

Maybe it was my tone or just the content of the mini-lecture that put a question into the young man's face. He sniffed at the air and went on walking, taking us ultimately to bungalow 11.

This was a smaller building with just enough room for Rufus's entourage, Fearless, and me.

Again CJ was seated with the accountant-looking brown man on his left and Ox Mason to his right.

"Can you give us some privacy, Mr. Hall?" Joe asked Fred.

An attitude of rebuttal dominated the guard's face but still he exited, closing the door behind him with some force.

"Fearless," Ox said.

"Mr. Mason."

"You're Fearless Jones?" Rufus asked.

"Yes, sir."

The little kingpin stood up from his chair and held out a hand.

As they shook, Joe said, "It's an honor."

"Thank you," Fearless replied. He would not lie about being honored by the gangster.

"CJ," I said. "I know this might be crossin' some kinda line but could we speak in private?"

The prodigy/tyrant smirked and then smiled.

"Germaine," he said. "Why don't you and Ox take Fearless here over to the pool room? I heard tell he beat Fast Eddie Fontanot one time."

"You sure, boss?" the accountant asked.

"Go on."

Alone in the bungalow, I had time to look around the room. The table and chairs were the same make as in public schools I used to work at as a custodian for the Los Angeles Unified School District. There was a window that had a shade pulled down with the window open. The breeze wafted in and the green-leaf branch of some bush moved in and out also.

Joe took a charcoal branch from a small box and began jabbing at a tan sheet of newsprint paper.

"What have you got for me, Mr. Rawlins?"

"Not much. The cops know that Seymour didn't kill Boughman but they're willing to let him be prosecuted anyway because they need to close the case. I know that you own the house where the murder occurred, that Jasmine Palmas was somehow involved in whatever was going on there, and if I'm not mistaken Seymour is your son and Jasmine his real mother. The way I see it, Boughman and Eugene Stapleton were involved in a negotiation to launder mob money but separately they planned to rob each other. Tony Gambol was moving the money and a woman named Avery was translating the cash into diamonds. I know that Avery was caught up in this business somehow and that Jasmine had to know something about it too.

"What I do not know is if you hired me to clear Seymour or to somehow reclaim the money that I'm told was stolen. Word on the street is that you're planning to leave the country, and I have it from pretty reliable sources that Jasmine has the same plans."

Joe was looking at me pretty hard toward the end of my report. Then he held up the newsprint to show a deft impression of me talking. His interpretation of my face giving the report was new to me but I believed that he got it right.

"Raymond was right about you," he said. "Nobody ever guessed about Seymour before."

"Why the name Brathwaite?"

"He was supposed to be adopted and I had a cousin named Saline Brathwaite who had a son that she lost to crib death."

"Celine? The French name?"

"No. Her mother, my father's sister, was not an educated woman. A doctor once had her using a saline solution for an eye infection and she just liked the word.

"You're right about me and Jasmine too; I mean, we had made a plan to leave. That's changed now. I mean I'll still leave if I have to get Seymour out of harm's way. But I'd rather he get exonerated and live his life as a scientist and a teacher. I'm proud of him."

"What's different now that's going to make you stay?"

"I thought my business could function with me out the pocket, but just me being in here for ninety days and it all goes to shit."

"It would have been nice to know some of this before you sent me out blind and with a target on my back."

"I guess I didn't see how all this other stuff concerned you. Raymond told me that you were connected to the cops, that you could work to help Seymour through them."

"But you could see my problem, right, CJ?" I said. "You call me in here to try and get the cops to back off from your son. But you don't tell me he's your son or that the house where the murder occurred is a place owned by you and used for underworld meetings. You don't warn me that the murdered man is a known gangster or that other bad men are looking for anyone looking into Boughman's death. You didn't say that the man found dead with him was a hit man.

"I had to move my daughter out of our house; our house that was broken into by thugs. I was kidnapped and had a man hold a gun to my head. The only reason I'm alive is dumb luck. I know you're a tough man and a dangerous man but I do not like getting played."

I stopped there. I wasn't really angry. I had known when Mouse came to the office that the road would be winding, rutted, and most likely, as Willomena Avery had said, a dead end.

"I understand, Mr. Rawlins," Joe said. "But you got to believe me when I tell you that I didn't think that you'd get caught up in Boughman's business. I thought you'd just use your influence with the cops. I *was* planning to leave the country but I got my own money. I don't have to steal from the Mafia to buy my way out.

"And on top of all that," he said, "even if I was gonna double-cross somebody it sure and hell wouldn't be you. You one'a the most dangerous men in Southern California."

"Me?"

"You," he said with conviction. "You got Saul Lynx and Whisper Natly in the office with you. Raymond Alexander willing to kill for you and you don't even know it. There's Melvin Suggs, special assistant to Chief Reddin, and then there's Fearless Jones, Christmas Black, that insurance millionaire got the whole French Foreign Legion at his beck and call. And if that wasn't bad enough I hear one'a your friends is that crazy Indian, Redbird. I had a business associate once sent five men after that red man—they never even found one finger. So, Easy, I want you to know that I would not set you up because I know what's what.

"I only wanted for you to help Seymour and I'm sorry if it got complicated. But don't for one minute think that I don't know what you can do."

"Did you know what Boughman was up to?"

"I knew Peter," Joe said. "I knew what he did and we've done business before but I didn't have anything to do with what went on there that night. Seymour didn't either."

"And you didn't know why Boughman was there?"

"I wasn't the one let him use the house."

"Do you think it was Jasmine?"

"She could have. Maybe she wanted to make some'a her own money. But I doubt it."

"What about Uriah?"

"Uriah's a rat-bastard, he sure is. But I don't see a little coward like him killin' a man like Boughman. That's much more something like Stapleton would do. Maybe Uriah told somebody that he saw you up with Jasmine. Maybe that."

"Yeah," I said, thinking about Gregory Chalmers and his friends. "What else don't I know, Mr. Tyler?"

Sitting down behind the school table, Charcoal Joe once again laced his fingers, making that equilateral triangle with his elbows. His eyes were pointed in my direction but he was looking inward, thinking about many things and wondering which of these he could share with me.

"I'm not an evil man, Mr. Rawlins," he said. "I just don't care. In my entire life I have only loved my mother, Jasmine, and Seymour. You know there ain't a man my color like me on this whole damn continent. And so when I do something I have to be absolutely sure that I know every side and every angle. But when Seymour got arrested all my careful planning went out the window."

I looked at the swaying shade and the leafy branch that peeked under it now and then.

"A white woman came to Seymour with a little red diary written in Yiddish," I said. "She told him to give it to Jasmine. He called his mother but she wasn't there. He called Uriah but he said that she was gone. So he went down to the Malibu house where Boughman was killed."

"Who killed him?"

240

"I'm working on that but let me ask you something else."

"What's that?"

"How is it people are using your house for their clandestine business and you don't know about it?"

"They all knew about the house, everyone you mentioned: Jasmine, Boughman, Gambol, Stapleton, and Willomena. Hell, even Uriah had been out there fixing the plumbing. Anybody could have used the place."

"Seymour tells me that Jasmine has gone missing."

"Not missing. I had my people take her somewhere safe."

"Is there a way I can talk to her if I need to?" At that moment I remembered that I'd had sex with Charcoal Joe's woman.

"You don't need to talk to her. She doesn't know anything about what happened."

Hearing the protectiveness in the gangster's tone, and understanding that he could turn on me at any moment, I decided to change tracks.

"You gotta mailman in here?" I asked.

"A what?"

"Somebody that delivers your messages to the outside world."

"Yeah."

"Can you tell me his name?"

Light dawned in the onetime mortician's eyes. His lips twisted at the memory of a sour taste.

"Tom Willow," he said. "The guard that showed you in here the first time."

"I hear that he didn't come to work today."

39

I cut Fearless loose and headed out on my own again.

One thing about being a detective is that your actions often seem repetitive and even arbitrary; like a little black ant zigzagging her way across the floor, seemingly aimless, maybe even lost.

My problem was that Charcoal Joe was so convincing. I believed him, and one thing that detectives and lawyers have in common is that they can never afford to believe anyone. So I decided to double back on my tracks and go to Jasmine's house even though Joe had assured me that she wasn't there.

On the way I began to experience a feeling in my chest. It was both electric and respiratory. The feeling pulsed outward through my limbs and contorted my face in the rearview mirror.

This emotion-based palsy made me shudder and flinch.

I pulled to the curb near Fairfax on Pico and took in a deep breath. Sitting in the driver's seat, quiet and alone, I began to understand the physical symptoms I was exhibiting.

I was, for the first time in a very long time, excited—like a child on the verge of a great adventure. Maybe it had something to do with Mama Jo's tea, but I was pretty sure that those chemicals had already worked their way through my system. I was set against a whole cadre of bad men, and maybe a woman or two. I liked that, because danger forces you to appreciate life; to understand its frailty, transience, and its incalculable value. But beyond drugs and danger, the thrill in my body was a delayed reaction to the separation between me and Bonnie Shay.

I loved Bonnie. I was part of her heart the way a dog is a member of the pack. She felt the same way about me. That's why she wanted to carry my baby with her into hiding. That was why I couldn't leave her. But Jackson was right; Bonnie was a permanent landmark and I was a wave on the ocean somewhere—on my way.

Letting her go freed me. The dog of my heart didn't want that freedom but my soul, whatever that is, yearned for it.

I was that tiny ant, mindlessly repeating the mantra of life like Niska Redman chanting silently morning and night, or a wild dog on a vast plain howling at the moon.

Nobody met me at the little gate to the lower home.

I knocked on Uriah's door but he didn't answer.

I climbed the many, many steps to the high house and Jasmine Palmas's door.

It was ajar.

Without considering it, I took out my pistol and girded for armed conflict.

The first body was lying facedown in the middle of the floor of the main room of the aerie. He was wearing the same lavender suit I saw him in when he was still alive.

I knew Tony Gambol was dead by the open wound in the back of his head. Before I did anything else I reached into my left-hand pocket and came out with a black pair of cotton gloves. After pulling these on I decided to have an extra cigarette that day.

I lit up and sat down on the sofa inhaling noxious fumes, studying the prone form of the deceased gangster, and thinking that this was why I had to accept the loss of Bonnie.

She was a queen, not by decree but by nature, trying to save her peoples; and I was a commoner down in the shit.

Gambol's body was stiff when I turned him over. I almost had to lift him off the floor to get him on his back. There was a small pistol in his left hand and more than six thousand dollars in his wallet. The gun had been fired but I doubted that he shot himself from behind.

The back door led to a small outside patio that looked down on the houses for a few blocks over. There was no blood on the wooden platform, no bodies below.

I went through the bathroom door and then the door to Seymour's childhood bedroom. This chamber was dark, but not dark enough to fully envelop Uriah Hardy's corpse.

He was laid up in a far corner of the small room, his eyes open wide, an innocent look frozen on his face. He was wearing a plaid house robe and had worn slippers on his feet. He'd been shot in the chest multiple times and was probably dead before the killer was through shooting.

The only thing he had in his pockets was a keychain. If his body had been found in an alley the police might never have identified him.

For some reason this grim revelation made me smile.

Jasmine's house had nothing else to reveal. There was a good chance that at least three people were in the house at the time of the murders: Uriah, who had been slaughtered by the others, and Tony Gambol, who was killed afterward by someone he trusted enough to turn his back on.

One of Uriah's keys worked on the door of his lowland abode.

He was a rat, as Rufus Tyler had said; more accurately, a pack rat.

There were newspapers stacked everywhere, some that dated back to the forties; and dozens, maybe hundreds, of *Life* and *Look*, magazines that prided themselves on telling stories with photographs. One drawer was filled with at least a thousand keys and another had dozens of discarded sunglasses of every size, shape, and hue. Broken lamps, a burlap potato sack filled with shoes—some of which were made by individual cobblers, like the old people in the deep South used to wear when I was a boy. He must have had three dozen chairs, four sofas, and a bed that might have come down from his grandparents.

I tried to imagine Uriah and the prostitute Augusta in that bed.

Under the bedframe was a box filled with nudist-colony magazines. At the bottom of that stack was a metal lockbox painted enamel red. I broke three of his four hundred or so butter knives before I could pry the box open.

Inside there was maybe twenty-two hundred dollars, expired driver's licenses dating back to 1947, the marriage certificate between him and Jasmine, and a passport for Mr. and Mrs. Leonard Bartel that, if it had ever been used, would have expired twelve years before. There was no picture attached to the document.

When I sat on the bed the springs squealed like an alley full of tomcats yowling after a bitch in heat.

A pictureless passport. The criminal element of black Los Angeles seemed to be leaving in droves. Uriah had secreted his escape document with his precious printed materials. He died over it.

I searched for an hour or two more. There was nothing else of use to me.

40

"Have you told anybody about Seymour staying with you?" I asked Fearless from a pay phone sixteen blocks west of the undiscovered crime scene.

"Nobody, Easy. You know I might not say the right things now and then, but I never talk when I'm not supposed to."

"How about him?" I asked then. "Has he been a lot on that phone?"

"Naw, man, there's a lock on it," he said. "Right on the number three. Man who hired me put it on when he couldn't talk his wife outta lettin' me stay here. He put on the lock but she give me the key."

That last sentence could have been the repeat line from some old blues song.

"I want you to stay close to him, Mr. Jones. Don't let him out of your sight night or day. I'll pay triple time for that."

When I got back to the office I was, once again, feeling like Alice falling down that rabbit hole. I had accomplished what I'd been hired for. A good lawyer would have probably proven Seymour could not have committed the crime, at least not beyond a pretty long shadow of a doubt. But now there were gangsters, cops, and mysterious women involved. And they were looking at me for a lost fortune.

It was almost enough that I could forget the loss of Bonnie Shay to a man who at one time saved my daughter's life.

_____

"Did you get Tinsford's note, Mr. Rawlins?" Niska Redman asked me when I came through our front door.

"Yeah. How you doin', N?"

"Fine. He said that he's going to need your help and Saul's too tonight."

"What are partners for?" I said, and then moved toward the hall-way toward my office.

"A police sergeant named Trieste called," she said before I could escape.

"What did he want?"

"He said that he needed to talk with you as soon as you got in."

"How long ago?"

"Fifteen minutes. The number is on your desk."

I glared at that number as if daring it to dial itself. I never liked talk-ing to cops I didn't know; I didn't like talking to most cops I was acquainted with. It was the duty of the police to keep men like me down and out, so scared that we were liable to make a slip, then to clap us in chains and lock us away from love, laughter, and light.

Keeping all this in mind, I dialed the number.

The phone rang once, made a funny crackling sound for a few seconds, and then buzzed twice instead of ringing.

"Station thirty-two," a man said in a brusque tone.

"Sergeant Trieste," I said.

"Who is this?"

"Rawlins calling for Trieste."

"What are you doing on this line?"

"Calling Sergeant Trieste."

"Where did you get this number?"

"Look, man, if you don't want to put me through that's fine. Tell Trieste or don't tell him but I called."

I hung up the phone feeling both triumphant and that I had dodged a bullet.

I had a lot on my mind. There was a cache of money in the trunk of my car causing men to kill and be killed with unsettling regularity.

It came to me that I should talk to the benevolent racist Tom Willow. He was Joe's mailman—the guy that delivered messages from and to the unique crime boss. Tom might know something useful to me. When I asked Joe about him a dark light had gone on in the artist's eyes.

Information only had one *Willow, Tom.*

"Hello?" a man with a slick drawl said.

"Hello," I replied. "Is Tom there?"

"Who is this?"

"A friend of Tom's."

"I'm gonna have to give him a name."

"Easy Rawlins."

"Hold on."

"Hello?" another man's voice said.

"Lookin' for Tom Willow."

"Did you just call me?"

"I don't even know who you are, man."

"Sergeant Bernard Trieste of the LAPD."

The phrase *it's a small world* is not always a blessing. I considered hanging up but couldn't see how that would in any way improve my relationship with the LAPD.

"Where's Tom?" I asked.

"Why don't you come over here to see me, Mr. Rawlins? I've been looking for you."

"Where are you?"

"1621 North Sacrosanct Drive, up in West Hollywood."

Damn.

There were four squad cars and as many unmarked police sedans parked on the street, in the driveway, and even on the lawn of 1621. The front door of the terra-cotta flat-roof, faux-adobe home was open. A uniform stood sentry at the sidewalk.

This cop was just another barrier in my way.

"Crime scene," he said, putting a hand on my shoulder.

"Trieste called me," I said. "Now remove your hand."

Anger and fear live right next to each other in the chambers of my heart. I was ready to run or kill.

"What did you say?" The police officer demanded.

"I said, mothahfuckah, remove your hand." Wow.

The stunned look on that white man's face was worth the risk. I don't think he had ever heard a civilian address him like that.

"Norman!" a strong voice called. "Norman!"

The second in command turned around. "Yeah, Sergeant?"

"Send that man up here."

"But he—"

"Send him up."

I am quite sure that moving aside for me was one of the hardest things that Norman had ever done. He wanted to make me bleed. I had the same designs on him. It's wild how people can come to hate each other without having even a passing acquaintance.

The man at the door was five-nine, in an avocado-colored suit. He was thin and his white skin had a tinge of brick red to it.

"Rawlins?" he asked.

"Yes."

"Why did you hang up on the relay officer?"

"Same reason I'd've broken Norman's jaw. People don't act right on the wrong days."

I expected some kind of quip but the thin sergeant smiled slightly and said, "I got something to show you here."

He walked me through the living room, down a short hallway, and into a fairly large kitchen. On the floor was the clay of a man surrounded by a goodly amount of coagulating blood. All he wore was a white T-shirt that was fairly well spattered with red; no trousers, no underwear. Also on the floor was a blocky milk bottle, its spilled white contents in sharp contrast to the darkening red. His eyes were open wide. His expression gave no hint that he knew what was happening when he died. The bullet had entered his back somewhere and knocked him forward, turning him as he fell. He was probably unconscious for a while before he was dead.

"Tom Willow," Sergeant Trieste said.

"And?"

"Do you know him?"

"No."

"Then why did you call here?"

"A man calling himself Willow rang my office and left a message saying that he had some information for me. He left the phone number I called."

"What information?"

"He didn't say."

"What about this?" Sergeant Trieste asked, handing me a clear plastic sleeve that enveloped a business card.

It was a WRENS-L Detective Agency business card with my name scrawled at the bottom.

"Where'd you get this?" I asked as innocently as I could.

"It was on the floor in his bedroom. Any idea how it got there?"

"I hand these things out by the dozen. When we got them printed we didn't put our names on them. So I always write mine in so people will know who to contact."

Trieste studied me then. My answers were too perfect.

"He was killed a few hours ago," he said.

"I was at Avett Detainment then."

"That's where Mr. Willow here worked."

"Not a few hours ago."

"So," Trieste said. "Do you know him?"

"I don't recognize him. I might have met him but you know, most white guys look the same to me."

Trieste gave me that wan smile again.

"Looks like Mr. Willow had just opened his refrigerator," Trieste surmised. "He was knocking back a draught from the milk bottle when someone shot him."

"That's what it looks like," I agreed.

"Do you remember him now?"

"No."

I noticed something then.

"His suitcase was packed," Trieste added.

"A lot of that goin' around. The vacation season sneaks up on you."

"You were at Avett when Tom Willow was on duty," the patient, self-amused sergeant informed me. "The administrator had him bring you down to see Inmate Rufus Tyler."

"This was that guy?" I asked the question with real wonder in my tone. Then I squatted down, pretending to want to get a closer look. I did want a better view; of the baby finger of the dead man's left hand.

Standing up again I felt a minor rush of blood from my brain. I said, "You know I think you're right, Sergeant. This was the man that brought me out to see Joe, I mean, Inmate Tyler."

Trieste was no longer smiling.

"This is murder, Rawlins, not some joke. What did this man say to you?"

"'This way. Bungalow eight. You have fifteen minutes,'" I said. "I certainly didn't give him my card."

"Why did they send you with him?"

"I wanted to see the prisoner and they called this man to take me that way."

"Did he know the prisoner?"

"Maybe he did. I really don't know."

"So you're telling me you don't know this man at all."

"If I had any idea of who killed your man here," I said, "I would lay it out next to the blood and milk. But the truth is I don't know anything about him dying. I don't even know why he didn't have his pants on."

It was at that moment the black ant of my mind doubled back on the million dollars in the trunk of my car. I couldn't have this cop wanting to search me and my vehicle.

I consider myself a man of fair intelligence. I know what secrets I should keep, and not to drive around the city with a million dollars in the trunk of my car; just like a married man knows that he shouldn't bed Eartha Kitt with his wife in the next room. But sometimes, when the real world comes knocking, all we can do is hold tight and hope the roof doesn't fly off.

"There was a letter that he was working on still in the typewriter," Trieste was saying.

"Oh?"

"It was his resignation from Avett."

While we spoke, policemen were sifting through the apartment; slamming doors and opening drawers, inspecting glasses and putting clues into little plastic bags.

"There was one thing he said," I told Trieste.

"What's that?"

"I told him that he seemed to have a great job and he said that he hated L.A. and was gonna move back to, um, North Carolina I believe. He said that he was going to open a commissary store out among the Negro tobacco sharecroppers."

Trieste was looking at me pretty hard. But at one moment his glance went beyond me to someone or something behind.

I turned to see a plainclothes cop standing next to youngish but balding white man who wore a short-sleeved yellow, button-up shirt and maroon Bermuda shorts. The man was peering at me and shaking his head.

I turned back to Trieste and said, "That's why you wanted me here?"

"Witness saw somebody leaving the premises."

"And if I was that man do you think I'd call up to see if he was still dead and then come back here to be identified?"

"Crooks are stupid."

"I guess them and the cops must make a matching pair then."

41

Once again mimicking my insect counterpart, the little black ant, I made my way back to Rodeo Drive. Précieux Blanc was closed when I got there. All of the merchandise had been removed from the windows; a standing precaution against the smash-and-grab class of thief.

It was getting late so I went to a pay phone and dialed my own office. Niska passed me through.

"Hello," Whisper said.

"I'm into something, Mr. Natly. When do you need me?"

"Nothing will go down until after eleven. Why don't we meet at Reuben's sometime before ten?"

"I'll be there."

An hour or so past sunset I made it over to Highland. Fearless answered the door to his posh servants' quarters and smiled.

"Easy."

"How's it goin', Fearless?"

"Just fine. Come on in, brother."

We sat at the square dining table. He had a beer and I a glass of ice water. After the pleasantries were over I asked, "Where's the college man?"

"In the back with Marybeth Reno, tryin' to forget what tomorrow might be."

"I'm here, Mr. Rawlins."

Seymour came out wearing a pair of new blue jeans and a black-and-white speckled dress shirt. Next to him stood the waitress Fearless had introduced me to two days before. She was wearing her new man's faded red T-shirt, nothing more.

"New clothes?" I asked.

"M got 'em for me this afternoon."

M.

"How are you, Miss Reno?" I inquired.

"Great. It's nice knowing real people out here."

"Do you mind if I have a few minutes alone with Dr. Brathwaite?"

"Not at all. Fearless was going to teach me how to play Chinese checkers."

On the apron of concrete between the servants' quarters and the garage, Seymour and I perched side by side against the hood of my car. There was a floodlight shining from a pole between the two structures.

"How's it goin', Mr. Rawlins?" he asked. "I mean with my problem."

"You don't seem too worried."

"Marybeth is very nice," he admitted, giving a shy smile and pushing on his glasses. "She only moved out here two months ago and has been kind of lonely."

"Do you know a woman named Willomena Avery?"

"No."

I took the photograph that Suggs gave me from my breast pocket and handed it to the young man.

"This is the woman that brought me the diary," he said. "I'm almost positive. Her name is Avery?"

All the young man's arrogance and trepidation were gone. Marybeth Reno might have been the name of some elixir on Mama Jo's alchemy table.

"A woman told me a folktale the other day," I said.

"This Avery woman?"

"Yeah," I said. It was hardly a lie. "She said that there was an owl that lived in a tree and that there was a green snake that was rumored to be able to climb trees. The owl worried that the stories about a climbing snake might be true, so she took her crystal eggs and hid them in the apple of wisdom. Does that mean anything to you?"

"Where did you see this woman?"

"At a jewelry store."

"What does it mean?"

"I wanted to know what you thought," I said. "You're the one with the big education."

"You think it might have something to do with the dead men in Malibu?"

"Could be. It doesn't mean anything to you?"

"No."

"Then maybe she was just talking," I said.

"Did you get that book for me, Mr. Rawlins?"

"Oh, yeah. I got it in the backseat."

Handing Seymour *The Feynman Lectures*, I had the feeling that something was off but I didn't know what and I didn't have time to figure it out.

I left Fearless, Seymour, and Marybeth to follow their own repetitious patterns.

I knew what I needed but not how to get at it. There were places I could go, people I could ask, but there was a problem with every solution. The best thing was to wait for the next day and to see what had and had not happened.

So I drove down to Reuben's Cafeteria on Ott just south of downtown proper.

The little yellow kitchen, owned by Reuben Patel, was surrounded by big picture windows. It gave off enough light to illuminate the entire block at night. Reuben was a black man from Charleston who had been a cook on a destroyer in the Pacific theater during World War II. He cooked and served at the little restaurant from 6:00 p.m. to 6:00 a.m. It was the place where those in the know could get a meal at an hour when no other restaurant was open.

Ren Tollman, a very large white man from Bangor, Maine, sat guard at the front door, and it was well known that Reuben never went anywhere without his .45 close at hand.

Reuben always had clam chowder on the back burner and his hamburgers tasted like they were homemade.

I was working on a bowl of chowder and a grilled cheese sandwich when Whisper and Saul came in. That was somewhere just past nine thirty.

We were all wearing loose dark clothes.

Both of my friends had eaten but Reuben didn't mind. Nine thirty was still early. His big crowd didn't come in until after midnight.

"How's your thing with Mouse going?" Saul asked after ordering his second cup of coffee.

"Hangin' by a thread and there's a storm warning on the radio."

"You armed?" Whisper asked me.

"If it's you askin' for help you better damn well believe I'm armed."

In the no-man's-land between South Central and downtown there was a little street named St. Croix that wasn't zoned at all. There was a produce distributer called Fruit Valley, a factory of some kind named Purvis Inc., a few three- and four-story brick buildings that gave no inkling as to their purpose, and a small hotel called the Lily.

Driving a dark gray 1959 Plymouth Fury, Whisper ferried us past the hotel and parked up the street. The car was not his and the license plates weren't from that car; I knew this without asking because Whisper was a very careful detective.

"Redd Roberts usually comes back around midnight," Whisper told us. It was the first time I'd heard the name of our quarry. "He got the top floor of the hotel. His half brother Paul is at the front desk."

"Roberts," Saul said. "Wasn't he the guy they had on trial for killing that woman in Compton?"

Whisper nodded and I felt in my pocket for my gun.

"What's the plan?" I asked.

"When he comes in we go around the block. There's a wall there that blocks an old alley. I cut a hole in it two nights ago. We follow that alley to a door that no one uses since the wall was put up. There's stairs that lead to the top floor."

"She's with him?"

"She'll be with him when he gets here."

"What's his game?" I asked.

"He gets a woman, breaks her all the way down, and then sells her to places keep a woman a slave."

"Wouldn't it be better to tell the police?" I asked. "I mean that way we save Lolo and put Redd away."

"I promised Keisha that I'd get her girl out with the least possible damage. The police can't promise that. You know if he's scared her enough Lolo might tell 'em that she wants to be with him."

"Maybe she does," Saul suggested.

"That ain't Redd's game."

And so we waited.

One of the many things I appreciated about my partners was that they didn't feel obliged to talk when there was nothing to say. There was no light to read by or radio on. Whisper knew what he was looking for, and so Saul in the front passenger's seat and I in the back just sat there letting our minds wander.

I was thinking about how I could find Willomena Avery. Maybe she would be at work the next day. But even if she was, I didn't know if I should approach her or follow. It was a very public place and her bodyguard was armed. She was dangerous on her own, I knew that much. She had killed Tom Willow.

"There he is," Whisper said at a few minutes past one.

A 1967 cherry red Cadillac deVille had pulled up in front of the Lily. A black man in a bright strawberry-colored suit got out, went to the driver's side, and pulled a woman to the curb. She was young and light-skinned, staggering and helpless. The man, Redd Roberts, slapped her for no reason that I could discern and then pushed her with some force toward the front door of the hotel.

When they were gone Whisper turned the engine over and drove around the block.

It was a dark lane with only one streetlight—and that was out. Whisper had probably disabled it that night or the night before.

He walked us to a plank wood wall, inserted a pocket knife at about four feet from the ground, and tilted the haft upward. A four-by-three-foot section of the wood fell outward and Whisper ushered us in.

He had attached a handle on the other side of the portal so that he could put the wall back in place while we did our business at the Lily.

Once we were sealed in, he took out a flashlight and we followed. The black door at the back of the Lily was once secured by four padlocked latches but they had all been cut.

We climbed four flights and then slowly opened a door labeled 5TH on either side. There was a short hall with red carpets and walls. Seeing the color, I wondered how long Roberts had been using that floor.

At the end of the hall a rangy man was sitting in a chair facing the other way, an elevator door to his left and a stairwell to his right.

With hand gestures Whisper told me and Saul to stay put. He

took a sap from his pocket and moved ever so silently up behind the sentry.

Tinsford laid a blow against the side of that man's head that made me wince. I knew it was anger at how his client's daughter had been treated but still I felt for the defenseless sentinel.

When Whisper threw open a door to his right, Saul and I were close behind.

Another red room. It reeked sickly sweet and of human body odor.

The girl, sallow-skinned Lolo Bowles, was naked, on her knees, facing us with a look on her face that was mostly confused. Standing over her, also naked, was Redd Roberts. He had a huge erection and a knife somewhere close to Lolo's throat. I could tell that he was high, probably on cocaine, because the erection didn't wilt at the sight of three armed men coming in on his play.

I noticed that there was music playing, "What the World Needs Now Is Love," sung by Jackie DeShannon. Between the smell, the knife, the erection, and the helpless child, I forgot for a moment my own problems.

"Get the fuck outta here mothah—" was all Redd had time to say; this because Whisper shot him in the throat.

Blood gushed out on Lolo's head and shoulders. She was so out of it that she didn't scream. Saul grabbed her and pulled her away from the fallen pimp but her head, both shoulders, and breasts were covered in red.

I wanted to wash her off, but a shot had been fired and so it was way past time to be gone.

42

Whisper drove us back to our cars, waiting in a dark corner of an empty parking lot three blocks from Reuben's Cafeteria.

Saul had a new case from the insurance consortium Harry belonged to and Whisper had to go to the airport to pick up Keisha Bowles, who was due in on the first flight from San Francisco. That left me to clean Lolo up and bring her to the private clinic Saul used up in Oxnard.

I put her into the shower of our office and rolled up my sleeves to wash the blood out of her hair and ears, off her face, shoulders, and breasts. She was pliable but moaning. After she was clean and dry the complaints got worse because the last dose of heroin was wearing off. She was crying pretty hard when I buttoned her into a plain brown dress that Tinsford had from the mother.

When Lolo was just starting to voice her complaints, I handed her a small glass phial filled with white powder that Whisper had vouched for.

Like an infant child she stopped her whining, distracted by the glass bauble, and asked, "You got a fix?"

"No, baby. You gonna have to do it the old-fashioned way."

I sat next to her on my blue sofa as she snorted and ate the powder out of the palm of her hand. When she was finished I used one of my cheap handkerchiefs to wipe the blood from her left nostril.

———

Lolo slept in the backseat on the hour or so ride to the clinic. I knew she was still alive because of the snoring.

The private hospital was located in the hills above Oxnard behind a high, white stone wall. The sanatorium was a group of large adobe buildings. Saul had called the night nurse, a big redheaded woman with a name tag that read NURSE MAX, who met us at the door of the main building.

"When's the last time she used?" Max asked.

"Maybe an hour and a half."

"Has she been sick?"

"Just sleeping."

"When will her family be here?"

"First flight from San Francisco is in at six thirty," I said. "Mr. Natly will have her up here as soon as he can after that."

"You'll have to wait until her family gets here," Max informed me.

Saul had prepared me for that.

Max was big and brawny for a woman but gentle as a kitten putting Lolo in the wheelchair. I walked next to the girl holding her hand as we rolled down a long, dimly lit hall of closed doors. Now and then there were cries and moans from the rooms. Whenever someone called out in pain, Lolo squeezed my fingers.

When Max was rolling her into one of the cell-like hospital rooms, Lolo said, "Will you wait with me?"

"I'll be right outside the door until your mother gets here," I said.

"Is Mama gonna be mad?"

"Not at all, honey. She's just worried but when she sees you every-thing will be all right. Believe me, I know."

Max went away to get things in order for the mother's arrival.

I sat in an ornately carved walnut chair in the hall, hearing the sporadic sighs and whimpers from the inmates.

I was thinking about Willomena Avery and Tom Willow. I was sure that he was the lover she was talking about in her journal, because of the thick platinum and sapphire pinky ring he had on when he died; that and the business card I'd given her. That ring was more than a year's salary for Tom.

Augusta had told me that Uriah wanted her to break into Jasmine's aerie, and Willomena had been seen multiple times with Tony Gambol and Peter Boughman. Tom Willow was Charcoal Joe's mailman and so he'd likely know about the Malibu house.

"Easy."

I opened my eyes to see Whisper and a tall, buxom black woman maybe just a few years older than I. She was wearing a fancily brocaded dress in the colors silver and blue. Maybe, I thought, she had just come from an upscale event when Whisper's call came in. She'd been too distraught and exhilarated to undress, so she just waited for the morning to come so she could go to the airport and fly down to save her child.

"This is Mrs. Bowles," Whisper was saying as I made it to my feet.

"Pleased to meet you, ma'am."

I held out a hand. After a moment's hesitation she shook it.

She seemed fragile, uncertain about everything she came into contact with.

I learned from Whisper a few days later that Keisha Bowles came from an upper-class family. Her white husband was a high-powered lawyer from an important San Francisco family. They met when she was at Radcliffe and he at Harvard Law. Neither side of the family approved of the marriage but love won out.

"Can I see my daughter?" Keisha asked.

Max came up from behind, opened the door, and ushered the big, brittle woman into the room.

"Thanks, Easy," Whisper said when they were gone. "You know it's not a whole lotta people that I'd trust with something like this."

"What time is it?" I had taken off my watch to wash Lolo and forgot to put it back on.

"Almost eight."

"Hello," a lovely and very feminine voice said into the receiver at my ear.

"Mary."

"Easy," she said. "How are you, hon?"

"I wish I was back in the desert lookin' for you."

"That bad?"

"I need eyes at the sides as well as in the back of my head."

Mary's laugh was strong and knowledgeable. She understood the nearness of death and could laugh at it as well as any man I knew when I was a soldier on the front lines of the largest war in history.

A deeper voice boomed somewhere behind her laughter.

"The ogre commands," she said.

The next thing I heard was, "That you, Easy?"

Melvin always got protective around Mary. In turns she had been a grifter, a con woman, a counterfeiter, and probably worse. But she was beautiful and, at least for the time being, in love with the surly cop.

"You heard about the murder of a man named Tom Willow in West Hollywood?"

"No, but I was in meetings most of yesterday."

"A detective named Trieste was the officer in charge."

"So?"

"You should ask Trieste if Willow had a gun."

"Why?"

"Because if he did I'll give you three-to-one odds that if you check it against the bullets you pulled outta Boughman and Brown, you'll find a match."

"Where'd you get that?" Suggs asked. He had to.

"Sittin' in a chair thinking about Boughman, Gambol, that Malibu house, and Willow. If he heard anything about that house around Tyler and his people at Avett, he might have decided to go into business for himself. And if he did that then he'd be a cinch for a hit."

The reasoning was thin but the words were true.

"So you're telling me this just so you can get your client off?"

"That's the job, Melvin."

"You don't want anything else?"

"Not from you."

"From whom, then?" Melvin had proper grammar when he needed it.

"Melvin," I said like a vexed piano teacher. "Did I not just hand you a murder suspect who won't argue back?"

"I'd like the money he stole."

"I don't have it, man. But you got a whole police department and a house full of clues. You don't need me to do everything, do you?"

"Bye, Easy!" Mary yelled from somewhere in the cavern of the room. "I'm going to work!"

"You let her have a job?" I asked Melvin.

"Even your friend Mouse wouldn't try and stop a woman like her."

"Where she workin'?"

"Santa Monica Public Library."

Thirty-two minutes later, by the nurse's folding desk clock, I made the next call.

"Avett Detainment Facility," the operator announced.

"Dorothy Stieglitz, please."

"Who may I say is calling?"

"Mr. Rawlins."

"Hold on."

The line clicked twice and maybe four seconds passed.

"I thought you were going to call my house," the assistant to the administrator said. She sounded happy to hear from me.

"I still plan to but this right here is business."

"How can I help you?"

"I need to speak to Inmate Tyler."

"I know that we seem pretty informal here at Avett, Mr. Rawlins, but prisoners don't receive personal calls."

"This is anything but personal. It's urgent."

There was a long pause and then, "Give me a number."

43

I gave Dorothy the office number of Nurse Max. Seventeen minutes later the phone rang.

"CJ?" I said upon answering.

"This is Germaine Lang," his jailhouse assistant said. "Mr. Rawlins?"

"That's me."

"Is this phone clear?"

"Like water from the tap."

A moment passed and then came the low rumble of Charcoal Joe. "What's so damn important, Rawlins?"

"I need to speak to Jasmine," I said. "On the phone'll be fine."

"Why?"

"If I can get her to answer one question I will be able to promise you Seymour's exoneration."

"What's the question?" he said. "I'll ask her."

"You can ask her what the question was after we've spoken."

"You work for me, Rawlins."

"I'm doing this for Mouse, so either give me a number or I quit."

First I sleep with his woman and then I spit in his face. I was the consummate professional.

"I'll have her call you," he said.

A few minutes later the phone rang again.

"Jasmine?"

"Mr. Rawlins. You wanted to ask me something?"

"Anybody listening on the line?" I'd learned something from Germaine.

"No. This number only has one phone."

"If you want Seymour to beat the charges you have to give me Willomena Avery's address."

"Why?"

"You can ask her that question tomorrow. Right now give me the address and don't tell her that I'm coming. You might not want Joe to know either."

"What makes you think I would have it?"

"Because when I said her name you didn't ask, 'Who?'"

"What does Willomena have to do with any of this?"

"Ask her tomorrow."

The back and forth went on longer, but in the end she gave me the address. I told her that if she warned her friend, Seymour would be the one paying the price.

Once I got to Santa Monica I took Highway 10 all the way to Pomona. I stopped at a downtown World Gas Station to get directions for 124 North Raleigh Street.

The forty-something white attendant had handsome features and would have been thought attractive if he were only five inches taller and did some push-ups and sit-ups now and then. His ears hugged the skull, and his mouth had tasted something bad a long time ago, never really recovering from the experience.

"Why?" he asked after I made the request.

This reluctance and impertinence was no surprise to me. I was a black man in a brown suit asking directions that would take me into the middle of a white neighborhood. That made no sense at all across a broad swath of white America in the 1960s.

So I reached into the backseat and pulled out a blue-leather notebook.

The gas jockey took a step back when I unzipped the folder. He probably worried that I'd come out with a gun. After he saw the sheaf of printed papers I presented, his natural frown turned into a confused sneer.

"Term life insurance," I explained. "My company, Omaha Security International, OSI, offers a million dollar policy for one hundred dollars a year less than the ones Mr. Andrews currently keeps."

"What?" the man said. His widening eyes were the color of walnut shell.

"I'm an insurance salesman. Life insurance my specialty."

"You?"

"Yeah. A customer of mine got divorced and bought a term policy from me to cover his alimony payments just in case he died. It was only for twenty thousand but it's the percentage rate says what's what. That friend works for Max Wellman." It was a name I made up on the spot. "Andrews works for the aeronautics industry and he's got twelve employees need to be insured because of their jobs. When he heard what I had to offer he said he wanted me out at his house today."

"A million dollars?" the attendant asked, for absolute clarity.

"Times twelve."

"How'd you get that job?"

"Went to the sales office and offered to work on commission. You know I usually sell to colored people but the only color Andrews cares about is green."

The attendant, his name tag said CORKY, traded directions for a detailed explanation on what to say to an insurance company if he wanted a job as an insurance salesman. Once he grasped the value of term life insurance he thought that if they let a Negro sell it, then a card-carrying white man like himself could make it rich. He might have been right.

————

The house was a modest whitewashed cottage between a two-floor brick monstrosity and a three-story apartment building with a facade of gray and brown stone.

After pressing the doorbell I stood there wondering about the case. For all intents and purposes I'd done the job Raymond contracted me to do. I was sure that Tom Willow had killed Boughman, because he was the connection between Joe and the other crooks involved—especially the diamond girl, Willomena Avery. The charges against Seymour would be dropped and Charcoal Joe could go away, or stay, with Jasmine while the young physicist taught *The Feynman Lectures* at Stanford or UCLA.

I was standing still at the front door but that little black ant was twisting this way and that in my mind.

It occurred to me that I could be implicated in the violent death of Redd Roberts. Maybe Lolo would remember the killing; maybe she believed she loved her captor. It was a bad situation but if Whisper hadn't shot him I probably would have. I couldn't fault my partner for better reflexes.

I pressed the button again.

No one answered but I remained there, remembering Roberts's red Cadillac and the red rooms of the fifth floor of the Lily. His blood cascading over Lolo was also red, as was the diary that Willomena, incognito, had left with Seymour. . . .

So was the box that contained the three-volume lecture series. . . .

"Mr. Rawlins," she said. I hadn't heard the door open. "How did you find my address?"

The jewelry store manager must have waited a full three minutes before answering the door. That was her mistake.

"What's your real name?"

She paused for a moment, frowning, but then she smiled and said, "Irena. Irena Król. It is Polish."

"Jewish too?"

Once again I managed to surprise her.

"Won't you come in, Mr. Rawlins?"

"You know," I said, "if this was just ten days ago I'd've taken you up on that offer. But ever since I got mixed up with this job I've gotten kind of skittish."

She was wearing a beige dress that had quarter-inch straps for shoulders, with a hem that came down an inch below her knees. Her thick hair was tied back and her shoes were dark red, a fitting punctuation for the end of my detective's revelation.

The little ant in my heart cried aloud for her sisters to come help.

"You want to stand out here?" Irena asked.

"There's a coffee shop I saw right downtown. Why don't we go there, where all I have to worry about is being considered suspicious?"

"Let me go change."

I reached out to touch her left forearm.

"You look fine," I said.

"I don't have to go with you."

"You gave Seymour that journal for Jasmine," I said. "But how did you get *The Feynman Lectures* back on the coffee table in her house without her knowing?"

The coldness in those eyes for some reason brought to mind the hole in the back of Tony Gambol's head. He had been looking for that collection of essays, but I'd bet he didn't even know it.

"Let's go," she said.

Cha-Cha's Grill and Diner had an almost vacant parking lot and most of the tables were empty.

We were seated, given big, one-sheet laminated menus, and served ice water in squat glasses. The waitress was about the same age as Irena but she looked two decades older. Her name tag read MISSY.

"No specials," she said. "We're serving the lunch menu now."

When Missy went away Irena asked, "What do you want from me, Mr. Rawlins?"

"I'm a detective, Miss Król. Detectives want answers."

"Król is not a Jewish name," she said, answering a question gone by. "But my mother was Jewish. She married my father to get us out of the ghetto. We attended Catholic mass but she taught me my letters at home."

"Have you decided?" The impatient waitress had returned while we were concentrating on each other.

"I'll have the pastrami sandwich," I said.

"Chicken soup," the woman known as Willomena Avery added.

For some reason our order bothered Missy. She was short with half-gray and half-brown hair, and wore an incongruously festive blue and yellow uniform. The look on her face would have gone well with Corky the gas station attendant. I thought that maybe breathing the heavy smog out in Pomona turned its permanent residents sour over time.

"Is that all?" she asked.

"Yes."

When she was gone again I asked, "Why did you kill Willow? Or should I call him John and you Julia?"

"You speak Yiddish?"

"This is not wartime Warsaw, Miss Król. There's a lot of people who speak your language in L.A."

"You are a surprising man, Mr. Rawlins. Are you working for Joe?"

"Is he looking for you?"

"I didn't think so. Not yet anyway."

"My job," I said, "was to help Seymour Brathwaite get out from under that murder charge. Were you there when Tom Willow killed Boughman and Brown?"

"No," she said, but it might not have been true.

"You loved him."

"Not love really, it was a . . . a terrible obsession. We were animals together, but when he said that he was going to kill Jasmine I had no choice."

"He thought she had Boughman's money?"

"Not the money. I told him that I had given her the diamonds."

"Packed neatly inside *The Feyman Lectures.*"

"Yes. How did you know?"

"That little fable at the end of your journal. You were talking about the lectures. I figure Jasmine gave you a copy to smuggle diamonds in. She had to ask Seymour for another. You carved out the pages to contain the diamonds."

"Yes."

"What I don't understand is how you got the diamonds when Boughman still had the money."

"The man who owns Précieux Blanc, Sol Hyman, was in on it. He'd get diamonds and then the bagman would turn over the money. The client always paid twelve cents on the dollar for the diamonds, and Sol took twenty-five percent of the profit. He'd been doing it a long time. Nothing ever went wrong before."

"What if Jasmine had opened the book?"

"Why would she? It had been gathering dust on her coffee table for three years. I switched the books from my box into hers so she wouldn't notice anything different."

The waitress came with our food.

I was hungry but Irena didn't touch her soup.

"So," I said after the disapproving Missy had gone, "I figure that you know Jasmine because you both worked for Doris back in the day."

"You're a very good detective, Mr. Rawlins. Yes, I worked for her. Doris always likes to have a couple of white girls on call. Some black men want that. Jasmine was my only friend. After she met Joe she quit the business and introduced me to one of her clients—Sol Hyman. We hit it off and I went to work at Précieux Blanc."

"Does Joe know you two worked together?"

"I don't think so. I was never sent to him. He only liked Negro women."

"But you and Jasmine were close. You went to her house sometimes when Seymour wasn't around. Once Jasmine told you about *The Feynman Lectures* being a holy scripture for physicists. That's what the riddle about the owl and the snake meant. Does Jasmine speak Yiddish?"

"Of course not."

"Then why give Seymour the journal for her?"

"She knows my people. They would have translated for her—in time."

"How did you get the lectures back on her table?"

"I called Doris and told her that Jasmine wanted a girl for Uriah. Then I made a date with Jasmine for the same time. When the girl came I went upstairs and switched out the books. I called the restaurant and told Jazz that my car broke down. When did you figure it out?"

"In that family it's a popular book. Seymour wanted me to bring his copy from his apartment and when I picked it up I noticed a difference in weight." I *had* noticed the difference but it didn't mean anything to me at the time. I lied because I needed Irena to believe that the jewels were in my possession.

She took a sip of ice water. I took a third bite out of my sandwich.

"Did Tom kill Gambol?"

"I didn't know Tony was dead. He called me at the store after the murders. He wanted to talk. Everybody was suspect when Boughman turned up dead with the money missing. I went to meet him with Tom. They were going to go talk to Uriah."

"Why?"

"They knew that he was always trying to steal from Jazz. They thought that maybe he was the one that robbed Peter."

"How did he get involved? Gambol, I mean."

"The money was moved through the track. It was due to come in on a special armored car, and then Tony would plan the time when it was passed to Boughman. Stapleton brought him in because he could tell us within twenty-four hours of the deal going down."

274

"I still don't understand how Uriah fits into all this," I said.

"Uriah knew that Jasmine moved money for Joe now and then. He was always breaking into her house and searching it."

"Why didn't she tell Joe?"

"Uriah was a client before she met Joe. But it was different with him and Jasmine. He told her that he loved her but she didn't take him seriously. Then he offered to marry her so that everything he owned—his house, his retirement—everything would be hers."

"And she took him up on it?"

"We were whores, Mr. Rawlins; disposable women. If a man offers you money and respectability, that's a powerful gift. He told her that he was saving his money to take her to Jamaica and buy her a house."

The old passport with no photo suddenly made sense.

"But she has Joe's baby and lives apart," I said.

"Uriah wanted to take care of her," Irena said. "But he didn't have enough money yet. So she still had to work for Doris."

"And that's how she met Joe."

"Uriah was heartbroken when she went with Joe," Irena continued. "He loved her but she realized that the man she needed was Joe."

I wondered if there was some course at Stanford or UCLA that explained and explicated the Economics of Love.

"Jazz felt guilty. That's why she had Joe make him her gatekeeper. She wouldn't share Uriah's bed, but she wanted to protect him because he was the first man that had ever tried to save her."

"But that just made him mad."

"I worked for her," Irena admitted. "I held packages she moved for Joe so Uriah wouldn't steal them and get himself—and maybe Jasmine—killed."

Feeling suddenly restless I asked, "You gonna eat that soup?"

Curling her left nostril, she shook her head no more than a few centimeters.

"Then let's get out of here."

I drove up into the hills without any specific direction in mind. We had no reason to trust each other but at least we acted like we did.

"So what happened?" I asked, even though I already knew.

"Tom."

"He made you steal from your friend?"

"I went crazy. One day, just two months ago, Jasmine had Tom bring over a satchel of money that one of Joe's men collected down at the docks. It was a small amount; maybe forty-five thousand dollars. I was supposed to deliver it to a man in Compton.

"Tom was handsome and so I offered him a drink. He kissed me and then opened the bag. I wasn't worried. If he stole from Joe he'd be a dead man. Then he kissed me some more and asked why didn't we run with the money? I told him the power Joe had and how no one ever stole from him and lived. He said he was joking . . . and then we were lovers.

"I didn't tell Jasmine. I should have told her.

"When Joe's customers made big deals where large sums had to be turned into diamonds, I used Seymour's book. Jasmine said that she never understood it and nobody wanted to read about physics. There was a big transaction coming. Tom knew something was up."

"How?"

"He was passing information from Joe to Peter and Tony. He knew it was something big."

"So Joe knew?"

"Joe knows everything. He always made things run smoothly because the police saw him as some kind of petty criminal, just a low-level gambler. But then Gene Stapleton came to me. He was the point man for the Cincinnati mob that was moving the cash. He wanted me to give him the diamonds when they came in. He said that he'd fix it so that everyone blamed Boughman. He promised me a hundred thousand."

"And what did you do?"

"I needed time to think and so I told him that because it was so much money, the diamond dealer insisted on bringing the stones personally to the meeting, that he would have a bodyguard with him."

"And so the Cinch decided to go in there with his three men," I said. "Kill the dealer and Peter, then run with all that money, the diamonds too."

"I was scared and I was angry. I was in love and, you know, when you love somebody you always think that their heart is like yours; that they could never betray you. So I told Tom. I didn't plan to at first but he could see it in me. I told him everything and, and . . . he said that we could do what Stapleton planned. We could steal the money and the diamonds. He said that we'd run away together. I didn't want to but . . . but between Stapleton and Tom the choice seemed easy."

We had reached a promontory. I pulled off the road and got out of the car. Irena came after and we leaned against the warm hood, looking down on the blanket of brown smog suffocating the inland town.

It felt as if we were under some kind of temporary cease-fire where the foot soldiers could climb out of their trenches without the fear of death.

I was already smoking before I knew there was a cigarette between my fingers.

"Can I have one of those?" she asked.

We smoked for a while in silence.

When she crushed the butt under her red shoe I asked, "So why did you turn against your boyfriend?"

She gazed at me as if the answer was written there on my forehead.

"I don't sleep well," she said at last. "In Poland, whenever I felt safe, next there came the fear. I knew that I was never safe and that my greatest enemy was feeling that I was.

"Then, three nights before Tom was going to rob Boughman, I woke up in his bed so nervous that I had to get up. I wanted to run but told myself that this was silly. There was no more war. I had met a man that I loved.

"I wandered the house thinking that any minute he would reach out for me and then wake up to come tell me that he loved me and bring me back to bed. . . ."

I gave her another cigarette and lit us both.

"When he didn't come I looked through his uniform for a cigarette. There was a letter folded in his shirt pocket, a letter he had written to Felicia Whitman—his fiancée in North Carolina."

She didn't say any more about the letter. She didn't have to.

"But even so," I said, "you went through with the robbery."

"What could I say to him? He had plans that didn't include me. He knew the setup and I still had to get away from Stapleton. The next morning I put the diamonds in the book and took it to Jasmine's. Then I brought the journal to Seymour. He'd never met me and I wore a scarf and dark glasses—I talked like an old Jewish grandmother."

"Why Seymour?"

"No one would suspect that he held the secret to the diamonds. I told Tom that I got nervous and sent the diamonds in the mail to Jasmine just in case Stapleton or Peter decided to take them from me.

"Then, on the morning of the tradeoff I gave Stapleton an address in the Hollywood Hills, telling him that that was where Boughman was to make the trade. I said that the dealer was going with his bodyguard and that they told me to stay away.

"From there you know. Tom went to Malibu six hours before the meeting. Peter was early too but only by a few hours. When Tom heard him at the door he hid in a closet. Peter was there with another man. They talked about how they would steal the diamonds. Peter said that they could hide in the closet. When the man with Peter opened the door Tom shot him. Boughman didn't have the money on him and so Tom beat him and then he lost his temper and killed him. He had just finished searching Boughman's car when he saw Seymour going toward the beach. Tom didn't know who he was or what house he was going to, but he called the police so that they would think a Negro had broken in."

"But why would you kill Tom?" I asked. "I mean you had the diamonds, you could have just run?"

"It was a mistake to tell Tom I sent the diamonds to Jasmine. If Boughman had had the money, that would have been all right but he didn't have the cash. He planned to rob me.

"Every day after he killed Boughman and Brown, Tom would ask me about the diamonds. I put him off by saying that they must still be in the mail. That worked until night before last. He said that he'd kill Jasmine if she didn't give us the stones. I had no choice."

The coldness in her tone was the announcement of the end of the cease-fire.

"When Stapleton came to the store he couldn't do anything because of the new security guard and the others. I told him that Boughman called at the last minute to change the meeting place. I told him I had no idea of what happened after that."

"And he believed you?"

"Not completely, I don't think. But why would I still be at work if I stole from the mob? And he was in trouble with them too. I wanted to get the diamonds and run, but Seymour was in jail and Jasmine was heartbroken. I wanted to help her if I could and I thought, if I lived, I could get the diamonds later. But now you have them."

"Yes," I lied. "I do."

"I could turn them into cash."

"How much?"

"Six hundred thousand, at least."

"What does your boss say about all this?"

"You mean Sol?"

"Yeah."

"I showed him the story about the murder in the paper. I told him that it was not only theft but also murder. Sol is a coward. He took a jet to Israel the next day."

"Smart man."

"What about the money, Mr. Rawlins? I have the connections to get the best deal and I know who to trust."

"Except for bad men and boyfriends."

"Can we make a deal?"

"You shot your last partner in the back."

"I won't shoot you." She smiled after saying this and I couldn't help but like her.

"I'm gonna drive you home and then go think on it," I said.

She wanted to argue but there was nothing to say and so we got back into the car.

When we were parked in front of her house I said, "Let me ask you something."

"Yes?"

"How did you get out of Tom's house without being recognized?"

"No one knew me there. Most of the time we went to my place. I put on his sweat suit and rolled up the pant legs and the sleeves. After I put up the hood you really couldn't be sure if I was a small man or a woman."

"And just one more thing."

"What?"

"Stapleton."

"What about him?"

His men came to my house right after I started looking into Boughman's murder. How did he know about me?"

"Tom said he overheard enough of what Joe said after you left to know that he had hired you. When Gene asked me the next day about what happened, I mentioned that I heard Joe had talked to you."

I didn't say anything but I'm sure that my face hardened.

"I was desperate, Mr. Rawlins. I thought I was going to be murdered."

"What's done is done," I said. And I meant it, too.

I stopped at Corky's gas station again and went to a pay phone.

"Hello?"

"Fearless."

"What's wrong, Easy?"

"You hear it in my voice?"

"Like a buoy in the dark, brother."

"I need you to do something for me, Fearless."

"What's that?"

"I want you to go to a house and take a book off of a glass table."

"That don't sound like somethin' to have the blues over."

"There's two dead men in the house. When you get there you have to make sure that they haven't been found yet. If it's clear, take the book then wrap it in brown paper, write my name on it, and drop it in the slot of my office. Definitely don't let Seymour see it."

I knew that Fearless took me seriously because he waited six or seven seconds before saying, "You got it, Easy. If I don't see no cops you can consider it done."

45

There was more money in the trunk of my car than most eight-ton armored cars ferried in a month. On a coffee table in the mausoleum of Jasmine's high house there was a boxed set of college lectures containing a cache of diamonds of equivalent value.

There had been five murders plus the incidental deaths of Stapleton's men. The murderer was dead. His killer was a woman scorned and desperate.

Redd Roberts was dead, but that hardly seemed to matter.

I pulled up into the driveway of my house, turned off the ignition, and sat there wondering about my next move. Some guy named Sol had secured the diamonds on credit, expecting a windfall, but now he was tucked away in Jerusalem or maybe Tel Aviv. The money belonged to the mob.

My lover was gone for good; deserting me for a crippled king in a wheelchair.

I like to think that I'm an honest man, but in the modern world you can't carry honesty very far without taking a break from time to time. Back then, in the sixties, two million dollars was enough for an entire lifetime of rent and meals, reasonably priced clothes, and, of course, gas for the car. I could send Feather to any university in the world and buy a house for Jesus and his family.

I put my fingers on the key still in the ignition, intending to fire up that engine again, then go to my office, pick up Feather, and drive as far away as I could get.

It was remembering the talk with Sarah Garnett that changed

my mind. I was all Feather had, and the road I wanted to embark upon might have some bumps.

My job was to keep Feather's life as smooth as possible. Money might have been useful, but the currency she needed was stability and love.

Plucking the key from the ignition, I climbed out of my Dodge.

I crossed the lawn to my front door thinking that maybe I should have used Saul and Whisper the way they relied upon me. Maybe their help would have made the road easier.

With teamwork and delegation in mind, I walked across the threshold into my soon-to-be ex-house.

"Mr. Rawlins," he said.

I looked up to see who my home invader was, recognized him, and said, "You lied to me."

"About what?" Charcoal Joe asked.

"You're the one who orchestrated the money exchange."

Ox Mason, standing behind his lord, shifted his shoulders menacingly.

"Shall we go into the living room?" Joe suggested.

"How'd you get out of Avett?" I asked Rufus Tyler when we were seated.

"They have a prisoner release policy," the prodigy explained. "If there's serious business or some tragedy, an inmate can get a pass for a day or so. That's at Administrator Bell's discretion."

Ox Mason was standing next to the sofa chair his boss inhabited.

"And what was this?" I asked.

"A little of both."

"How so?"

"Two million dollars has gone missing, and I'm the one that assured the transaction would be completed without incident."

"I thought Sol Hyman had signed for the stones," I said. I shouldn't have. It was like showing a cardsharp your hand before discarding and drawing again.

. "How did you know . . ." But before the question found its subject, realization dawned and he said, "Willomena."

"Miss Avery and I had a conversation."

"She was involved?"

"It was your postman—Willow."

"And where is he now?"

"In the morgue keeping Boughman and Stapleton's men company," I said. "Uriah and Tony Gambol are also dead. Money and blood are constant companions, it seems."

"Mr. Hyman left the country as a precaution against early death," Joe said, telling me what I already knew. "But the people he deals with will come to me for the cash. Willomena was not familiar with that part of the deal."

Joe stared at me a moment or so. I felt that I had crossed a border into a land where the laws I abided by were not enforced.

"Why are you here, Mr. Tyler?"

"I need to know what you know, Mr. Rawlins." His smile was almost innocent.

"Like what?"

"Was Jasmine or Seymour involved in the theft?"

"No."

"You're sure?"

"Yes."

"Why are you sure?"

"Willow figured out what you were into. I don't know how. Maybe some delivery you put him on. He killed Boughman and his man, stole the money, and laid hands on the diamonds."

"And where was Willomena in all this?"

"She was making the delivery. Being Southern, Tommy refrained from killing her but he scared her pretty good."

Joe's nose twitched.

"Who killed Tom?"

"Does that have something to do with your money?"

"If Tom stole the cash and stones then his killer probably took my property."

My soul-searching in the driveway had paid off in an unexpected manner. I might have been able to hide from the white men that lost the cash, but a black gangster like Charcoal Joe would have gotten to me sooner or later. Too many people knew my involvement in the moving parts of the thefts.

"What if I told you that I might be able to find your two million?" I said.

"Then I'd believe that you were the one that killed Tom Willow."

"Would that matter?"

"He was from North Carolina like my people were."

"And that makes you loyal to him?"

"Not one bit. Now where's my money?"

"I didn't kill Willow but the cops will probably know who did. If I play it right they'll lead me right to your money and never even realize it."

"That's a whole lotta *if*."

"What if I told you that I'd give it to Jasmine within the next two days?"

"Is that what you're telling me?" Joe asked.

"What would the return of your money be worth?"

"The man or woman who delivered it could take, say, seventy-five thousand from the cash."

"Two days," I said.

46

Sitting in my dinette watching the darkness gather on the street and in the sky, I was reminded, as I often am at twilight, of the miracle of being a man. For me the journey was nearly over. All I had to do was give Joe's money to Jasmine and cross my fingers about Roberts, Redd.

The phone ringing did not surprise me. I turned my head to look at it on the kitchen counter but stayed in my chair at the eight-sided table.

It rang thirteen times and then stopped.

A minute went by and the caller tried again. Thirteen more rings and then the hang-up. That was a clear message, whether it was meant to be or not, so when the racket started up again I raised the receiver to my ear and said nothing.

"Rawlins?" a man with a deep voice said.

I maintained the silence.

"Don't get me mad, man," the caller warned.

"Who is this?" I asked.

"Hold on."

The phone banged down and there was a powwow of men's voices in the background. The wait was about half a minute. I used that time to take a few deep breaths.

"Why haven't I heard from you, Mr. Rawlins?" Eugene Stapleton asked.

"I told you I'd call when I got something."

"What you got so far?" His tone was both light and deadly.

"Tom Willow, a prison guard, stole the money and the jewels. He must have had a partner because by the time I got there he was dead and the money was gone."

"You don't say."

"The story about the murder should have been in the late edition. If not it'll be in the morning paper."

"Well then," he said, as ho-hum as a spider spinning his web. "I guess I better pack my bags and head for the hills, huh? Maybe I can get a job as a dishwasher in Columbus or a stevedore down on the Galveston docks."

I believed that he had considered these professions recently . . . but something had changed.

"I don't know what to tell you, Mr. Stapleton."

"No? Then let me tell you something. I got your partner right in the next room."

It's rare for me to be caught off-guard about intelligence when on a job. I'm the detective. I know what happened and who was involved. My job is looking for the right skeleton key for the locked door before me; but not that night on the phone with the Cinch. What partner could he have meant, Saul or Whisper?

"What are you talking about?"

"I'm saying that you got the diamonds and I have the girl who can change them into cash."

Irena Król. Either he figured out where she lived or she came to him with a desperate scheme to get enough money to disappear from a world tainted by her love of Tom Willow. Maybe Joe had called her and made some demand and she ran to Stapleton—the lesser of two great evils.

"Mr. Rawlins."

"What, Gene?"

"You can't get anything near the value of those stones. People are looking for them and there's no nigger fence in the world that could sell them. I got the bank teller. You got the passbook."

My first thought was to say yes and make a meeting with the

man. He'd go there and I'd go to Jackson Blue's while Melvin Suggs kept the appointment.

"She told me all about you two," Stapleton said when I hesitated.

"Oh?"

"She told me about how you were lovers and that you got her to betray Tom Willow. You must have put some serious voodoo on her."

I couldn't go to Melvin. If he confiscated the money I'd have both the mob and Charcoal Joe after me.

I couldn't go to Mouse either; not with two million dollars under the table. Raymond was about to retire and that temptation might have overwhelmed even his love of Charcoal Joe. I had no desire to get involved in that kind of war.

"What do you suggest?" I asked.

"Why don't you come over here and we'll talk about it?"

"Why don't I just drive off a cliff and get it over with?"

The gangster chuckled.

"What do you want?" he asked.

"Gimme the phone number where you're at."

"Why?"

"Because I have an idea that will cover all the bases, but I'm not gonna stay in this house to wait for another visit with your men. You ask Willomena who she thinks would buy the diamonds and then we all meet at that bank or jeweler's tomorrow afternoon. I'll call later on tonight for the particulars."

"That's a pretty good plan," he said, impressed. "We split the money in the room and go our separate ways."

"That's the gist of it."

"Damn," he said and then, after a full minute of silence, "Okay."

I was hoping that Melvin was at work but no one answered his office line. So I called his home.

"Hello," he said in a voice a full octave lower than was his norm. He didn't sound sleepy.

"That Mary keepin' you up, Melvin?"

"You know I love you, Easy, but this callin' every day has got to stop."

"The gun work out?"

"Yeah. It killed the men down at the beach house and only his prints were on it, on the bullets too. The prosecutor dropped the charges against your client."

"That must look pretty good on some report somewhere," I speculated.

"It'd look better if I had the man who killed Willow. It'd be a month-long vacation in Bimini if I could find that money."

"Can't help you there," I said. "But you could do me a good turn."

I heard a kissing sound and a satisfied feminine hum over the line.

"What, Easy?" an impatient Melvin said.

Once I had the address I went to the safe at the WRENS-L offices and withdrew six thousand dollars of my money. I also took a very special, unregistered .25 revolver and a powerful, steel-jacketed flashlight that Saul kept in his closet.

I considered calling Fearless but he'd done enough.

I thought about waiting until morning and going to see Joe but this, I felt, would ultimately put me at cross-purposes with him.

The second stop was the Torrance Arms Hotel on Wilshire a few blocks east of Western.

It was nine minutes after nine by the clock on the wall when I walked into the main lobby of the small hotel.

A pretty young Asian woman looked up from the registration desk. The tilt of her head and shoulders asked if I had a question, but before I could approach her a man said, "Mr. Rawlins?"

Five-eight at the height of his manhood, he was skinny everywhere except his stomach, which bulged out over the beltline. When buying his suit off the rack he had to decide whether he wanted the shoulders to fit or the jacket to button.

He decided that the open-sports-coat look best suited him.

White and blue-eyed, to match his lapis lazuli–colored suit, the man moved with the necessary arrogance that all policemen donned before going out in a world that both hated and feared them.

"Yes," I said. "Officer Smiley?"

"Follow me."

We walked up three flights of stairs to the fourth floor of the Torrance. The hall wanted to be fancy but the carpeting was thin and the teal walls needed a new coat of paint.

At the end of the hall was suite 401A. Officer Smiley knocked twice and then twice again.

Another detective, this one taller with more substance to him, opened the door. He wore a red polo shirt and blue jeans. The only way you could tell his affiliation was the badge dangling from the front of his belt and the gun in the clip-holster on his side.

He was standing in a small room made for entertaining. There was a dining table where the cops had been playing dominoes and a portable bar stocked with quart bottles of scotch, rye, and vodka.

"This him?" the new man asked.

Ignoring his partner, Detective Smiley pointed at a door to the left and said, "He's in there."

I walked up to the closed, cream-colored door, considered a moment, and then decided to knock.

"Come in."

Gregory Chalmers was sitting on a single bed wearing a white T-shirt and a pair of white painter's pants. He was leaning against the wall at the head of the bed watching a small television against the opposite wall.

There was a rerun of an episode in the series *The Life and Legend of Wyatt Earp* playing. Wyatt and another man were facing each other at the denouement of all TV westerns, the showdown.

Seeing me sat Gregory up straight. He crawled on his hands and knees to the foot of the bed and turned off the TV.

Then he stood on bare feet and asked, "What are you doing here?"

I was so concentrated on my mission that I hadn't thought about how the mob lieutenant would react to seeing me. Less than a week ago he'd planned to kill me, and then, through guile and sheer luck, I capsized his entire life.

"I'd like five minutes to talk," I said. "If I had ten I'd kick your ass too."

He was the same blocky man that had me hog-tied and nearly slaughtered, but there was something different about him.

"Can I have a seat?" I asked, waving toward a blond chair that sat before a plain pine desk.

He lowered back down to the mattress and I pulled out the chair. He was watching me closely because we both knew that I wasn't kidding about the extra five minutes.

"Okay," he said, "talk."

"I want to know where you think the Cinch would be holed up with two or more."

Gregory broke out into a grin, then closed his mouth and shook his head.

"No?" I said.

"Look, man," he said. "I might talk to the cops about a thing or two if it means getting out from under serious felony charges. But why the fuck would I help you?"

That's when I realized what was different.

"You shaved off your mustache, huh?"

The quick switch of subject confused the bad man.

"You think a bare lip and some white clothes is a disguise?" I asked.

"They made me wear this shit" was his reply. "Said that if I ran, that I'd stand out in the crowd."

"Three thousand dollars," I said.

"What?"

"Three thousand and another three if the Cinch is where you tell me."

"Bullshit." His sneer was that of a man who used his lip hair for punctuation.

I reached into the right-hand jacket pocket of my gray suit and pulled out a stack of sixty fifty-dollar bills, fanning myself with them.

His square face froze like that of some exotic cat that had seen a multicolored bird land on a branch just above. He licked the bare lip and began to nod.

"Okay," he said.

"I know what you're thinking, Greg. You think you'll give me the address of some old apartment or the house of a girlfriend you don't like anymore. Maybe you'll send me to the back room of some pool hall or bar where your friends would beat me to death just for being stupid."

He squinted at the glare of the truth.

"But know this," I continued. "If I don't find Stapleton by the end of the night I'll call suite 401A and tell Officer Smiley that you have a nest egg somewhere in this room. You and I both know what that fat-gut cop'll do."

Greg's eyes opened wide looking for a way around the threat.

"But if I find what I need I'll be back tomorrow, at the latest the day after, and give you another three."

After a long silence he said, "You know grabbing you like we did it wasn't personal, right?"

The address Greg gave me was on Oxnard Street a few blocks down from Sepulveda Boulevard. That was in Sherman Oaks, an upscale neighborhood in the San Fernando Valley. The two-story house bordered a large park. Greg said that Eugene liked it that way so he'd have a quick exit if things went south.

"He's got a gun stashed at the bottom of an oak not thirty feet from the back fence," said the man who once was going to murder me. "So if he has to jump out of bed and run quick he'll have a piece waiting."

The back fence was wood and high but the gate was only secured by a simple iron latch.

If Stapleton still had his way there'd be two men with him; one for the back door and the other for the front. There was a stand of bamboo that partly blocked the gate.

Greg really got into the description once the money was in his hands.

I drove past the house at a little after ten that night. There was a single light on upstairs and a man on the front porch. The sentinel was sitting in shadow but I knew where he was by the now-and-then glow of his cigarette.

I drove three blocks down, stopping at a corner phone booth. There I dropped a dime and dialed some numbers.

"Yeah?" he answered.

"Mr. Stapleton."

"Tomorrow at four," he said. "There's a bank called Teller's a block and half up from Wilshire on Beverly Boulevard. It's after business hours but the guard will let us in."

"No," I said.

"Why not?"

"I want business hours. I want bank guards and loan officers all around the place. You know I'm not goin' into any closed vaults after hours with a man like you."

"I can't get in touch with him now."

"I'll call you at ten tomorrow morning. Make it work."

Before I could hang up a car horn blared.

"Where are you?" Stapleton asked.

"On the street. At a pay phone." After a moment had passed I said, "Ten o'clock in the morning," and then hung up.

After our brief conversation I took a drive over to Coldwater Canyon to check out the real estate. I needed to move soon, and I had to let Stapleton settle down after my ultimatum. I was pretty sure that the house I reconnoitered was his hideout; mostly because of the half-hidden guard and the dark Lincoln parked at the curb in front of the house.

At a few minutes before one in the morning I was moving through the dark trees of the park behind the Cinch's hideaway. I wondered yet again about Mama Jo's latest elixir.

The chemical impact of the tea was finished, but the memory of being able to concentrate on one thing while leaving other thoughts and concerns behind had somehow changed the way I experienced the world.

This was not necessarily a good thing. The only thought in my head was Stapleton and Irena. They both knew about the diamonds and he was using her to get at me. I had to do something about that, and if that something meant going into a white neighborhood and facing three armed men, then that was what I was going to do.

Other concerns, like good sense and safety, took a backseat.

Using the squat pocketknife, I teased the iron latch on the back gate open. Crouching down, I moved silently behind the bamboo and then across the yard, watching the back door as I went.

There was no guard outside and none that I could see through the glass of the back door—which was locked. Maybe the Cinch only had one man to help him.

There was a path down one side of the house that led to the foot of the stairs to the porch.

What I had going for me was that the sentry on the front door didn't use the porch light, thinking that he could see anyone coming from the street while they couldn't see him. But with smoking so much a second nature, he forgot that there was light there too.

I took the chance of peeking around the corner because I didn't think he'd see my dark face in the gloom. I'll never know if my supposition was accurate because the guard was asleep in his heavy redwood chair. He was slumped backward and snoring softly. I backed away and took off my shoes.

The plan was simple, if flawed. I gripped the lantern-end of my long-handled flashlight, tiptoed quickly up the stairs, and hit the guard as hard as I could on the pate of his head.

He slumped down a little more and I hoped that he wasn't dead.

I left my shoes where they were and tried the front door. I figured that the door was either unlocked or the sentry had the key in his pocket.

It was unlocked and I walked into an entry hall that led to a living room and then to the kitchen. In my right hand, gloved ever since I entered the park, I carried the long-barreled .25 pistol. I chose this weapon because it was unregistered and made the least noise of all my guns. I found a small lamp on a table and took the chance of turning it on.

It was a well-appointed kitchen with copper pots hanging from the wall, and a drain board filled with the supper dishes all clean and lemon-smelling. On the dining table there was an eight-ounce brown glass bottle with a white cloth next to it. I sniffed at the cap, felt a moment of dizziness, and put the sweet-smelling chloroform back down.

I tried to remember the week before on the first Monday in May, when I was happy and expectant, almost married, and innocent again.

Irena was in the house somewhere, most likely. So was Eugene Stapleton.

There was a Fisher AM/FM radio sitting on a window ledge next to the dining table. Across from there was a pantry door that opened into a room just large enough for a man to hide in.

Without giving it too much thought I turned on the radio and went into the pantry, leaving the door only slightly ajar.

"I Was Doing All Right," by Dexter Gordon, was playing on the radio. It surprised me that Stapleton was a fan of black jazz.

There came the thumping sound of half a dozen barefoot footsteps and then, "Ira?" It was Eugene Stapleton calling from outside the kitchen, probably the living room.

A few more steps but then they stopped. I could see the table and lamp clearly. I wondered if Stapleton had worked out my simple-minded strategy; if he would shoot through the yellow door and end my career right there.

Then he appeared, stark naked, reaching for the radio.

"Ira," he called out and I threw open the pantry door, pointing my pistol at his chest. He was very hairy with a powerful physique.

"Hold it right there, Cinch," I said boldly.

On TV shows like westerns this always seemed to work. All you had to do was point the gun at an unarmed man and demand he surrender; he grumbles, puts his hands in the air, and you go home to a pot roast and the plaudits of lovers and friends.

But TV did not take into account forty-plus years of substance abuse and psychological trauma.

Eugene Stapleton's eyes opened wider than seemed possible and his face glowed red. He reached over to a shelf on his right and grabbed an honest-to-God meat cleaver.

Then he roared.

I don't mean that he cried or screamed or hollered. That man roared like a lion that hadn't eaten in a week.

But I had the gun. I was the man in charge.

Stapleton kept bellowing as he moved toward me. I shot him because of the sound, which was frightening down to the core of my being. I pulled the trigger four times, fell down to the left, and saw the cleaver dig deep into the doorway just behind where my head had been a second before.

Stapleton, bleeding from four wounds to his torso, tried to pull the small ax out of the doorjamb. The first pull almost succeeded but then his strength drained away. He fell to his knees and I got to my feet.

Stapleton looked up at me and with labored breath said, "Where did you come from?" He ran his right hand over his hair, streaking it with blood, then fell sideways onto the multicolored linoleum floor.

48

In for a penny, in for a pound, a woman that everyone knew as Aunt Louise used to say in the Fifth Ward of Houston, Texas. She lived in a recess between Foreman's Bar and Sailors Last Baptist Church. The only furniture she had was a chair and a high stool that she used as a table. Her protection from the hot sun and pouring rain was the overlapping eaves of Foreman's and Sailors. Aunt Louise gave advice for free but most of the poor people that came to her would leave some bread or beer. I used to spy on her conversations from the alleyway behind, trying to get the wisdom of both the questions asked and the advice given.

I thought about the penny and the pound as I wondered if someone had heard the shots fired.

I suppose I could have called an ambulance for Stapleton but I was pretty sure that he was dead; and, anyway, I didn't think of it.

The chloroform would have been used by the Cinch and his minion to keep Irena quiet.

I unlocked the back door, in case someone came and I had to run. Then I took the chloroform and white rag to dose the unconscious man on the front porch. After retrieving my shoes I went through the rooms on the first floor but found nothing.

Upstairs I searched what must have been Stapleton's room and another bedroom that hadn't been used. The third door revealed Irena, tied to a chair and unconscious.

I turned on the light. She was clad in a satin slip and reinforced bra. There were burns up and down her arms. I figured that her tormentors gagged her while applying the cigarette butts. They wanted the diamonds but only got my name.

She was moaning and moving her head until I let her breathe a little chloroform. Then I went through the back door, the gate into the park, and down a path I had already traveled to my car on a quiet block.

I drove back to the hideout, pulled up in the driveway, entered the house, untied the unconscious Irena, and carried her down to my car.

On the drive to Pomona I had to stop once to dose Irena again.

We got to her house at about three in the morning. I pulled up into the driveway, jimmied the back door with a crowbar from my trunk, and carried the narcotized Polish killer to her bed.

I had no proof that Irena had killed Tom Willow and I wasn't bothered if she got away with it.

It felt good putting her in her own bed. She'd wake up in the late morning with memories of being tied and tortured. It would feel like a miracle to find herself delivered from that hell, and I liked the thought that at least once in my life I was the author of such a feat.

I never found out how Irena ended up Stapleton's prisoner. She might have been trying to betray me, or maybe the Cinch was after her all along. Regardless, I was almost finished with the case. I went to Tommy's on Beverly and ate two chili dogs and a pint of cheese-and-chili fries. I washed these down with three pineapple sodas, then bought a cup of coffee that I nursed till sunrise.

I rang Jackson Blue's doorbell at 7:04. He answered already dressed and ready for the corporate world.

We drank coffee and he smoked at the kitchen table until eight.

"Daddy!" Feather yelled from the doorway.

My daughter ran to me and jumped into my lap. She hugged my neck and said all kinds of sweet loving things that a younger child might have voiced. She'd been afraid while in exile at the Blue residence.

After dropping Feather off at Ivy Prep, I went to my office to retrieve the diamonds.

"Easy," Whisper said as I was looking at the brown paper parcel that Fearless had left me.

"Hey, Tinsford."

"Did you hear about the Lily?"

I put what was known as the Feynman Bible under my arm.

"No."

"There was a fire. It started on the fifth floor."

"Anybody hurt?"

"One fatality. No one else injured."

"Coroner's report?"

"The building was wood," he said. "It burned to the ground. The unidentified body had been burned down to the bones and crushed by the weight of burning timbers. It was ruled a homicide but only because the fire was arson."

"Were you planning to kill him?" I asked.

"No. But when I saw how high he was I figured I couldn't take the chance."

"Okay," I said, and we never discussed the subject again.

One of Niska Redman's pink slips on my desk said that Rufus Tyler called with an address on Don Carlos Drive in View Park and the initials *JP*.

———

I called Fearless but he didn't answer. Then I jumped in my car and made my way to an area that was sometimes called the Black Beverly Hills.

The three-story house was on a crest overlooking an undeveloped area that was large enough to be a city park. Two serious-looking black men in dark suits stood at the top of the driveway. They put up their hands and I stopped.

It was a warm day so my window was already rolled down.

"What's your business?" one of the guards asked. He had sideburns that detoured into a mustache on their way down.

"Easy Rawlins for Jasmine Palmas," I said with a smile. "Joe sent me."

"We expected you yesterday." The guard had nothing against me personally; he just didn't like people.

I elected not to answer his criticism and so, after a stern look, he stood aside and I pulled up next to the house.

The second bodyguard walked me to the door and knocked for me. I suppose he wanted to make sure that I was Easy Rawlins and not the next candidate for the latest in a long string of beatings.

The door opened and there stood Fearless Jones, wearing a pretty nice off-white suit.

"Easy," he said, smiling broadly.

"Fearless."

"Is it okay, Mr. Jones?" the guard asked.

"Better'n that, Larry, better'n that."

The doorway led into an expansive and very modern living room that had its own bar and an outer glass wall that looked down on Central Los Angeles. Jasmine was there sitting in a conch-shaped white leather chair, wearing a one-piece bodysuit comprised mostly of swirling shades of turquoise and pink. Seymour was on the other side of the glass wall, standing on a deck and looking down on L.A.

Jasmine rose out of the shell like Black Aphrodite.

"Easy." She smiled graciously, walked up three stairs from her sunken part of the living room, and kissed my cheek. Then she gazed into my eyes.

I hoped that my nostrils weren't flaring.

"You called Seymour?" I asked.

"Yes. Then I invited him and Mr. Jones to come here to wait for you."

She was holding my hands with both of hers.

"Do you want something to eat or drink?" she asked.

"I haven't been to bed in two days. Let's take care of business and then talk about hospitality."

49

The garage for the ultramodern house on the hill was larger and cleaner than any carport I'd ever seen. The floor was white cement and the walls cured wood. With the exception of a few oil stains, it could have been a recreation room waiting for a carpet and a few chairs.

Jasmine and I were alone and the doors were all closed. I pulled out the sacks of money that Boughman had stolen, and then I handed her *The Feynman Lectures*.

"Is this why you wanted Willomena's address?" she demanded.

"Indirectly."

"It was her?"

"Boughman was planning to run with the money. Stapleton wanted it too. Somehow Tom Willow got into it and she was just another fly in the honey."

The expression on Jasmine's face made her a good match for Charcoal Joe's reputation.

"She's been kidnapped, tortured, and betrayed," I said. "Believe me when I tell you that she's paid the piper already."

I could see that I was, in her eyes, still within the aura of the saving of her son.

"If you say so, Mr. Rawlins. I'll let it be. Have you already taken your money?"

"I thought I'd let you do that."

She counted out my fee and gave me a small satchel to carry it in.

When the transaction was done I was ready to go but she touched my chest, arresting me.

"About the first time we met," she said.

"That was somethin' else."

"I'm not a whore."

"Neither me."

This sense of equality made her smile.

"I heard that you and Rufus were leaving the country," I said. "Now he tells me you plan to stay."

"We realize that Seymour deserves to have a family he knows."

This seemed a good note to end on, so I moved to leave.

"Joe will want to know who stole the money," she said.

"It was the Cinch," I said.

"Do you know where Joe can find him?"

"No. No I don't."

"Mr. Rawlins," Seymour called as I was opening the door to my car.

"Yeah, Seymour?"

He approached me wearing the clothes that Marybeth Reno bought for him.

"Where's your girlfriend?" I asked.

"At her job," he said. "We're getting together later tonight. I, uh, I wanted to thank you and to apologize for acting like I knew so much or whatever. I mean . . . you saved my life out there. My mother told me."

I made an assignation with Fearless and then drove down to the Torrance Arms, where I gave Gregory Chalmers three thousand dollars. He was surprised by the gesture. When he'd heard about the death of his former boss he'd suspected me, but there was nothing to connect me with the killing.

When he gave me a questioning stare I said, "I'm a man who believes in paying his debts."

I picked up Feather and drove her home. There we took turns in the bathroom and then dressed up for dinner.

We met Fearless at 7:15 at the Brown Derby Restaurant on North Vine Street in Hollywood.

Feather loved Fearless even though she'd only met him twice before in her short life. We talked and ate steaks, told stories about the old days, and relaxed.

Just before Feather's strawberry shortcake dessert came I handed Fearless a small brown paper bag containing ten thousand of Charcoal Joe's dollars.

"You already paid me for my time, Easy," he said. "And then there's that car."

"Seymour wouldn't be in his house if it wasn't for me. I wouldn't be at this table if not for you."

I didn't tell Feather about my plans to move us. I didn't tell her about her grandmother's neglect. Time enough for the barbs and arrows. For the next few weeks everything would be about her smile.

The following Monday I walked to work thinking about Bonnie. I was late that morning because Feather had lost a notebook and we had to search the entire house before admitting it was nowhere to be found.

I drove her to school and then came back home. The walk to work was a pleasure.

"Good morning, Mr. Rawlins," Niska Redman said.

"How are you, Miss Redman?"

"Fine. He's waiting in your office."

"Who is?"

"Mr. Alexander." The timbre of her voice contained that riled-up tone that most women get around the lovable bad man.

He was sitting in my chair, smoking a cigarette. I took the visitor's seat and said, "I hope you don't have any more jobs for me, man. I don't think I could survive another."

"No, baby, I sure don't. Here I find you work and you don't come to me when there's two million dollars to be had."

"It turned out to be Joe's money, Ray. I'd do the same for you."

"But he lied to us."

"No. He wanted to get his son off the hook but there was money involved too."

"That's okay, Easy. I don't mind. I just thought I'd drop by because Joe aksed me to tell you that a dude named Gregory Chalmers was killed at the Torrance Arms Hotel. They found him shot to death at the bottom of the fire escape out back. I guess someone promised to spring him and then they shot him instead. Joe says that that was for tryin' to steal mob money and that you don't have a thing to worry about."

"Not a thing" was my rejoinder. "And even if I did worry, that wouldn't stop that hammer comin' down."

About the Author

Walter Mosley is the author of fifty books, most notably fourteen Easy Rawlins mysteries, the first of which, *Devil in a Blue Dress*, was made into an acclaimed film starring Denzel Washington. *Always Outnumbered*, adapted from his first Socrates Fortlow novel, was an HBO film starring Laurence Fishburne. Mosley is the winner of numerous awards, including an O. Henry Award, a Grammy Award, and PEN America's Lifetime Achievement Award. He has just been named the 2016 Grand Master by the Mystery Writers of America. A Los Angeles native and graduate of Goddard College, he holds an MFA from the City College of New York and now lives in Brooklyn.